Puffin Books

The Fire in the Stone

He picked up a small piece of ⸻ ⸻
slowly in the light. Green, blue and green, and a few needle-points
of red. It was opal all right– 'the fire in the stone'. For
fourteen-year-old Ernie Ryan, a dream had come true.

Living with his alcoholic father in a primitive dugout in the
harsh and lawless opal fields of inland Australia, Ernie had either
to fend for himself or starve. But when his precious cache of opals
is stolen and he sets out with a friend determined to find the thief,
his dream becomes a series of nightmares.

The Fire in the Stone was commended by the Australian
Children's Book Council in 1974 and has also won an Edgar Allan
Poe award from the Mystery Writers of America as runner-up for
the best juvenile mystery of 1974.

Colin Thiele

The Fire in the Stone

Puffin Books

Penguin Books Australia Ltd,
487 Maroondah Highway, P.O. Box 257
Ringwood, Victoria 3134, Australia
Penguin Books Ltd,
Harmondsworth, Middlesex, England
Penguin Books,
625 Madison Avenue, New York, N.Y. 10022, U.S.A.
Penguin Books Canada Ltd,
2801 John Street, Markham, Ontario, Canada,
Penguin Books (N.Z.) Ltd,
182–190 Wairau Road, Auckland 10, New Zealand

First published in Australia by Rigby Limited 1973
Published in Puffin Books 1981

First published in the USA by Harper
and Row Publishers, Inc, 1974
Published in the USA in Puffin Books by arrangement
with Harper and Row Publishers, Inc, 1981

Made and printed in Hong Kong by
Sheck Wah Tong Printing Press Ltd.

Set in Plantin Roman 10/12
by Syarikat Seng Teik Sdn. Bhd.,
Kuala Lumpur, Selangor, West Malaysia.

CIP

Thiele, Colin Milton, 1920–
    The fire in the stone.

    First published, Adelaide: Rigby, 1973.
    For children
    ISBN 0 14 031360 5

    I. Title.

A823'.3

Chapter One

Ernie knelt on one knee with his hip pressed against the tunnel wall. He swung the pick hard. The sharp point drove an inch or two into the tough sandstone and broke out a handful that fell at his feet. It was slow going. There was little enough space in the tunnel, and Ernie had to work with his body crouched, getting power into his strokes with the swing of his shoulders.

The line of potch* ran down the working face in front of him. Ever since he had come across it he had been following it steadily, burrowing away on his own like a solitary mole with a secret. And why not? On the opal fields miners kept their eyes open and their mouths shut; they weren't in the habit of making speeches if they thought they were on to something.

He knew that many of the greatest strikes had been made by following thin wavering lines like this to the end — or, better still, to a point where two lines met. Long long ago they were probably cracks in the stone that filled with silica, sometimes an inch or two wide, sometimes as thin as a razor blade. For thousands of years the process of settling and hardening had gone on until the cracks themselves became stone too—a different kind of stone that was usually white and milky and worthless. Potch! But now and again it turned into fire—blue fire, green fire, red fire. Then you had opal. Then you had treasure and riches.

Ernie stopped working for a minute and crawled back to the cross-drive where he'd left his water-bag hanging on an

*Potch: A vein of rock, valueless in itself, in which opal is sometimes found.

1

old wire spider. It was cool and pleasant in the drive because there was a good draught of air moving through to some other shaft. He put the water-bag back, wiped his sweating forehead with his arm, and crawled into his tunnel again. He could see by the position of his candle that he'd managed a foot or more during the afternoon shift—good going without a jack-pick or compressor. He smiled at the thought of old Red Ned O'Keefe, one of the oldest gougers on the fields, swearing and ranting at the way men mined these days: with bulldozers and gelignite and jack-picks and elevators. Softies! Milk-sops! Chicken-miners! Not like the old-timers who did it all with picks and bare hands. Three feet a day.

Ernie was glad that Red Ned would have approved of the way he was mining. Nothing but a gouge and a shovel. He reached up for the candle, pulled out the spider that held it, found another spot further along, and hammered the spike into the stone again. It always paid to have light falling right on the face you were working; you never knew when a bit of colour was going to jump out from the point of your pick. So you worked carefully near the potch; slowly and carefully.

For a long time there was no sound but the thudding and scratching of the gouge, the small splatter of falling fragments, and the hiss of Ernie's breath. The candle flame swayed and curved like a finger-high dancer at his elbow—a bit of a show-off in a pale yellow dress.

When the pile of mullock at his feet was as high as a wheel-barrow, he took the spade and started shovelling it back into the main drive. If he hadn't been able to do that he wouldn't have done any mining at all. One man on his own was hopeless. Ernie Ryan, fourteen years old and no great shakes for muscles, would have been worse than hopeless. Shovelling the mullock into a drum, hauling it to the shaft, climbing up thirty or forty feet to the windlass, winding up the bucket, emptying it clear of the shaft, lowering it, climbing down again, and repeating the whole process. Over and over and over. Never get anything done that way. 'One man's got whiskers on him,' Red Ned used to say. 'Always need two. Got to have a mate. One up, one down. That's the way to get opals. Partnerships.'

Ernie would have had whiskers on him too, if he had been using a windlass and drum on a normal drive. But he was only scratching. Fooling about in a worked-out claim that had been honeycombed by a dozen fossickers before him and finally abandoned. All he was doing was putting in another drive and throwing the mullock back into some of the old tunnels. It worked for a little while if you weren't serious about it; and there were hundreds of stories to urge you on about the fortunes that had been missed by an inch. You could never tell about opal. The fool or the new-chum was as likely to find it as Merlin the Wizard or even Red Ned. 'You never know! You *never* know. Not till it's in your hand. That's the beauty about opal. Like a lottery. But you've got to be in it.'

Ernie was in it all right; the sweat on his face showed that. Not that he really thought he'd ever find anything. But the Christmas holidays were long, the heat outside was fearful, and life underground was cool. So he'd scrounged about among the abandoned claims until he'd found one that looked easy to work, pointed his finger at a spot on the side of one of the drives, swung hard with his pick, and christened it 'Ernie Ryan's Chute'. That had been three weeks ago; weeks of hard hard work. Often enough he'd been on the point of giving it up, but there was nothing except heat and boredom above him, so he kept on.

And then one day, suddenly, there was a line of potch. Useless stuff, but it livened up the game. An omen, he told himself. A sign. 'That way,' it said like a finger pointing.

Ernie worked steadily for another hour. His candle was almost gone by then —nothing left but a disc of white with a sad little flame guttering inside the spiral wire of the spider like a prisoner behind bars. It was getting late. Although he didn't have a watch, he knew that the long afternoon must be waning. Time to knock off. He had been chipping away at the line of potch in the bottom corner of the tunnel, almost at his toes. He had followed it stubbornly for days, and now it looked as if he would have to dig down beneath his feet if he was going to keep up with it.

He eased his pick back and sat on his heels while he wiped his forehead with his arm again. He felt tired and despondent. Another day gone. Blasted potch. It glinted up at him, hard, smooth, milky—and useless. On the spur of the moment he swung back and brought the pick down hard. It was an act of spite, a way of getting his own back for all the frustration. The point of the pick drove in deep, close beside the seam of potch, curving a little behind it. At the same time there was a grating sound like metal scratching on glass. He heaved on the handle, levering upwards against the rock. The pick refused to budge, as if stuck behind a hard lump of stone. He heaved again, savagely. It gave way suddenly, and there was a splintering of potch where the point tore out chunks as it came through. It was a careless angry movement that fitted Ernie's careless angry mood. He wasn't even watching properly.

He pulled the gouge up for another final onslaught, scattering some of the bits he had rooted up at his feet. At the same instant he sensed something there, and his heart jumped. Colour! A stab of red no bigger than a beetle's eye, and a glint of blue-green shadow. He caught his breath. 'Opal! My gosh, I've found opal!' The pick clattered beside him as he pulled the spider feverishly from the side of the tunnel and knelt down in the corner of the

4

drive, the candle flame an inch from his eyebrows. He picked up a small piece of stone and turned its broken edge slowly in the light. Green, blue-green and a few needle-points of red. It was opal all right. Gem opal.

Without knowing it he was talking to himself in a hushed whisper. 'My gosh! Opal! Real opal!' He picked up another piece and held it close to the light. He was surprised to see how much his hand was trembling. This time there didn't seem to be much colour—mainly milky potch with a hint of green in one corner. He scrabbled about amongst the uprooted bits, holding up piece after piece. Some were dull stone, some glowed with vague promise, one or two glinted fiercely as they were turned. Although he was sitting down now Ernie felt his heart pumping more violently than it had in the heat of his hard work with the pick. 'I've done it,' he kept saying under his breath. 'I've found opal. I've found *opal*.'

He picked up a chunk of stone as big as a lemon and held it close to the flame. It looked like common rock at first, but there was a texture about it that made him pause. He pulled over the pick and chipped off a corner of the stone against the point. This time there was hardly any need to turn it in the light; he was shaking like someone in a fever long before he saw the full flash of it. Bold clear shafts, red and blue-green, changing and leaping from instant to instant like frozen fire locked in the stone.

The candle wick sputtering in its final pool of molten wax brought Ernie back. He only had a minute or two left. Once the light went out he would have enough trouble finding his way back along the tunnel in utter darkness, without trying to crawl about on his hands and knees deciding which stones were precious and which ones were useless mullock.

He suddenly realised that he didn't even have anything to put his specimens in. No bag, no tin or bucket, not even a lunchbox. So he picked up the stones he'd gathered together in a little heap at his knees and crammed them into his pockets—a dozen bits on one side of his pants and two or three of the bigger ones on the other. He seized the pick and chipped gently and urgently around the hole in which he'd made his find. When he'd loosened a good deal more he scraped out all the pieces and ran them hastily through his fingers. There was more good colour everywhere, but he had no time to sort it all out now. On the spur of the moment he took off one of his boots as quickly as he could and scooped the stone into it until it overflowed. Then he grabbed the spider and started scrambling back along the drive. He was astonished at the weight in his pockets; it felt as if his thighs had been shackled with convict cannon balls.

He hadn't gone more than ten feet when the candle finally spluttered out and he was left to grovel along in total darkness. He found it suddenly unnerving. A terrible sense of claustrophobia swept him—a feeling of being trapped underground forever, with no sense of direction, no knowledge of where he was, no hope of escape. He began to crawl forward faster and faster, more and more desperately, his breath wheezing and hissing between his teeth, his arms and knees aching, his thighs weighed down with tons of iron. A ridiculous urge to shout out for help swept him and then, worse still, a need to get rid of the weights around his legs, to empty his pockets, to throw away the boot full of rock he had been clutching to his chest, and to crawl on fast and free.

A vague glimmer in the drive ahead saved him just in time. It was the bottom of the shaft from which the tunnel led off at right angles. He crawled forward to it, heaving and sucking in his breath in great gulps, until he could stand upright at last, clutching the ladder that led up to the surface.

6

For a long time he stood there, gradually calming his pumping heart and taking a grip of himself again. Then, slowly and painfully like an old man, he laboured up the shaft. As he did so a great change came over everything. The gloom fell away behind him like the dark underworld it was, and light poured in more and more strongly from above until, when he stepped up out of the shaft on to the surface again, he found himself standing in a golden world of afternoon sunshine. It was warm and bright—and human.

He looked around quickly to see if anyone had seen him come up. His elation at his find came flooding back now that he was safely above ground, but it was mixed with fear and suspicion that someone else might sniff out his secret. In his mind's eye the opal he was carrying was already shining through the leather and cloth, his boot and his pockets alight with it, so that the first person he met would be sure to ask in astonishment, 'What on earth's up with you, Ernie? Look, your pants are on fire! And why are you carrying a burning boot?'

But there was no one in sight; only the distant movement of a truck in a golden haze of dust on the Alice Springs road, and the faint *phut-phutting* of a petrol motor on a hoist somewhere out of sight. Ernie felt secure. A glow of satisfaction and excitement filled him as he hitched up his sagging pants and set off for home.

Chapter Two

The opal fields lay six hundred miles north-west of Adelaide, midway between Port Augusta and Alice Springs. A flat, bare landscape it was for the most part, with undulations here and there and flat-topped hills and breakaways and wind-swept plains. An old old land, eroded and wrinkled, worn down over endless ages, peneplain on peneplain, until even the hills were remnants of ancient plains. And in the sides of the slopes, cut into every knoll and knob, were doorways and entrances and burrows as if the whole place was inhabited by five-foot-high rabbits walking about on their hind legs.

These were the dugouts—cheap convenient homes that were warm in winter and cool in summer and never needed painting. Every room was hacked out of the natural sandstone, the walls and roof often beautifully marked and stippled in natural colour—cream and ochre and red-brown—as if interior decorators had been called in to deck out the place in mottled patterns.

Some of the dugouts were big and luxurious, with lots of rooms and all kinds of conveniences: a private electricity supply, modern kitchen utensils, stereo players, carpets and rugs, comfortable furniture, and bookshelves cut into the walls. They had an air-shaft driven down through the hill above them for ventilation, and a fine front door at the entrance, with a bell or fancy knocker. All they lacked was water. Even those who struck it rich still had to ration their supplies and buy it at thirty cents a drum—if they could get it.

For in the wide parched land all around them water was almost as precious as opal, or so the people said. The Government's solar still did its best to turn the salty underground water into fresh as fast as it could; but even at a ration of twenty gallons a week for each person it was hard to keep up the supply without having to bring in water tankers from great distances over some of the most boneshaking tracks in Australia.

Though some of the dugouts were big and their owners wealthy, most of them were small and bare. And some were no more than little burrows or squats where a man could crawl in like an animal and sleep. Ernie's was like that. He often felt ashamed about it, especially when he was supposed to be doing some reading or writing for homework, but his father never seemed to get around to enlarging it. In fact, his father never seemed to get around to doing anything about anything. They had been on the opal fields for five years now—he and his father—and they were still living in the same crude way. 'Emergency accommodation' his father had called it. 'As soon as we get settled we'll enlarge the place and put in some mod cons.' But they never did get settled and they never did have any mod cons.

It was the same with opal gouging. When his father found out that mining was hard work with little promise of reward, he seemed to lose his enthusiasm. And, perhaps because he was easy-going and lackadaisical himself, he always chose the wrong kinds of partners who did more talking than digging and more drinking than talking. When they did find a few dollars' worth they spent it in celebration and were often worse off afterwards than before—besides being poor, they had a headache as well.

So after five years on the fields Robbie Ryan was known as a harmless old shyster, and his son Ernie as an unlucky kid. But because there wasn't much time for pity on the fields, and because many of the people there had fled to Australia from far worse terrors and tyrannies overseas, Ernie had to make the best of it. And if at times his father was too poor or too lazy or too unlucky to supply food in the dugout, then Ernie had to fend for himself or starve. It was as simple as that.

But Ernie, walking home from the mine with his pockets bulging, wasn't even thinking of the past. His mind was far too full of the present. It was calm and hot. The sun was setting on the western horizon and the late afternoon rays shone through the haze in long sloping planks of light. In the centre of the little town ahead of him there was life and bustle. A car and a couple of utilities were dashing in towards it from various points on the plain, rolling clouds of brown-yellow dust swirling up and hanging above them like a fine yellow mist. Several more vehicles were coming up the slope near Post Office Hill towards the Miners Store, and a tourist bus had just pulled in beside the motel.

For a moment Ernie marvelled at the change that was coming over the place. Five years before, when he and his father had first arrived, the only buildings above ground had been the school and the school teacher's house. And a few years before that there hadn't been anything. Now there was a modern motel, a police station, a large store, a bank, fuel dumps, and all kinds of buildings of the strangest shapes and designs. In almost every direction, too, he could see great mounds of earth where bulldozers were rooting about like monstrous terriers in search of opal. The machine age had arrived on the fields. Compressors were roaring every day and jack-picks were stuttering underground. Even the time-honoured old windlass and hand winch had gone, and motor-driven hoists stood like spindly scaffolding above the shafts.

Yet Ernie didn't mind the change. There were more people to see, more things to watch, more kids in his class at school; and there was more opal being found, and more buyers on the fields. And, he guessed, more secrets being kept. That was one of the biggest changes. In the old days if someone made a lucky strike everybody soon knew about it; there were drinks and celebrations, and slappings on the back, and roisterings into the night. But not now. Secrecy, and fearful precautions against theft, and careful watchfulness were much more likely and much more necessary.

That was why Ernie didn't want to meet anyone tonight. It only needed a sharp eye and a loose tongue to set his story going up and down the bar at the motel within ten minutes. Luckily no-one was likely to take much notice of a fourteen-year-old lad shambling along on his own, even if he did seem to be walking as if he had a couple of melons stuffed inside his pants. Especially when they realised that it was Robbie Ryan's kid.

So Ernie came down undetected and struggled on to his dugout at last, his legs aching and his thighs chafed sore by the angles and edges of the stones bulging in his pockets. It was dusk by the time he limped through the entrance, brushed aside the hessian curtain that served for a door and flopped down on a chair beside the rickety table made of packing-case timber. But he was glad to be there. He was home. And he was alone— with his secret. There was no sign of his father. He had gone down to Kingoonya with a friend two days before to pick up some goods from the transcontinental railway. But though it was only a couple of hundred miles each way and some people did the round trip easily in one day, his father was likely to take a week. At the moment he was probably arguing in the pub without a thought for Ernie or anyone else.

Ernie didn't mind. He preferred to be alone, at least

until he'd had time to think things out. And his first job was to sort through the stones in his boot and his pockets.

He got up, took two or three boxes from the corner of the dugout, and stood them one above the other in the doorway so that no one could walk in unexpectedly and take him by surprise. Then he brought out a square piece of masonite he'd scrounged from the back of the Miners Store the week before, laid it flat on the table, and started emptying his pockets. He was very thorough about it, even turning out the lining; then he up-ended his boot and thumped it on the board as if trying to clear it of centipedes or scorpions.

When he was sure he'd finished, he got up, lit the lantern, and brought it over to the pile of stone. He took his father's snips and his own pocket knife and began working over the pieces one by one. Although he had never made an opal find before he thought he knew what to look for. A dozen times during the past few years he'd seen buyers at work, flicking through a miner's parcel—putting a price on the lot but always looking for the few pieces of precious gemstone to make up for all the milky stuff between. And often enough he'd brought in the results of a weekend's noodling: bits of colour gathered together from bulldozer cuts or old mullock heaps, and sold for a few dollars to the highest bidder.

First he put aside the best pieces that were plain to see, where a broken edge showed strong clear colour. There was no point in risking damage to stones like that; he'd heard scores of stories about silly asses who had cut away half a fortune by trying to see how far the colours ran. Next, he took the big promising bits that were coated in mullock so that it was hard to see what they really were. There was no doubt about the lemon-sized lump he'd chipped with the pick: as he rubbed and polished it the colours leapt in the lamplight until they fairly blazed at

12

him. All the trembling excitement he'd felt in the tunnel came back to him again as he turned it this way and that to make the colours play. He found himself guessing the weight—two ounces at least, maybe even more. And how much was it worth? A thousand dollars an ounce? He felt like Midas gloating over his gold.

He worked slowly through the whole parcel, clipping the surfaces and edges gingerly with the snips when he was quite uncertain, but stopping fearfully as soon as he found colour. Now and then he rejected a lump altogether when he failed to find even a trace, but for the most part everything he'd brought up seemed to have at least a brush of green. When he'd finished with the last piece and scraped up the tiny fragments from the board he suddenly realised how tired and hungry he was. His eyes were strained and sore from long intense gazing within an inch of the lamp, and his body ached to the bone.

He looked about for something to put his treasure into but he couldn't see anything that was suitable. In the end he took down a biscuit tin they'd been using for sugar, tipped the last of the sugar into an empty pickle bottle, and carefully put his find into the tin. It was an old relic from home, with a dent in one side and a picture of a purple thistle on the lid—probably painted there long ago by his mother. He pressed the lid down hard, stood uncertainly for a minute while he looked about for the best hiding place, and finally slid the tin far under his bunk in the corner of the dugout.

It was dark outside now, and quiet—a vast Central Australian quietness that seemed to lie endlessly over the world and stretched upwards to the huge star-pricked sky. When he had first come to live on the fields the night silence had frightened him, but now it was part of life and he liked it.

He ate his tea slowly. Camp pie from a tin, margarine

13

spread sloppily on stale bread, and a tin of stewed fruit for dessert. Then he took off his remaining boot, lay down gratefully on his bunk, and closed his eyes.

Although he was tired he didn't sleep well. Long before morning he was awake again, stewing things over and over in the darkness—strange mixed-up thoughts, fleeting ideas and sad little memories of his childhood: the house in Adelaide where he'd lived until he was nine, the terrible arguments between his mother and father that went as far back as he could remember, the shock when he came home from school one day to find that his mother had gone away—'cleared out for good' as she said in a note to his father—and finally his father's decision to go up to the opal fields to try his luck and get away from it all.

Ernie never forgot the trip up from Adelaide in the old Landrover his father bought. It broke down constantly and they had to spend three nights camping beside the track. To Ernie who had never travelled further than the Adelaide Hills it was a new world. Hundreds of miles of red red road, rough and corrugated and pot-holed, going on and on through the stunted scrub; hour after hour of driving without sight or sound of another human being; only the chug of the engine and the bump of the trailer coming along behind them, an occasional kangaroo that had escaped being shot 'for sport', and once a goanna skittering across the road with his long tail streaming behind him.

And there were the stops by the roadside when he had lunch with his hat on like his father; and the queer unnatural feeling of night coming on with nowhere for him to go—no house or kitchen table or electric light or bedroom or mother. For the first time he realised what the world was. The sky above him at night made him feel smaller than the head of a pin, and the shadows in the scrub terrified him. But when he woke up in the morning the light was bright, and his father standing beside his sleeping bag was as high as the sky.

And then all day there were plains of saltbush as far as he could see, and more plains beyond that, till the Landrover was smaller than a fly crossing a football oval. Not even any fences. He couldn't imagine how a stretch of land could be so big. And it was all part of Australia.

But at last, at long long last, they arrived—emerging from the dust haze like ancient explorers out of the waterless land. His father, who had been there before, bucked up at the sight of the mullock heaps. 'There it is, Ernie. Look at it. No other place like it in the world.'

'Where, dad?'

'Here. There. All around.' His father waved his hand vaguely in a circle. 'This is it.'

'I can't see anything.'

'Course you can't see anything 'cos there's nothin' much to see—except the new school over there, see.'

'Where are the people?'

'Under the ground.'

Even though he was only nine Ernie recoiled at that because 'under the ground' was the phrase his mother had always used about people who were dead. But his father soon jollied him along.

'We'll camp here for the night, Ernie. And tomorrow I'll find a spot for a dugout. Then we'll be settled in a wink.'

But it was a long wink. Ernie hadn't realised how many weeks of hard digging it would take to gouge out even a couple of tiny rooms. And neither had his father. So the wink stretched into a year, into two years, into five years, and still their place was nothing but a squat in the hillside, a camp, a little hotch-potch.

Those years had been hard for Ernie. Five years of dirty sweat-marked books at school, five years of heat and cold and wind and dust. Five years of loneliness. The teachers

15

said he was a loner. It was probably true. He kept to himself and had few friends: Nick Andropoulos, perhaps, and Stan Henderson, but even these were hardly bosom companions and often came and went with others. Only with Willie Winowie, a thin little Aboriginal in his own class, did he seem to have some real affinity; but even that was a strange friendship of silence and few words.

One of his teachers wrote 'colourless' beside Ernie's name in the school records, and most people would have agreed that it fitted him. He wasn't bright and he wasn't dull, he wasn't good and he wasn't bad, he wasn't tall and he wasn't short. He wasn't even interesting to look at—just middling. No marks or scars, no freckles, no big teeth or ears. Muddy sort of irises around the pupils of his eyes and mouse-coloured hair. Average. Terribly average. A bit like his father.

Because Ernie had nothing to read, because he was shy about visiting anyone else, because his father was often away, he did the only thing he could do—he roamed the countryside. Before long he knew every claim and every shaft for miles around, fossicking and noodling at weekends as far as the Eight Mile. And before long everyone knew him. 'That Ryan kid, always bumbling about on his own or noodling with the boongs.' Strangely, if Ernie did feel partly at ease with anyone at all it was with the Aborigines at the Reserve. Perhaps their miserable humpies, the hovels or the wrecked car bodies some of them called home, were so much like his own that they could expect to understand each other. But though he moved freely through their camp he seldom stayed long, unless Willie Winowie had a new pup to show him or a secret place he wanted Ernie to see.

Sometimes Willie went off to visit relatives on a walkabout, and then Ernie wasn't likely to see him for weeks. That was what often happened during the school holidays.

That was what had happened this time, until Ernie had gone off gouging on his own. That was why there was a biscuit tin full of opals under his bunk.

Chapter Three

For hours Ernie lay on his bed , thinking. By the time the sun rose he knew what he had to do. It was no use going along to the first opal buyer he could find and saying, 'How much will you give me for this packet?' People would soon get to hear of it and then they'd want to know where he'd been mining, did he have a Miner's Right, was the claim registered. There were legal things to be cleared up before he did anything else.

As soon as he'd had breakfast—from a tin—he set off to see Dan Davies whose counter served as everything from post office to claims register. Ernie hated leaving his tin behind but he knew it would be madness to walk about with it in open daylight. All the same there were plenty of stories about ransacked nest-eggs, or buyers bashed in their motel rooms, or bulldozer drivers who left their finds hidden overnight under their heavy dozer blades only to find all the opal ratted away during the night. The thought of all this was too much for Ernie. He'd only gone a few yards when he turned back, hid himself inside again, opened the tin, and took out five or six of the best pieces including the big lemon-sized lump. He wrapped these up in a bit of rag and put the bundle in his pocket. Then he hid the tin under his bunk again and set off.

A hot wind was rising from the north. It was beginning to whip up the dust all over the fields and drive it in blasts across the plain. When a sudden gust struck a fresh mullock heap the loose dust plumed up in puffs like smoke from exploding shells, and long running clouds of it streamed along the roads where the wheel tracks had ground everything into a fine powder. It was already very hot. Those miners and their families who hadn't gone south for the summer, or for the school holidays at least, were keeping out of sight underground. There wouldn't be much movement above ground today, not before the sun went down.

Ernie was glad of this. It would mean more privacy for him. He reached the post office feeling hot and dried out, and pushed in. He knew Dan quite well, which was a blessing because he didn't have to go through the agony of finding a way to talk.

'Good day, Ernie.'

'Good day.'

'Scorch the hair off your chest today, I reckon.'

'Yes.'

'Where's your dad? Haven't seen him around.'

'Down Kingoonya. Coupla days.'

'That where?'

'Yes.'

Dan paused. The opening greetings were now finished and it was time to get down to business. 'You want something?'

It was a crucial moment for Ernie; he still didn't really know how to start.

'That . . . that old mine of Bordini's—you know the one?'

'Old Tonio's?'

'Yes. Is . . . is it abandoned now?'

'Hasn't been worked for a long time.'

'No.'

'Tonio and his brothers are working out at the Eight Mile now.'

'I know.'

'Have been for a year or more.'

'Yes.'

Dan scrabbled about among papers and books. 'You going to do a bit of gouging? Or your dad?'

Ernie was cautious. 'Might. If it's okay.' He knew that a slip of the tongue could get him into deep water. He couldn't reveal that he had, in fact, been mining the old Bordini claim for three weeks or more.

'Better make sure,' said Dan. 'If old Tonio still reckons he's working it he'll stick a knife into your ribs if he finds you poking your nose around down there.' Dan laughed. 'Apart from getting yourself two years' jail or a six hundred dollar fine for poaching.'

Ernie shifted from one foot to the other and fidgeted with a biro on the counter. He didn't like the way the conversation was going.

'You can only have one claim at a time, can't you?' he asked.

'Sure. But Tonio's got three or four brothers. They could each have a claim registered.' Dan was still scrabbling about.

'But they're supposed to work it all the time.'

Dan laughed again. 'Sure, every mine, eight hours a day. Half the time you wouldn't know whether they were putting in eight hours or eight minutes.' He finished his fussing. 'Anyway, it should be okay for that one.' He took up his pen and put on his official face. 'You want to register it?'

'Yes.'

'In your dad's name? He'll have to give up the one he's got.'

Ernie had foreseen this danger, but now that it was upon him he didn't quite know what to say. 'I . . . I . . . see, dad's not home.'

19

'Does he know about it?'

'No. It's . . . it's just for fun.'

'Some fun.'

'Better than sitting up top, roasting.'

Dan agreed with that point at least. Ernie pushed his feet far back behind him and pressed down nervously with his elbows on the counter. Then he put the vital question he'd had on his mind all night. 'Could . . . could I take out a claim myself?'

'You?'

'Yes.'

Dan eyed Ernie quizzically. 'How old are you?'

'Fourteen.'

'How you gonna work it, even if you can?'

'What d'you mean?'

'This eight-hour-a-day business—when school starts?'

Ernie felt that things weren't going well. 'Couldn't I work it just for three or four weeks? Till school starts. No law on how long you have to keep a claim, is there?'

'No.'

'Well then?'

Dan pursed his lips even more and made a kind of kissing noise. 'You're a sharp young rooster, Ernie. Can't see why not.'

He looked very businesslike and cleared the counter for action.

'Right then. Full name?'

'Ernie Ryan.'

'Ernie or Ernest?'

'Oh. Well, Ernest I s'pose. Yuk!'

'Got another name?'

'Yes, Ryan.'

'No, I mean a second name.'

'Oh that. Yes, it's awful.'

'What is it?'

'Kilkiernan.'

'How d'you spell it?'

'K–i–l–k–i–e–r–n–a–n.'

'Where the devil d'they get a name like *that* from?'

'Mum did. It's a place in Ireland somewhere. She and dad were always fighting about it.'

Dan went on writing for a minute. 'You got a sketch?' he asked suddenly.

'Sketch?'

'Supposed to have a sketch. Of the claim. Supposed to show the north point, the measurement of the sides, and the distance from other pegs. Has to be square, with sides no longer than a hundred and fifty feet. Date of the pegging and the number of the Miner's Right has to be put on each peg.'

Ernie looked at Dan suspiciously. 'You're having me on.'

'Not on your Nellie.'

'Bet you most of the miners don't do it—not in South Australia. They just dig where they like.'

'They'll be sorry then, if it comes to a court-case. Could lose all their opal.'

Ernie's face had fallen as long as a carrot. 'Gee!'

Dan looked at him suddenly again. 'You got a Miner's Right?'

'No. Dad's got one.'

'You better have one too, then. Cost you fifty cents.'

Ernie dug feverishly, painfully aware of the parcel—the illegal parcel—in his pocket. 'Might just have.' He counted out the money laboriously in small pieces. 'Just short. Only forty-seven cents.'

Dan was genial and good-natured. 'Your lucky day. I'll dob in the three cents for you.'

Ernie was embarrassed at having to be grateful, but he did his best to mumble some thanks. Dan issued the

21

Miner's Right and got back to the business of registering the claim.

'You'll have to put that number there on every peg. But you'll have to give me a sketch too.'

Ernie was livening up a bit under Dan's encouragement. 'Wouldn't there be a sketch anyway—from Bordini, in the first place? I only want the same place that he had.'

'Guess you're right.' Dan hesitated. 'Still be safer if you had one of your own. Wouldn't take long.'

Ernie had done so well that he didn't want to risk trouble now. 'All right, then. But it'll take a while. I'm not much good at drawing.'

'Just a rough one'll do. You ought to see some of 'em; kill you, they would.' Dan laughed. 'And it'll cost you ten dollars.'

Ernie stopped short. '*Ten dollars?*'

Dan looked pained. 'Didn't you know?'

Ernie was on the point of saying that he didn't have ten dollars and had rarely had ten dollars in his life. But a warning note of shrewdness sounded in the back of his mind just in time.

'I'll . . . I'll have to get it for you. I haven't got ten dollars with me now.'

'I know.' Dan was thinking of the forty-seven cents. 'But that's okay. Give it to me later.' He paused. 'And you needn't bother about the sketch.' There was a mocking tone in Dan's voice as if he didn't really believe that Ernie would ever come back. Ernie blushed and felt stubborn. 'All right. I'll be back for sure. This arvo.'

'Be jake. See you then, Ernie.'

Ernie took his Miner's Right and escaped outside. He still felt mildly angry at being treated as if he was a silly kid; but at least he'd managed to clear things up properly. He had a full legal claim to the old mine—or would have when he paid the ten dollars. He'd have to think of a new

22

name for it—maybe Bordini's Bonanza or Ryan's Riches.

But the first job was the ten dollars. He knew there was no money in the dugout, not a cent. Whatever there might have been his father would have taken to Kingoonya where most of it would now be lying in the publican's till. They'd be running up some more debts at the Miners Store when he got back, that was certain; but this would only add to the big unpaid bill that was there already.

There was only one way to get the money for the registration fee. He would have to sell a stone, a small one. Apart from the big overseas and city buyers, there were several local dealers who lived on the fields and bought small parcels all the time. One of them, Herb Henderson, knew Ernie fairly well, so there ought to be no problem.

Ernie was about to make for the Hendersons—a big nine-roomed dugout in Post Office Hill—when he suddenly changed his mind. Instead he set off for a recently-abandoned bulldozer cut down on the Flat; it had yielded a fortune to a couple of young Greek miners a month or two before, when everyone else had said they were crazy for mining in a place like that. Ernie went straight to the mounds thrown up near the cut and started noodling on the inner slopes. The wind had risen still more and the dust swirled about him, sometimes in sheets so thick that they seemed to flap past him solidly like wings. The heat was fierce and he was glad of his old Army Disposals felt hat for protection.

He searched diligently for about an hour. Anyone who saw him must have thought he was mad, or else so destitute with his good-for-nothing father off on a bender again that he had no way of keeping himself from starvation except by noodling desperately every day. But Ernie wanted them to see him. Now and again, when there was a lull in the wind, he stood up and looked about, hoping to see a utility or truck going past. Then he went on searching.

In a way the wind helped. Most of the best noodling finds were usually made after a good blow-out or a flash flood, when the hidden stones that had been missed by the miners were unexpectedly exposed. Ernie found four or five bits of colour, though only one of them was good enough to even warrant a glance from a dealer.

When he thought he'd been there long enough he knelt down on the side of the mullock heap and took the rag-wrapped bundle from his pocket. He opened it up carefully, quickly took out one of the smallest pieces with real colour in it, and put the parcel back into his pocket. Then he scratched about for a few more minutes, rubbed the new piece in the dust along with his noodling finds, and set off for the Hendersons.

Luckily Mr Henderson was at home. 'Hullo, Ernie,' he said. 'Come in. Can't hardly see you for dust.'

'Thanks.'

Ernie knew that he could be a sour and hard man, especially after an argument or a bad deal, so he got straight to the point. 'I've found a few bits, Mr Henderson. I...I was wondering if you'd...'

'Sure, sure. Let's have a look at 'em, Ernie.'

Ernie opened the palm of his hand and tipped the pieces on to a bench by the door. 'It's not much.'

Mr Henderson flicked the stones apart and turned them over with a little spike he was holding. The noodling bits he discarded with barely a glance; but he stopped short at the good piece, picked it up, turned it over carefully, and then went to get his glass.

'Mmmm,' he said. 'Not a bad chip this one, Ernie.'

'No, not bad.'

'Where did you find it?'

'Just mucking about.'

24

Mr Henderson smiled. 'Don't give anything away.'

Ernie shuffled sheepishly but said nothing. Then came the question he was waiting for.

'What d'you want for it?'

It was always the same, and he never knew how to answer it. He wished buyers would speak out right from the start and say what they were prepared to offer. But they never did. It was part of the haggling that the Greek and Italian and Yugoslav miners seemed to like, but most Australians didn't.

Mr Henderson waited for a second with the stone in his hand. 'Well?'

Ernie fidgeted. 'Would . . . would you say thirty dollars?' He felt certain it was worth fifty at least, but he didn't want to get into an argument and spoil his chances.

Mr Henderson was hard. 'Give you twenty-five.'

'Okay.'

Ernie knew he was being duped. Tonio Bordini or his brother Mario would have laughed in Henderson's face, picked up the stone, and walked out in disdain. But Ernie's only thought was the registration fee; that was more important than anything else just now.

Mr Henderson took a bundle of notes from his pocket and counted out the money. 'Ten, twenty, twenty-five. There you are, Ernie.'

'Thanks, Mr Henderson.'

'You're doing all right—nearly as good as the boongs.'

Perhaps because of his friendship with Willie Winowie, Ernie always felt uneasy when white men on the field called the Aborigines *boongs* or *abos*. It sounded as if they were sneering at them.

'Old Normie's been making a hundred dollars a week lately, noodling. Better than half the miners who're digging their guts out.'

Ernie was still uncomfortable, but he didn't want to

25

seem rude. 'Bit hot, noodling,' he said. 'Day like today.'

'You can say that again.'

Ernie was edging for the door. 'Anyway, thanks Mr Henderson.'

'See you, Ernie.' He held the door open as Ernie walked out. 'How's your dad?'

'He's down at Kingoonya.'

'Good spot for a holiday.' Ernie could hear Mr Henderson still laughing at his own joke as he shut the door.

Outside, Ernie pulled his hat down hard, lowered his head as if butting against the wind, and set off through the swirling dust. Ten minutes later he had paid the registration fee and officially become a miner. He had intended going on to the mine to see if there was any more colour where he'd made his strike, but by now such a full-scale dust storm was sweeping the fields that walking in the open was almost impossible. As he struggled back to the dugout his face and chest were peppered with stinging grit until the skin smarted. He had to keep his eyes closed most of the time, guiding himself by instinct as much as by sight. Everything beyond a few yards from him was obliterated by a rushing wall of dust, as if the fields were caught in the slip-stream of a vast jet engine that was blasting the earth away.

He'd known dust storms before, dozens of them. Sometimes in school dust as fine as sifted flour seeped through the windows, doors and floor-boards and settled over everything. In places it lay on the floors and cupboards in tiny ripple patterns like sand on the beach. It found its way into everyone's hair and ears, and mixed with perspiration to make muddy paddyfields on desks and work books.

But Ernie had never seen dust like this—a moving wall. Half choked and blinded he struggled into his dugout at last, blocked the doorway as best he could with boxes and

26

hessian, and lay down exhausted on his bunk. Despite the whine of the wind outside he found his little corner soothing and sheltered. Before long he was asleep.

Chapter Four

Ernie woke up once or twice but each time it was so dark that he couldn't even see the door of the dugout, so he guessed that it must be the middle of the night and went back to sleep again. But at last the vague whiteness of early morning began to seep through the hessian in the doorway and he got up and went outside. The hot north wind had blown itself out and the weather was fine; a cool change must have moved through during the night because a faint breeze was coming in from the south, and there was even the suggestion of a cloud or two far to the south-west. 'Fine day,' he said to himself. 'Beaut.'

To celebrate, he decided to have a morning wash—one dipper of water from the drum at the doorway, one cracked cake of soap, a shallow swishing of hands in the tin basin, and a quick dab on each cheek. But it made him feel better and gave a special flavour to the day; squandering a pint of water was a kind of celebration, like buying a bottle of champagne.

He knew what was at the bottom of it. He was a miner, and he was rich. He had a Miner's Right and a registered claim of his own. And he had just struck the jackpot. Ryan's Riches! Bordini's Bonanza! He had fifteen dollars in cash in his pocket, several hundred times that much in opals under his bed, and heavens knew how much more still waiting to be mined.

The thought of the mine made him hurry. He scrabbled

27

about for something to eat but there was nothing left in the dugout so he decided to call in at the Miners Store on the way. It was lucky that he had the money from yesterday's sale or he might have starved; his father evidently didn't think there was any need to worry about him.

Before he left, Ernie took out his tin again and worked over his find once more in clear daylight. Although he was disappointed at some of the bigger stones there was some beautiful colour among the medium-sized and smaller pieces. One or two were magnificent—pin-wheels of fire, broad splashes of orange and blue, peacock flashes. And then there were the lovely stones in the piece of rag in his pocket, including the big lemon-sized leader. Ernie put his hand in his pocket as if to add these to his collection in the tin, but suddenly changed his mind. They could stay where they were. So he shut the tin, pushed it far back under his bunk again, battened down the dugout, and set off.

Although it was still early in the morning there was a bustle in the Miners Store when he got there. Three or four miners were waiting to be served, stomping about in their dusty boots, several Aboriginal women wanted tobacco, a tourist looking ridiculous in long trousers and a white shirt was fussing over some engine oil, and old Red Ned O'Keefe was grizzling about the poor quality of rope these days. Ernie felt like laughing, especially at the tourist who kept saying that he had to hurry because he was due back in Adelaide and there'd be trouble if he was late. As if it mattered! That was one thing you learned on the opal fields: you put time back in its proper place. Made it your servant, not your master. You did what you wanted to do today and left the rest until tomorrow. Or the next day. You forgot about timetables and hooters and punch-cards, and nine o'clock and five o'clock, and buses and trains, and news reports, and split-second change-overs in factory

28

shifts and TV programmes. You ran your own lives.

That was what kept so many people on the Fields, despite the hardship and heat and dust and flies and the long wait for better luck. Because here they felt free. Nobody to push them about, nobody to wave clocks in their faces. Only the sun to do that. From all over Europe they came: Greece and Italy and Yugoslavia and East Germany and Poland; some fleeing from pasts they couldn't forget, some from the present that was too insistent and too close. And some were Americans and Australians from big cities where there were so many people that they'd almost suffocated. No wonder the opal fields were unique; they were the last frontier.

Ernie waited while the tourist finally got his oil and disappeared down the road towards Kingoonya in his own private dustcloud. Some of the men laughed. 'Damned southerners! Always in a hurry.'

Red Ned disentangled himself from his coil of rope like a Greek god wrestling with a snake. 'Nuts!' he said gruffly. 'I hope he gets corns on his car-seat.'

Ernie laughed. He liked old Red Ned; there was something very big and honest about him, something solid. Even though he was getting old now, and his hair was like white cotton-wool, he was so straight and strong that he looked as if he could still dig a shaft by hand, four feet a day, like the great old miners of the past.

Ernie bought biscuits, crisps and other supplies, and stood outside for a while, eating. Four vehicles were standing nearby—two Landrovers, a car, and a utility—caked in dust. It lay over everything, red and yellow and cream-coloured, on bonnets and hub-caps, roofs and grilles, tail-lights and fenders. It lay in small narrow dunes on windscreen wipers, and formed miniature mounds on brackets; it had been dusted like talc through hinges and hubs, doors and boot-lids, covers and engines. It bore finger-prints on dash-panels and trouser-prints on seats. It was the trade-mark of the opal fields.

Two of the dogs belonging to the Aborigines got into a fight just then and distracted everybody; they rolled across the road in a snarling ball of dingo-coloured fur shot through with flashes of teeth. The two women rushed out at them, shouting and beating, and finally managed to separate them. Ernie threw each one a piece of biscuit to settle them down, but it nearly started another brawl. So he decided to go his own way.

It was a pleasant walk to the mine. After the recent heat it looked as if the temperature would be bearable for a day or two at least. Ernie carried an old canvas gelignite bag with him this time. It held a fresh supply of candles and matches, a water-bottle, a scraper, some string, a bit of lunch, and a few other odds and ends; but he was hoping that he would need it for a different purpose on the way back.

As soon as he reached the mine he slung the bag from shoulder to armpit with the piece of string, took a good look around, and started to descend the shaft. Nobody appeared to have noticed him. At the twenty-foot level he almost lost his hold for a second and it occurred to him that he was stupid for going off secretly like this on his own without letting anybody know; if he fell and hurt himself nobody would have any hope of finding him and he would be left to starve miserably to death. He dismissed the thought.

Once down, he crouched on his knee, lit one of the candles, and started crawling forward towards his chute. He moved eagerly now, all the excitement coming back to him as he neared the spot again. Near the intersection of the main tunnel with his own drive he found his water-bag lying on the floor in a wet patch of mullock where most of the water had leaked out slowly past the cork. He picked it up angrily, shaking it near his ear to gauge the amount that was still left. He found the old wire spider on which he had left it lying nearby; evidently in his haste he hadn't hammered in the spike properly and the weight of the bag had pulled it out. He replaced it as best he could and continued on. Now that he was nearing the end of his own drive he was desperately anxious to explore the hole that had yielded his opal; he was willing to spend all day widening and deepening it, digging all round it if necessary, to see whether there was any more colour to be found. Perhaps he had only scratched the surface; perhaps a stone like the *Olympic Australis*, as big as a loaf of bread, was still hidden there waiting to be prised out of its matrix.

The tunnel was getting lower and he realised that he hadn't been clearing the mullock back as far as he should have. He was panting and wheezing, as much from excitement as from exertion, when he finally reached the end of the drive. He held up the candle to get a good look at the working face and the corner where he'd been digging. Then he stopped short. There was a huge hole in front of him. For an instant he was convinced that he'd followed the wrong tunnel, and he half turned to go back. Then he looked again, carefully. No, this was his chute all right, his pick lying nearby, his shovel, his water-bag back there. He held up the candle in bewilderment and looked around again. Suddenly, with a rush that almost made him shout aloud, the meaning of it all flooded in on him. 'I've been robbed! I've been robbed!' He crawled to the edge of the hole and held the candle closely against the sides. It was ragged and uneven, about three feet across and perhaps a little more than two feet deep. Whoever had done it had obviously been in a hurry because a lot of the mullock had just been thrown back on to the floor of the tunnel, leaving very little room to manoeuvre.

Pushing and scrabbling forward, Ernie crawled right

31

down into the hole itself, then heaved himself up until he sat on the rim, with his feet in the hollow. He stood the candle on the mullock nearby and began sifting through all the loose stuff methodically. Most of it was rock and worthless potch but here and there he found traces of colour. A few chips even gleamed with real depth, but on the whole they looked like what they were—pitiful leftovers, remnants and accidental bits broken off from the big ones that were gone.

Ernie took the gouge and picked steadily around the edge, probed the sides, dug out and enlarged the bottom. There was nothing more to find. The slide he had been following for days which had led him to his treasure had petered out. The thing he didn't know was whether he had left a great deal behind last time, and whether the thieves who had bandicooted his claim had made a rich haul or not.

He felt sure they had. The stuff that was at home in his biscuit tin was almost certainly the beginning of bigger things. He felt suddenly very angry; angry with himself for not having stayed on to finish his find, for not having brought spare candles or at least a torch, for not having returned yesterday despite dust-storms and heat. Now it was too late. If had allowed a fortune to slip through his fingers he would never know—and even if he did he would never be able to get it back.

His anger was followed by despondency. He collected the few bits of colour he had found and put them in his pocket. Then he took his gouge and shovel, his canvas bag and candle, his water-bottle and other odds and ends, picked up his old water-bag on the way, and retreated slowly back to the main shaft. Despite the brightness of the day his climb up the shaft was slow and gloomy.

The more Ernie thought about it the more he seethed. It was monstrous. He had registered the claim—and paid ten dollars to do it. He had taken out a Miner's Right. And, having found opal, he'd had it ratted out in front of his nose. No wonder some miners guarded their mines with rifles; no wonder they threatened to drop sticks of gelignite on top of poachers' heads. It was all they deserved.

He had only gone about half a mile when he met Willie Winowie. He looked smaller and thinner than ever, as if perpetually underfed. His dusty black hair, as tousled as a mop, matched his dusty black face. There even seemed to be dust on his eyelashes which showed up clearly because he had a habit of looking down at his feet whenever someone was talking to him, But he was friendly and quiet, and his teeth were white between his lips when he laughed.

'Good day, Willie,' Ernie said. 'You back?'

'Yea, just back.'

'Where you been?'

'Over Anna Creek.' Willie shuffled. 'Visiting Uncle Jacko.'

'Stockman?'

'Yea, stockman there.'

'Where else you been?'

Willie jerked his head westwards. 'All about the place.'

'Walkabout?'

'Walkabout a bit.'

Ernie fell in beside him and they walked on in silence for a while.

'Where you heading now?'

Willie pointed forwards with a nudge of his head. 'Camp. Got medicine to take home. Baby's sick.' And he took a small bottle of white pills from the pocket of his shorts and showed them to Ernie.

'From the Flying Doctor?'

'From the hospital. Sister Williams.'

They walked on silently. Ernie liked Willie, and he felt that Willie saw him as a friend. There was a quiet under-

33

standing between them that didn't need a lot of talk. Ernie knew he could come and go between his dugout and the Aboriginal Reserve as much as he pleased without looks and questions from Aboriginal Affairs officers or policemen. Although he didn't visit the Camp very often he knew he had open entry to it as Willie's friend, whether walking past by chance or calling for some definite reason. That was why he barely glanced about as he came up.

The Camp was a harsh bare place. Willie's father and mother, three smaller brothers and a sister, together with three other relatives and their pet dogs all lived in a tin shed on the Reserve. In the winter months they had a fire inside too—but no chimney. When Ernie felt like complaining to his father about having to do homework by lantern light on an old carton or packing-case in the dugout, he thought of Willie who couldn't even dream of doing homework anywhere in the Camp.

Some of the Aborigines on the fields slept in the open, some had humpies of hessian and iron, and some used wrecked car bodies. Willie's Aunt Merna slept in a burnt-out Humber Snipe.

Ernie went up to the tin shed with Willie and waited outside while the others talked about the medicine for the baby. He knew Willie's father quite well and had often seen him doing odd jobs at the motel; but it was his brother, Uncle Winelli, who was the best fun. He had a wide smile and always greeted his friends loudly and cheekily.

'Good day Ernie! Why you not down the mine today?'

'Be cooler than up here, that's for sure,' Ernie said.

'Harder work though,' answered Uncle Winelli shrewdly, 'don't you reckon?'

'Maybe.' Ernie looked at him sharply. 'Why aren't you down the mine yourself?'

Uncle Winelli laughed and his teeth flashed. 'Not me.

34

Too dark down there.'

Several other Aborigines came out of the shed and sat down on the shady side near Ernie. One was old Yirri, Willie's grandfather, whose face was so wrinkled that it looked like black corduroy, and whose wizened white hair frizzed over his face and the nape of his neck like frost. There was something about old Yirri's face that always caught Ernie's attention—it looked so old and wise and dignified. Even as an old man he walked powerfully: his body still strong and full of muscles. He put some of the younger men to shame. But Ernie was never as much at ease with the old man as he was with Uncle Winelli. There was something about Yirri's past that came through—the tradition of thousands of years perhaps, when his ancestors walked like kings and hunted the giant diprotodon before the great lakes dried up and turned into vats of salt.

'You dig opal?' Yirri asked, pointing to Ernie's gouge and shovel.

'Finished,' Ernie said, shrugging resignedly.

'All finished up?' repeated Yirri.

Uncle Winelli's laugh rose in the background. 'Plenty work, I reckon,' he said. 'Too much.'

Ernie agreed. 'Better off noodling.'

Uncle Winelli slapped his thigh and roared. 'Plenty better off—noodling.'

Willie came out of the shed and stood uncertainly beside Ernie for a minute. 'Where you going now?' he asked.

'Home,' said Ernie. 'Want to come?'

'If you like,' Willie answered.

'We'll go by the store. I have to buy a bit.'

Willie carried the shovel as they set off, Ernie's boots and Willie's bare feet clamping and padding by turn over the stones and dust.

It was noon by the time they reached the store. There was a notice in the window offering a reward of two hundred dollars to anyone giving information about the person who had attacked Mr Toshi Hiramatsu, a Japanese opal buyer, in his motel room; the attacker, the notice said, had escaped with a large parcel of uncut stones. Outside the motel a few people were leaning and yarning, and some Aborigines were sitting on the cement, drinking wine. Several of them, including Willie's Aunt Merna, had had too much. They were arguing in loud voices, waving bottles about above their heads and telling their companions to shut up. Two middle-aged white women who must have come up from Adelaide that morning went tutting past saying, 'Isn't it dreadful,' and, 'That's what happens with a weak Government.'

Aunt Merna heard them and tried to get up. 'Pull . . . pull your snooty heads in,' she shouted after them angrily. Her feet missed the edge of the cement slab as she stood up and she overbalanced backwards with a crash. For a minute she lay there half-stunned, but after a while she struggled back into a sitting position again and started to look about for her bottle.

Ernie could see Willie watching his aunt with a queer sad look, so he jollied him into the store. 'Come on, we'll get some lunch; anything you like.'

Willie was sheepish. 'You sure, Ernie?'

'Sure I'm sure. I've got money to pay for it.'

So they picked out some canned meat and fish, some preserved fruit and biscuits, and two bottles of soft drink. Then they sat down in the shade of the store, opened a tin of fish with the little key, and had lunch.

Sitting down there like that at the level of the road Ernie could see how stony and dusty and pitted with pot-holes it really was. And this was the main street. Every time a car or a utility or a big loaded semi-trailer turned the corner from Alice Springs the dust bowled down at them, swarmed over the low buildings opposite and went drifting off on the breeze towards Post Office Hill. Yet that was how it was. That was how he would remember it for the rest of his life. If ever they put down bitumen the place would never be the same.

The crash of a broken bottle and shouts of abuse came from the drinkers in front of the motel. Ernie and Willie jumped up and ran forward to see. At the same time a big man with a huge paunch came rushing out of the main doorway, yelling and cursing. A dirty shirt hung loosely over his shorts, and he wore a pair of flopping sandals on his feet. It was Bubblegut Bistro, as the boys called him—odd-job slushy about the place.

'Get the hell out of here,' he shouted. 'Blasted boongs! Take your booze somewhere else to swill.'

Aunt Merna and one of the men rose waveringly to intercept him but he brushed them aside. 'Out of it! Go on! Get! Get!'

He stepped forward sharply and trod hard on the broken bottle; a jagged triangle of glass sliced up the side of his sandal and cut deep into his foot. Drops of red blood splotched the concrete. He drew a quick breath, looked down at the blood, and swung at the group around him.

'Look what you've done now, damn you! Finish up killing a bloke.' And he lunged about at them so furiously that this time they scattered, staggering out in all directions across the roadway.

Ernie and Willie were only a few feet away from Aunt Merna now, and Ernie put out his hand as she tripped. But she pushed him aside angrily. Ernie looked inquiringly at Willie. 'Shall we try to take her home?'

Willie shook his head. 'Only turn nasty. Better to let her go.'

The big man had taken off his sandal and was trying to staunch the blood with a rag. He looked up and saw the two boys.

'You too!' he yelled. 'To blazes with you, all you boongs.'

Ernie bridled. 'What did you say, mister?'

Bistro looked up, his hand holding the sopping rag that was dripping blood.' You're all tarred with the same brush. So get!'

'No!' said Ernie, amazed at his own bravado.

The big man made as if to lunge at him, but paused. 'If I weren't bleeding to death from them bottle-bashers I'd kick you up the quoit.'

A utility came roaring up suddenly from the Flat in a swirl of dust and very nearly skittled the lot of them.

'Out of the way, young 'un,' the driver yelled at Ernie. 'Don't want to play the lead in a funeral, do you?'

Ernie was suddenly furious with everything and everybody. 'Ah, belt up,' he shouted. 'Go and practise for your own.' He turned to Willie. 'Come on; let's get out of this.'

But Willie hesitated. 'Think I better go home.'

'To the Camp?'

Willie nodded.

'What for?'

Willie hung his head for a second. 'Better tell Mum about Aunt Merna. Better tell Uncle Winelli, and Grandpa Yirri.'

It was Ernie's turn to hesitate. He began to see things he hadn't been aware of before. 'No good?' he asked simply.

'Bad,' Willie said. 'Bring trouble.'

Ernie picked up his things. 'See you then,' he said.

As he toiled off to the dugout Ernie wondered about people. They were forever bringing trouble on themselves or on others. Even out here with just a handful of them in the desert it was the same. Robbery, violence, poverty, racial abuse. Men could never get on with one another. Were never likely to.

Chapter Five

By the time Ernie reached the dugout he was almost exhausted. He flung down the gouge and shovel and lifted his canvas bag over his head; the string scraped the side of his face as he did so and his ear throbbed momentarily with pain. For a second he looked back at the Flat as he stretched his aching shoulders, and the feeling of angry frustration over Bistro and the Aborigines left him.

It was a beautiful afternoon—fine and warm, with a long breeze and not much dust in the air. The whole place looked peaceful: colours running over the plains and hills—straw and ochre and red-brown in the foreground, smoke-blue haze and lilac in the distance. Colour touched everything—the humped bulldozer mounds that were flung up untidily here and there where the big machines had rooted about like monstrous pigs, the strips of road and winding tracks like lashes across the land, the sudden gashes of gullies and washaways, the play of shadow on the slopes, the dark entrances to dugouts like eye-sockets in the hillsides, the glint of metal from galvanised iron tanks, the bare surfaces of stone and the pock-marks of the mine shafts with light-coloured mullock heaps all around. And over it all, over the whole vast quiet land to the edges of distance, was light. Airy light. It stretched away on all sides and rose up to meet the huge curved sky. When you looked up at it like that, Ernie thought, or gazed across at the hills on the horizon, you felt like a midget. It did you good to feel like that sometimes. Maybe people ought to look around a bit more than they did, people like Bubblegut Bistro for instance. It might teach them something.

Ernie turned, pushed aside the hessian curtain, and entered the dugout. He stopped short in the doorway, blinking. For a second it was hard for his eyes to adjust from the bright light to the gloom inside, but he could see that something was wrong.

The packing-case table was lying on its side and the two bunks had been pulled from their corners. For the second time that day Ernie had a sickening feeling of fear and assault; it was almost as if someone had attacked him personally, searched his pockets, gone through his things with rough, uncouth hands. It swept him in a flash, the same sort of stunned surprise, the sudden leap of fright, that he had felt in the tunnel at the mine.

'The tin! The tin!' He ran forward to the corner where his bunk had been, falling on his knees, scrabbling about wildly, searching everywhere. But he needn't have bothered. Even as he groped feverishly in the shadows he knew that it was hopeless. The tin had gone. Everything. The whole place ransacked. All his opal, thousands of dollars worth, stolen. His breath caught in a kind of sob as he knelt there bitterly on his knees. For a long time he didn't even move. A surge of fury and hopelessness raged over him; he was torn between an urge to rush to the police and to fling himself down on his bunk and cry his eyes out.

But it was useless. You didn't kill your enemies by thinking—especially when they were unknown—and you didn't get your money back by snivelling. So he got up at last and started straightening things up a bit, pushing the bunks back and setting up the table again. As he picked up the last packing-case something clattered from it and fell at his feet. His heart gave a leap. Opal! But it was a false hope. Just a scraggy piece that was mainly potch—so poor that the thief probably hadn't even bothered to take it.

Ernie turned it over bitterly. It was hard times when even thieves became fussy.

Ernie tried to imagine how it had happened. In the first place someone must have seen him at the mine, or noticed his bulging pockets that afternoon when he came up the shaft. Or maybe someone had heard that he had taken out a claim at Bordini's old place. He felt a pulse of fearful doubt: perhaps Dan himself . . . No, that was ridiculous. But Dan could have told someone else. Blurted it out accidentally to some greedy shyster who had put two and two together. Or even the Bordinis themselves who had always believed in the mine but hadn't made a strike—and now probably resented anyone else working it.

Whoever it was, someone had discovered his secret and ratted his find. And having done that, especially if they'd made a good haul, it was simple logic to expect that there must be more in Ernie's dugout. The galling thing was that it must have been done in broad daylight. There wouldn't have been much risk in it since everyone knew that Robbie Ryan was away on a bender and his son was a bit of a dill who wouldn't really know Arthur from Martha. And there weren't any occupied dugouts nearby because the only three families in the same area had all gone South for the school holidays. In fact Ernie and his father were supposed to be keeping an eye on things for them.

Ernie smiled bitterly at the thought. Good sort of watchdog he was; couldn't even look after his own. He was aware that his eyes were watering and his nose was getting ready to run so he felt in his pockets for a bit of rag and realised with a pulse of pleasure that he still had some pieces of opal wrapped up and safe. It was the first pleasant thing he'd felt since discovering the robbery in the mine. Even then it was little enough, a consolation prize. But it was better than nothing.

Rather than unwrap it in daylight he fossicked about for another piece of rag and finally tore a bit from the thing they called a tea-towel. For he was suspicious of everything now; if someone could discover his secret so quickly, who might not be watching him at this moment. Ears in the walls and eyes in the holes in the rocks. There were a dozen hiding places near the dugout that could easily be used to keep watch on him.

The longer Ernie stayed inside thinking, the clearer two things began to be. First, he had to get rid of his remaining little packet of opal; second, he had to make as many urgent inquiries as he could to find out if anyone had been seen walking about nearby that morning.

The opal was the problem. He couldn't keep on carrying it about with him. He'd never be able to sleep easily at night any more, and even during the day he'd be forever worried that it was going to drop through a hole in his pocket or be stolen from him in an organised brawl or a secret attack. It might even be dangerous, a risk to his life, if the thief guessed that he still had good opal hidden away somewhere. But what to do with it? He would never again risk leaving it in the dugout or burying it in a hidden niche outside. Nor would he entrust it to anyone else he could think of—not even his father. Certainly not his father.

In the end there was only one answer. He would have to sell it. And although it was rare for people on the fields to use the new bank because all opal deals were made in cash, he decided that the bank was the only thing. For if he exchanged his opal for cash he would have to carry the money with him too, or hide it away somewhere. So he'd be back where he'd started from.

By now it was mid afternoon. The thought of having to spend another night with fear hanging over him was too much. He made up his mind. Without even bothering about the curtain of the dugout he walked off quickly

42

down the hill towards the Flat and then headed up to the town. At the motel he asked nervously for Mr Toshi Hiramatsu. It was the hardest thing he had ever done, facing the sudden gazes behind the counter, but the reality of the little bundle in his pocket drove him on.

He knew what his question had done. It was like a searchlight switch. Instantly the eyes of everyone there were focused on him. And not only eyes, but thoughts and speculations. Why should Ernie Ryan, scrawny fourteen-year-old noodler, bum kid of a bum scavenger, be asking for such a big buyer? What did he want with him? Did he have opal to sell, real opal? There was this story going around that he'd taken out a claim on the old Bordini mine. But that was only a couple of days ago; he wouldn't have had time to scratch out even a dunny hole by now. Not a kid on his own. And dumb too. Unless he'd been at it long before and hadn't taken out a claim till now. Which was illegal.

In a place like this, isolated, polyglot, jealous, with desperate rags-to-riches hopes in everyone's mind, rumour swept through the fields like a virus. Standing there in the limelight, shifting uneasily from one foot to the other, Ernie was never more conscious of it than now. He remembered the stories he'd picked up in the schoolyard — wild, distorted yarns, most of them — but they seemed tame compared with the things he was reading about himself in other people's faces now.

'Mr Hiramatsu's out,' Maria Fellini, the girl behind the counter, said. She was curt, offhand.

'Oh!' Ernie was bowled first ball.

'Down at the hospital getting his head fixed,' she added after a pause. 'If it's bad the Flying Doctor'll have to take him to Adelaide.'

Ernie suddenly remembered the notice about the attack on Mr Hiramatsu. 'Oh,' he said again.

43

'Is notta too bad, I theenk,' Maria's mother said. 'Justa bumpa on d' head.'

'Oh,' said Ernie for the third time.

Mrs Fellini looked at him shrewdly. 'What you wanta wit' heem, hey Ernie? You maybe looka for deesa reward?'

'Reward?'

'Yesa. Two hundred dolla.'

A great light went up in Ernie's mind. 'No, no! Oh gosh, no. I don't know nothing about *that*.'

'You donta know nussing?'

'No, nothing. Cripes no.'

'You no see nobody— in d' nighta?'

'Me?' Ernie was aghast.

'The man had a knife,' Maria said. 'Bistro saw him running away but he couldn't get a proper look.'

'We needa d' witness.'

'Not me,' said Ernie fervently. 'I didn't see any bloke with a knife.'

Maria looked at him disdainfully. 'You wouldn't. What d'you want with him, then—with Mr Hiramatsu?'

Ernie shuffled and looked round uneasily. 'I'll... I'll come back later then.'

He turned towards the door but just as he stepped forward it swung open and the Japanese buyer walked in. He was wearing a bandage around his head, but apart from looking pale he seemed well enough. Ernie was plucking up courage to speak when Mrs Fellini did it for him.

'Meesta Heeramutsu. Theesa boy, theesa Ernie Ryan, he wanta speak wit' you.'

The buyer paused momentarily, then indicated the way up to his room. 'Pleasure,' he said in his strange Japanese tone of speech. He led the way with quick short steps, fumbled for a moment at the door with his key, and invited Ernie in. He touched the bandage on his head. 'I was attacked,' he said simply. 'Last night. Sorry.'

He indicated a chair but Ernie was too nervous even to notice, so they both continued to stand. 'What you wish?' Mr Hiramatsu asked.

'Are . . . are you still buying opal?'

Mr Hiramatsu had obviously not expected the meeting to be about opals. His eyes opened perceptibly wider. 'You have opals? That why you here?'

'Yes.' Ernie looked more uncomfortable than ever. 'Don't you want them?'

Mr Hiramatsu collected himself. 'Yes,' he said quickly, 'Yes, I buy—if good.'

Ernie took the rag bundle from his pocket and looked about for something to put it on.

'Here,' said the buyer, indicating a small table near the window, 'will do here.' He put up the blind and let the sunlight stream in. Ernie tipped the whole packet on to the hard surface and Mr Hiramatsu drew up a chair.

'Ha,' he said, poking about among the stones with a spike like a nail-file, and peering intently. 'Ha.' He took up the big lemon-sized lump, held it close to his glasses, and rotated it slowly. 'Ha, ha,' he said. Then he took a jeweller's tool that looked like a kind of folding scalpel from his pocket and gently, very gently, pared away a fraction of the rough surface from various parts of the stone, pausing now and then to hold it up for scrutiny again. 'Ha-ha, ha-ha,' he said several more times. Ernie sensed that he was mildly excited but was trying to give the impression that he wasn't. When he'd finished with the scraper he took out a polishing cloth and rubbed certain spots very vigorously, peering at them from time to time. Periodically, between polishes, he held up the whole stone and inclined it at different angles to the light.

While all this was going on Ernie was trying to sort out his ideas about price. The big stone that was causing Mr Hiramatsu so many contortions was obviously of good quality. And it was heavy, two ounces at least. But it seemed to be mostly blue-green in colour; only at one end was there a broad show of red, the play of flame that flared suddenly like tiny embers of real fire. On the other hand, this was a Japanese buyer, and the Japanese were not so excited about red opal, not like the Europeans—especially the West Germans — who put high priorities and high prices on it. So allowing for everything, say he put six hundred dollars an ounce on it. No, seven hundred. Seven hundred an ounce for the big one, and say it weighed a bit over two ounces. Fourteen hundred dollars. Say fifteen hundred in round figures.

Then there were the other smaller pieces. They were all fairly good, naturally, because he'd only picked out the best ones to put in his pocket that lucky morning. One or two of them were glorious. Thank heavens he'd had the urge to do that or these would have gone too. Say all of them together made up another ounce. Good quality pieces—five hundred dollars an ounce. That made two thousand in all. And if you wanted to finish up with two thousand you started bargaining at two thousand five hundred.

The outcome of all this mental arithmetic made Ernie realise what he'd lost in the robbery. Although the stones in the tin would not have averaged such high quality, there was so much of it—three pounds weight at least. Even at a hundred dollars an ounce it added up to another five thousand dollars. And as for the stuff ratted from the mine, who knew its value now, except the thief? Ten thousand dollars worth perhaps.

Ernie's sums in the head were interrupted by Mr Hiramatsu. For some time he had been ha-ha-ing among the smaller pieces, flicking them about with his metal spike and occasionally holding one up to the light. Now he seemed to have finished his inspection.

46

'What you ask for this parcel, Mr Ernie Ryan?' he was saying. 'How much?'

Ernie took a breath. If it hadn't been for his previous experience from noodling, and for the stories he'd heard a hundred times about some of the monumental hagglings and dealings on the fields, he would have been tongue-tied out of his wits. He tried to sound casual about it, but his voice seemed to get stuck at first and then blurted out squeakily like a broken clarinet reed. 'Two and a ha . . . grmmmmmm . . . two and a half thousand.' It sounded as timid as a sparrow's cheep.

Mr Hiramatsu looked up sharply and smiled a wry smile of patience and experience.

'You put high price on, Ernie Ryan,' he said. 'Where you get these stones from, ey?'

Ernie immediately went on the defensive. It was the sort of question that would never have been asked of a grown-up miner, even if the answer was well-known to everyone. It rather branded Ernie as a boy—or a thief.

'From my mine.' Ernie purposely made himself sound huffy and offended.

'Is all right,' said Mr Hiramatsu quickly. 'From last night I am, what you say, suspicious. You understand?'

Ernie wasn't very willing to try. 'None of your stones there, I'll tell you that.'

Mr Hiramatsu smiled. 'No. Certainly none of mine,' he agreed. 'Will offer you twelve hundred dollars,' he said almost in the same breath and scarcely changing his expression.

Ernie was vaguely aware that he was in the Big League now, and he was somewhat appalled at the rough way grown-ups played. If it hadn't been for his five years on the fields and his knowledge of the way opal business was done he might have surrendered like a lamb and accepted the offer. The robbery had hardened him too. He had lost a fortune that morning, and so he wasn't going to be sold short this afternoon.

'I won't take less than two thousand,' he said, and was astonished at the calmness of his voice.

Mr Hiramatsu leaned back in his chair, eyeing the stones on the table from a distance. 'Is a good parcel, quite a good parcel,' he said magnanimously. 'But plenty poor stuff between too. Is not worth two thousand.'

'The smaller pieces aren't poor stuff,' Ernie said defensively. 'Most of them are beauties.'

'Some are quite nice, yes.'

'And the big stone is solid opal—over two ounces.'

'Quite big, yes, but not pure. Some cloud in it you see. Some matrix. Colours will not play so well.'

Ernie was on weak ground because he didn't know whether the Japanese was right or not. Quite likely he was. But he couldn't let his doubt show.

'Two thousand,' he said again, but it sounded weak somehow, like a dumb kid in the schoolyard repeating ''Tis, 'tis, 'tis,' or ''snot, 'snot, 'snot' over and over again.

'Is not worth two thousand,' Mr Hiramatsu said quietly and patiently. 'Much will be lost from it. In the cutting.'

Ernie could feel a stalemate setting in, and he hated stalemates. It was the same at school; he could never argue successfully with the teacher, or even with the other kids. He'd far sooner let them have it their way as long as they left him alone. Only the thought of the robbery and what it had cost him rankled in his mind like a new wound and kept him arguing.

'Not much will be lost; it's all pretty pure.' He was trying to sound like an expert but he felt more and more like Ernie Ryan in front of the headmaster.

'The big stone, no. Much must be cut away—especially here.' Mr Hiramatsu leaned forward, touched the stone in

48

one spot with his scalpel, and inhaled resignedly on his cigarette.

Ernie tried to remember what Mr Herb Henderson had told him about the Greek and Italian and Yugoslav miners who haggled for days and then picked up their parcels and marched out indignantly, or who went from dealer to dealer asking five times the market value of the stone in the hope that they'd eventually find someone silly enough to pay it. But Mr Hiramatsu didn't look very silly. He'd made scores of visits to many different opal fields, and he played the game like an expert. 'Twelve hundred dollars,' he said calmly.

Ernie was suddenly angry. He was certain the parcel was worth more than that. If this was the best offer he could get here then he'd sooner go to Mr Henderson. At least he'd get an honest opinion there. He'd only come to the Japanese because international buyers had a reputation for offering better deals than the local ones. They could afford to take more of the poor stuff with the good. And it was an unwritten law that a buyer had to take the packet as a whole; there was no such thing as picking the eyes out of it and leaving the cheap bits behind.

That was why Ernie was offended now. His parcel was good; there was very little potch and milk in with it. And because the average quality was high, so should the price be.

'That's the best offer?' he asked. 'Twelve hundred?'

'Is top price,' said Mr Hiramatsu quietly.

Ernie took his rag and went to wrap up his stones. 'Thank you, Mr Hiramatsu,' he said with a kind of cold grown-up politeness. 'I'll have to go somewhere else.'

But Mr Hiramatsu leaned forward quickly in his chair and put out his hand. 'Wait,' he said. He looked at Ernie carefully. Then he butted his cigarette in the ashtray and stood up. 'I have lost all my best stones from two weeks' buying,' he said slowly, 'last night in the robbery. I must have more now. So I will pay a higher price, much higher, than this worth.' He prodded the table. 'More than they pay anywhere else.'

Ernie shifted one foot. 'How much?'

Mr Hiramatsu seemed to be studying him very closely through the round lenses of his glasses. 'Fifteen hundred dollars.'

'Seventeen hundred and fifty,' Ernie said so involuntarily that he started with surprise at his own voice.

'Sixteen hundred,' said Mr Hiramatsu.

Ernie couldn't believe his ears. 'I'm haggling,' he thought to himself incredulously. 'I'm actually haggling with him, and I'm doing all right.'

'Well?' Mr Hiramatsu was standing looking at him.

'Done.'

It sounded like an auctioneer, not like Ernie's voice at all.

'You are hard man,' said Mr Hiramatsu, smiling.

Ernie had the feeling that his companion still seemed very pleased with himself, despite the increased price he'd paid.

'Cash or cheque?'

'Cash,' said Ernie sternly as if he did this sort of thing every day of his life. He felt that everything was getting more and more unreal.

Mr Hiramatsu picked up the locked briefcase he had been carrying. 'Last night I am lucky that the thief gets only opal, not money,' he said as he turned the keys in the double locks, opened the case, and took out several wads of notes. There were bundles of twenty-dollar bills, ten wads of ten, each bundle worth two thousand dollars. And there were other bundles of various denominations, bigger and smaller, lots of them, until Ernie's eyes bulged. He had never seen so much money, not even in a bank.

Mr Hiramatsu counted out sixteen hundred dollars and handed it to Ernie. Then he held out his hand and they shook vigorously. 'Thank you, Ernie Ryan,' he said. 'It is good business I do with you.'

Ernie was having trouble trying to control the notes which wouldn't bend properly so that when he finally got them into his pants pocket the wad bulged out like an umbrella opening.

'People will think you have a boil on the leg,' Mr Hiramatsu said. He took a strong rubber band from his case and handed it over. 'This will hold.'

Together they finally managed to get the wad into Ernie's pants without leaving too much of a bulge to attract attention. 'I'll keep one hand in my pocket,' Ernie said. 'Then no one'll notice.'

He turned at the door. 'Thank you very much.'

Mr Hiramatsu gave a small bow of courtesy. 'Is pleasure,' he said.

Ernie hurried out with his left hand in his pocket, a strained expression on his face like a boy searching desperately for the lavatory. He kept looking straight ahead of him, especially when he walked through the foyer, so that he wouldn't have to speak to Maria or anyone else. They were sure to be bursting with curiosity.

Once outside in the afternoon sun he was strongly tempted to keep going. It seemed the best way of keeping his secret. Mr Hiramatsu would certainly not tell a living soul what he had paid for the opal, and how else could anyone find out? But after a while he realised that the money had to be put somewhere; he couldn't keep it in his pocket, and the ransacking of the dugout had shown how hopeless that was as a hiding place. So he turned round and went over to the banking agency.

Hugh Driscoll looked surprised when Ernie told him he wanted to bank fifteen hundred dollars, but he busied himself at once with forms and a pass-book.

'Struck it rich?' he said without really expecting an answer. 'Is this for yourself or your father?'

'For me,' Ernie said quickly. 'And will you keep it to yourself please, Mr Driscoll?'

Hugh put on his most honest face. 'Never divulge our clients' business,' he said as if he was offended. 'It's bank policy.' He brought the forms over to the counter. 'How old are you, Ernie?'

'Fourteen.'

'We'll need a specimen signature. New account, see.' He pushed the forms across. 'Sign where the crosses are.'

Ernie pushed his tongue hard against his teeth as he wrote his name in his best handwriting. It was the first bank account he'd ever had, so he wanted the thing to look right.

'Right you are, Ernie.' Hugh took back the forms and started to fill in the details. 'Your proper name's Ernest, I guess?'

'That's right.'

'Ryan?'

'Yes, Ryan.'

'Got a second name?'

Here we go again, thought Ernie. Mum and Dad should have had their heads read when they dreamed that up. 'Yes, I've got one.'

'What is it?'

Ernie took a breath. 'Kilkiernan.'

'Kill *what*?'

Same reaction, same look of unbelief, same wisecrack. Even the teachers at school couldn't believe their ears. He wondered why people wanted second names anyway. Never seemed any use to anyone.

'Kilkiernan.'

'Spelt?'

52

'What?'

'How's it spelt?'

'Oh. K–I–L–K–I–E–R–N–A–N.'

Hugh Driscoll got it right second try. He banged a couple of rubber stamps about and then took the brand new pass-book and bent back the pages for the first entry.

'Fifteen hundred dollars?'

'Yes.'

'You got it with you now?' There was a note of disbelief in his voice that angered Ernie.

''Course I have.'

Ernie hastily took the bundle of notes from his pants pocket and pulled off the rubber band. The stiff new notes flipped back like the open pages of a book. He was about to hand over the whole pile when he remembered that he wanted to keep back a hundred in cash, so he started to count off five twenty-dollar notes. They kept sticking to one another and he was all fingers and thumbs. Hugh Driscoll waited patiently with half a smile on his face while Ernie wrestled and fussed with his money.

'What you trying to do? Count 'em all?'

'Won't be a second,' Ernie said desperately.

'Tell you one thing,' Hugh said conversationally. 'This'd be about the only place from Sydney to the black stump where a lad like you'd be likely to bung down fifteen hundred dollars on the counter. I'll say it is.'

Ernie was in such a hurry to separate the five notes from the wad before this kind of talk went any further that he wrenched agonisingly at the last one, and the whole bundle went scattering over the floor like a pack of cards.

'Ah, struth!' Ernie dived after them on his knees.

'What, throwing 'em away now?' Hugh Driscoll couldn't resist the joke. 'Oh well, easy come, easy go.'

Ernie came up at last with a great untidy bundle like a schoolboy picking up scrap paper in the yard, and piled the notes on the counter in a heap. 'I hope they're all there—all except five.'

Hugh straightened them out a bit and started counting. He sorted them out in bundles of ten, two hundred dollars to a bundle, and added on the odd hundred at the end.

'Fifteen hundred dollars,' he said. 'Dead right.'

Ernie folded the remaining five notes carefully and put them in his pocket. They fitted snug and flat—no angles or bulges.

Hugh made the entry in the pass-book and stamped it. 'There you are, Ernie. And thanks for the business.'

They were only just in time. As Ernie turned to go, Maria Fellini and a friend walked in, goggling at him curiously.

'When was *he* doing in here?' he heard Maria ask as he went out, and was relieved to hear the guarded reply: 'Private business.'

The pass-book was more awkward to get into his pants pocket than the five notes, but he managed it at last even though it stuck up in the lining like a gun at the hip.

Everything still seemed quite unreal to him—the first find, the two robberies, the sale to Mr Hiramatsu, the bank balance, even the book in his pocket. But the afternoon sun was real enough, and the Miners Store, and the solid hills, and the dust over the Flat. And as the reality of the natural world came back to him he remembered that he had only dealt with one of the two jobs he had to do.

He still had some questions to ask.

Chapter Six

Ernie calculated that he had left the dugout at about six o'clock that morning, and returned at about noon. The thief must therefore have gone into it during that time, probably early rather than late because he would certainly have been keeping watch from a hiding place, waiting for Ernie to leave. He'd probably ransacked the place soon afterwards—before seven most likely.

So Ernie set out on his task. Detective Ryan at work. Private Investigator. His goal was to visit every dugout, and the two or three places that were above ground, on his side of the town. He worked out a standard question: 'Excuse me, you didn't happen to see a man around our way early this morning did you?' But he soon learnt that asking the same question over and over was a thankless business. Half the families were away anyway, and those that weren't had been asleep or at breakfast or busy down below at that hour of the day. That was the trouble with people who lived like rabbits, he realised. With ordinary houses you could expect that anyone nosing about would be glimpsed from the bedroom, or seen through the window, or spotted during the washing up. But not from a dugout. The inhabitants would need a periscope poking up through the top of the hill to sight an unwelcome stranger cruising about, or to torpedo a thief. After two hours he hadn't discovered a thing. Nobody seemed to have been out on the flats or slopes that morning.

It was after five o'clock by now so Ernie decided to give up and go home. Some of the miners were knocking off too; here and there he could see their utilities heading back towards the motel, the dust billowing and boiling out behind them like a golden-brown smoke screen. He could imagine how they'd tackle their first schooner at the bar; throats on them like limeburners' boots, as Hugh Driscoll used to say.

He toiled up towards the dugout, aware of a blister burning like mad on his heel. He'd have to get some plaster on to it tonight or he'd know all about it by tomorrow. He was concentrating so hard on the pain that he was hardly aware of his arrival until he brushed aside the hessian screen and marched straight into the dugout. For a second the gloom tricked him as usual and he stepped forward uncertainly. Then a shadow moved suddenly right in front of him; it was a man, bending over by the table, with his back to the door. Ernie leapt backwards, his nape tingling and his eyes wide, certain that the thief had come back and, having been caught in the act, would fight with knife and gun.

'Whoo!' said Ernie, tripping and tangling himself in the curtain.

'What the hell!' The man spun round in alarm and straightened up.

'Oh, it's you.'

'Dad!' Ernie's voice was a rush of exasperation and relief, all at once. 'Dad, what the heck are you doing?'

His father seemed nettled. 'What the devil d'you think I'm doing?' He pushed sourly at one of the bunks. 'Straightening up the place. What you been up to in here?'

'Oh, *that*?' said Ernie lightly. 'That's nothing much.'

'I like that,' his father said. 'Looks as if a willy-willy has been through the place.'

Ernie was so unconcerned about anything except the fact that the shadowy figure in the dugout had turned out to be his father instead of a knife-plunging opal poacher, that he nearly overplayed his hand. 'What you been doing?' he heard his father say again.

'Oh, just working on an idea I had. Did you have a good trip?'

His father took a while to answer. 'Not a bad old spot, Kingoonya.'

'Held up, were you?'

'The clots on the railway didn't send Harry's gear. Had to wait three days. Just killing time.'

Ernie knew that a pile of time would be lying dead in the Kingoonya pub, along with the bottles in the back-yard. But he didn't say anything.

'You...you been gettin' enough to eat?' his father asked at last, guiltily.

'Yes. Been okay.'

'You buy this stuff?' He pointed to the biscuits and the new cans of food from the store.

'Yes.'

'Book it up, did you? Struth, we must have a nice old bill there by now.'

Ernie felt his anger growing. 'No, I didn't book anything up.'

His father looked furtive. 'You didn't *pinch* the stuff, did you?'

'Ah, dad, what'd you take me for?'

'You pay cash, then?'

'Yes, I paid cash. Every bit of it.'

His father licked his lips, started to speak, then hesitated uncertainly. 'Been noodling?' he asked at last.

'Done a bit of noodling—off and on.'

His father seemed enormously relieved. 'Can't beat you kids. You and the boongs. Do a damn sight better than half the blokes sweating their guts out down the holes.' He laughed ingratiatingly. 'Hundred dollars a week the boongs make, some of 'em. Beat that. Bust it up on booze.

Red Ned. How'd you be? Easy come, easy go. Feel like changing places sometimes—with the boongs.'

'Don't keep calling them boongs.'

His father stood up, flushed and astonished. 'Well, for crying out loud.'

Ernie was suddenly exasperated. For the first time he began to see things about his father that he had never seen before. But they both dropped the subject then. His father pushed the rest of the furniture back into place and started to fill the lantern with kerosene for the night. Ernie lit the primus stove and opened a tin of stewed meat for tea.

'What you going to do tomorrow, dad?' he asked.

'Have to give Harry a hand for a few weeks. Get his new gear going.'

'He going to pay wages?'

'Twenty dollars. Rations thrown in. Worth taking, the way things are. No-one's on to opal. Place is about as lively as a dead fish.'

Ernie stirred the stew slowly over the hissing primus. 'Dad,' he said after a while. 'Why don't you give the old Bordini mine a go—you and Harry. Lot of opal came up all around there. Good stuff too, thousands of dollars worth.'

His father wrinkled up his nose as if he'd detected a bad smell. 'Bordini's? Yuk! Place is like a rat hole. Riddled with dead drives.'

'Make it all the easier.'

But his father was emphatic. 'You can't tell me those wops would have left her unless they were damn sure she had as much colour left in her as a mullock heap. Not Italians, no sir. Especially not the Bordinis.'

'Doesn't follow at all,' Ernie said. 'Look at old Mr Palladis; and George Andropoulos; and Mike Buzenskis and his brothers. They all went back to old mines and made fortunes. You can never tell with opal. You said so yourself.'

His father felt he was being conned into a corner. 'No point in talking,' he said angrily. 'I've already got the one at the Eight Mile pegged. Can't register claims all over the countryside.'

Ernie felt strangely cheeky. 'Don't have to; *I've* got the Bordini mine booked.'

He was so pleased with himself that he burnt the stew. A strong smell of burning warned him and he whipped it off just in time; but he missed the pleasure of seeing his father's expression.

'You what?'

'I've got it registered. In my own name.'

'What you want to do a damn fool thing like that for?' His father was raising his voice, but it was a swashbuckling kind of loudness as if he was really stage-playing his protest. Ernie pushed a plate of stew across to him and sat down to his own.

'If you and Harry can't mine it, I thought I might do a bit myself.'

'Don't be so darn stupid.'

'Why not?'

'You know why not. That's man's yakka.'

'I could still do a bit.'

'Not on your own, you couldn't. There's more fellows finished up underground for good by working on their own than anyone's willing to admit, that's for sure.'

'Well, I'll get someone to help me, then.'

'Who, for instance?'

'Stan Henderson or Hoppy Schmidt.'

'He'd be a lot of good.'

'Who, Hoppy?'

'You'd most likely finish up like him yourself, with a busted hip and skewy leg. Only have to fall down a shaft

59

once. That's all he did.'

'Well, there are plenty more who'd give it a go.'

'Sure.'

'Nick Andropoulos would, and Buzza Minkvitz. They're the same size as me. And . . . and Willie.'

'Willie who?'

'Willie Winowie.'

'What, that boong kid? Wouldn't know how to hold a shovel. Don't know what work is, them boongs.'

'He works at school.'

'Be just like the rest of 'em down at the Camp. Only get off their broads to collect Social Service, or maybe go noodling if they have to—when they're busting for a bottle of red hot bombo.'

Ernie pushed his plate back angrily and got up. 'You don't even know them,' he said. 'Willie's no different from Stan or Nick or Hoppy or me.'

'Well why doesn't he get cracking and get the hell out of that Camp then? Enough to turn you up, all those damned dogs and kids and relations all cooped up down there.'

'Because that's where his parents are. That's why the kids are there. Same as Nick lives with his. Same as me.'

His father was suddenly quiet, but Ernie didn't even notice, he was so full of himself. 'Kids have to depend on their parents. And a pretty raw deal they get sometimes too.' He paused. 'Not that it's Willie's dad's fault, or Uncle Winelli's, or old Yirri's. They've lost all their land, and the animals have gone. We've grabbed the lot. Except a Reserve like a cemetery. And a few tin huts. And a couple of wrecked cars. Big deal.'

'Ah, shut your trap. You're getting too big for your boots, that's the trouble.' His father got up angrily and went outside.

He was still standing by the doorway looking down over the Flat when Ernie went out a long time afterwards and stood there too. They didn't say anything. The sunset was fuming and smouldering like a vast fire across the west. Imperceptibly the flare of crimson and orange and red deepened and changed. Sultry black bars stretched and spread along the horizon, the colours above them lost their fierceness, sank and faded. Twilight became shadow, and the air seemed to grow soft and dark like invisible black down. Here and there a light came on below them, or winked and died. And above everything, in the infinite sky, the stars blazed in thousands, more and more of them as the darkness grew intense, till the Milky Way was like a bracelet of diamonds a million miles long.

'Just look at that,' said Ernie's father at last in a quiet voice.

'It's beautiful,' Ernie said.

'It's true, what some fellow said. If we could see the stars only once in a hundred years from one particular spot, people would come crowding from all over the world to see the miracle. We never appreciate what we've got. Not when it's too familiar.'

'Same with everything,' said Ernie. 'Same even with people.'

The next day was Sunday. Ernie got breakfast ready for the two of them and then went looking for partners. His father had said he could work the Bordini mine as long as there were always two other lads on the shift apart from himself. So he called on Stan Henderson and Hoppy Schmidt and Nick Andropoulos. But he didn't have much luck. Hoppy was away on holidays and Stan had taken on a job on a water truck. Nick was willing to come but he had to go to church first.

'You come too,' he said to Ernie.

'Me?' Ernie said. 'Ah, give it a go.'

But Nick was firm. 'Fair's fair. I come gouging with you, you come to church with me.'

61

'Hardly the same sort of thing,' Ernie said.

'Take it or leave it.'

Ernie gave in reluctantly. 'The things I do for some people.' He looked at his old shorts and dirty boots. 'I'm not even dressed.'

'I'll lend you a shirt,' Nick said. 'Come on down.'

Half an hour later he and Ernie were sitting sedately in church between Con Andropoulos—Nick's older brother—and his two small sisters. Ernie hadn't been inside for a long time and he was surprised at what he saw. The church had been enlarged and it was now a beautiful big dugout; not huge, but large enough to hold two neat blocks of pews, with a small centre aisle and plenty of head-space under the domed roof above them. The altar was glorious—set in a deep niche cut out at the front of the church and inlaid with coloured jasper picked up by the priest and his helpers. It matched splendidly with the mottled sandstone of the roof and walls—cream-coloured as they were, with stipples of brown and ochre where oxides or clay or other impurities had marked the stone. Here and there the long scores of the jack-pick could still be seen on the walls and roof like builders' trademarks. It must have taken a lot of hard work, Ernie thought, to pick and shovel and barrow out a gallery big enough to make a church. Even a little church.

On the right-hand side he could see the entrance to the priest's living quarters where he slept and worked and read his books. And beyond that, he knew, was a separate private entrance. During the service Ernie couldn't help gazing at the walls and their workmanship. What a thrill it would be to have a drive like this in the Bordini mine— down at the opal bottom, where you could stand up with space to spare above your head and shine a bright light all round for signs of tell-tale colour or potch or long slanting slides from roof to floor in front of your eyes. You could have it lit with electricity till it shone as bright as the salt mines he'd read about in some book at school. But there'd never be opal mines like that. There was too much mullock to shift, and too much chance. You might dig out a mountain and find no more than a pin's head of potch.

The bulldozers had proved that. Though some had unearthed a fortune, a lot of them had huffed and gored up the ground like mad bulls for a trickle of pocket money. No wonder some of the miners had howled and stomped when the Government suggested that they should back-fill the dirt they'd thrown up all over the place. The expense would kill them, they said; and anyway it didn't matter a wallaby's ear whether the ground was straightened up afterwards or not. It was such a desert as it was that a few mounds tossed up at random would liven things up a bit. The priest was giving the benediction and looking at Ernie a little strangely. Ernie had the feeling that he'd brought attention on himself by missing too many of the responses. But at least he'd kept his bargain with Nick.

'I'll have to pack some lunch first,' said Nick. 'And you'd better give me back my shirt.'

'Sure,' said Ernie, tugging it hastily over his head. 'Sorry. I forgot all about it.'

'Won't be long,' Nick said. 'Come on in and wait.'

Ernie fiddled with Nick's torch while he waited. 'We'll have to go down and see Willie,' he said. 'Dad reckons we always have to have three of us there at the one time.'

'D'you reckon he'll come?'

'Sure he'll come.'

'I don't know.'

'He will if *I* ask him.'

Nick put some cake and sandwiches in a bag. 'Got something to drink?'

'Water-bag'll do,' said Ernie.

Willie wasn't at the Camp but they found him noodling

on Lippinsky's old 'dozer cut. 'Come on,' said Ernie. 'You're a partner in Bordini's old mine. With Nick and me.'

Willie was sceptical, but they jollied him along till he agreed to come.

'Don't like it much,' he said. 'Mining under the ground.'

'Might make a fortune,' Nick said. 'Ernie reckons we will.'

'Tell you what,' Ernie said when they reached the shaft at last. 'We'll just spend the day exploring. There are lots of drives. Then tomorrow we'll start.'

'No windlass,' said Willie simply.

'No hoist or nothing,' Nick added. 'You going to chuck up the mullock with a shovel, Ernie?'

'Sure. Only thirty feet.'

'Joke, joke! What you going to do, then?'

'Just scratch a few drives. Plenty of old chutes to put the mullock in.'

'Come on, then. Who's first down?'

Ernie put his foot on the ladder. 'Maybe I'd better be. I know my way around a bit down there.' He descended a few steps and shouted up at the others. 'And don't kick any gibbers down over the edge when you're stepping across. I don't want 'em on my head.'

'Ought to have a helmet,' Nick said. 'Safety first.'

'Safety second is the way you move,' Ernie called back. 'Come on— and bring your torch.'

Nick followed Ernie, and Willie came last, climbing down lightly and quickly in his bare feet.

At the bottom of the shaft they squeezed and jostled for a minute in the narrow space. Ernie lit two long new candles and gave one each to Willie and Nick. Then he crouched down to enter the tunnel. 'This way,' he said unnecessarily. 'And follow me pretty close. Okay?'

'Okay.'

And they set off like a little priestly procession waving lights and candles on the way to a sacred celebration. Or a tragedy or funeral. In a way perhaps that's what it was—or at least the beginning of it.

Chapter Seven

Back at the dugout Ernie's father was in a very bad mood. He was having an argument with his partner, Harry Kernich. Actually Harry was more like an employer than a partner because he owned most of the equipment they were using; he was only giving Ernie's father a job out of the goodness of his heart because they'd been mates years before.

'I tell you, Harry,' Ernie's father was saying, 'I'll have to get more than twenty dollars a week. I've got over a thousand dollars on tick around the place and they're starting to squeeze me hard.'

'Sorry, Robbie,' Harry said. 'But I'm not in much better shape myself. Machines cost money, you know that. And I haven't had a decent strike in years.'

Ernie's father turned his anger on the machines. 'Madness, all these bulldozers,' he growled. 'You've got to be a millionaire before you can start. In the old days all you needed was a pick and shovel.'

'Not too many millionaires around these parts,' Harry said laconically. 'I reckon every other bulldozer's on the never never; three or four blokes club together to put down the deposit and hope they'll find enough opal to pay it off.'

'That's got whiskers on it.'

'Sure has when you don't find opal.' Harry opened another one of the cans of beer he had brought with him, passed it over, and got one for himself. 'You know how many 'dozers there are on the fields now?'

Ernie's father wiped the froth from his upper lip. 'Dozens of the things,' he said. 'Roaring and huffing half the night.'

'Best part of a hundred.'

'Struth.'

'Millions of dollars' worth.'

'And then they've got to run 'em. That ain't peanuts.'

'Say that again.'

'A hundred dollars a day, some of 'em.'

Ernie's father rolled his eyes above the can he was holding up to his mouth and swallowed in the wrong direction. He coughed and spluttered. 'And they reckon the little bloke's still got a chance!'

Harry shifted his bottom on to a more comfortable piece of rock.

'It's not only the 'dozers either, that cost the dough. Think of all the other gear—hoists and compressors and transport.'

'I'm thinking.'

'Even gelignite. You know what Archie Palladis reckons he's spending?'

'On gelly?'

'Yes.'

'Wouldn't have a clue.'

'Forty dollars a week.'

Ernie's father nearly choked for the second time.

'*Forty dollars!*'

'That's what he says.'

'He must be blowing up the whole State.'

Harry tossed his empty can on to the heap. 'Goes to show, don't it? You need capital these days. Like I said.'

66

Ernie's father snorted. 'Capital. Plant and equipment. The little bloke might as well pack up and go home.'

Harry agreed. 'It's a pity, though,' he added. 'They ought to keep the big syndicates out of here. Out of gem-stone mining. They can go after the other stuff—iron ore and nickel and oil and whatnot. But we don't want 'em here. Opals ought to be for the likes of us. For the little fellows.'

Ernie's father finished his drink and leant back gloom-ily. 'It was best in the old pick and shovel days, that's for sure. Everybody equal. All battlers together. Pity it couldn't be that way again—crawling around like a lizard with a candle. Plenty of times I nearly trimmed me eyebrows—peering too close, looking for the colour.'

'You can never put the clock back.' Harry got to his feet slowly.

'The only blokes who're making money are the ones who're selling stuff to everyone else—the store and the pub.'

'Always the way. I should have opened up a joint like that in the first place.'

'Too late now. Big business. Half the place is in debt to them. Tens of thousands of dollars.'

Ernie's father got up too. 'Yea, and I'm one of 'em,' he growled. 'Soon won't even be able to buy a half-inch tack. And I'll have to think of Ernie; he'll be starting school in a week or two. Be wanting a fortune's worth of books again I s'pose.'

Harry started to walk off down the slope. 'Cheer up, Robbie,' he called back. 'Tomorrow's the day. That's when we'll make the big strike.'

'Yea,' Ernie's father muttered. 'My thumb under the hammer, that's the only strike I'm ever likely to make.'

Harry waved and called something else, but it was lost in the wide space of air and swarming sunshine. Robbie

67

Ryan was acutely aware of his surroundings again—a kind of golden peace that seemed to fit in very well with Sunday afternoon. For a long time he stood at the door of the dugout as he always liked to do—looking down at the Flat—before going inside to get ready for tea.

Ernie was astonished at the size of the old Bordini mine when he really came to explore it. He had always known that there were lots of connected drives and shafts in the area, but he hadn't realised how far they went. Normally a miner didn't make deep lateral drives because it was too hard to drag all the mullock out over long distances to the vertical shaft for disposal. It was quicker to sink another hole.

Ernie had never had the courage to push far into the drives on his own, but with Nick and Willie for company he led off boldly. Luckily all of them were fairly small for their age and they moved down the tunnels freely. The drives on the fields were rarely more than three feet high and the men usually worked in a tight, crouched position. Sliding back the drums of mullock to the shafts was a back-breaking job, even when you had a hoist there to take them up to the top. Now and again the tunnels opened up, of course, where someone had chased a slide up into the roof or down below the floor, and then you could even stand upright. Ernie liked these spots best; they gave a feeling of space where you could have a breather, instead of that enclosed, suffocating feeling in the narrowest parts of the drives where it seemed as if the whole earth was going to close in on you, squeezing you tighter and tighter until you were trapped, and died horribly. Claustro-something-or-other the teacher had called it once.

As far as Ernie knew, the only shaft with a ladder left in it was the one he had always used, so they put down markers before they left the main tunnel to explore any of the side drives. The ladder was a rarity in any case; normally the miners rode the hoist up and down. This must have been an emergency arrangement in case of a breakdown. Ernie was glad it was there at any rate like a bridge back to safety from the underground labyrinth they were in.

'Cripes it's dark in here,' Nick said as they paused for a rest.

'Wouldn't want to lose your lights. Send you off your crumpet in five minutes.'

Ernie agreed. He remembered his own experience on the afternoon when he'd made his strike.

'Don't like the dark,' Willie added briefly. 'You know which way, Ernie?'

'Sure.' Ernie wasn't as confident as he sounded, but he knew that a leader always had to seem certain. They went on for a while until suddenly the gloom began to lighten and a faint smudge of light showed up in front of them. 'Shaft up ahead,' he called.

When they reached it they found it was so narrow that there was barely enough room for the three of them to stand upright.

'Drill shaft, by the look of it,' Nick said.

Ernie ran his hand along the smooth round sides. 'No ladder.'

Willie pointed quickly above his head, accidentally jabbing his elbow against Nick's ear as he did so. 'Clouds.' Far up, as if seen through the wrong end of a telescope, was the circle of daylight at the top of the shaft; and another telescope-end beyond that again was a moving bit of something that might have been clouds.

'You've got eyes like binoculars,' Nick said begrudgingly. 'But you'd need wings to get out of this one on your own.'

'Could do it, I reckon,' Willie said.

'You'd need a rocket,' Ernie said.

'Well don't try, either of you.' Nick was solid and practical. 'You'd get half way up maybe, and then what? Either sit there, or fall back down on your broad like a drum of mullock all over the place. And then we'd have to drag you back to the other shaft with a couple of busted ribs or legs or something, and hoist you up the ladder. Be great.'

'I'd still like to see where this shaft comes out,' Ernie said. 'How far from the other one.'

'You can see that from the top.' Nick crouched down to get back into the drive. 'Come on, let's go back.'

'More exploring to do first,' Ernie said. 'Plenty of time.'

So they spent the next hour fossicking about. In one of the lateral drives they came on a large hollowed-out area the size of a room, with traces of potch in shining little spicules on the walls.

'Wowie,' said Nick, holding up his torch. 'They must have thought they were on to something here.'

'Didn't do any good though,' Ernie said. 'Not as far as I know. Didn't ever hear of the Bordinis striking it rich.'

'You can never tell with that sort; they'd never let on.'

'Hard to keep a secret in this place though.'

'Mr Bordini left it,' Willie said quietly. 'Must think this one's all finished up.'

Willie spoke so seldom that his comment seemed to gain added weight from the silence all around it.

'Fair enough,' Nick agreed. 'They wouldn't have gone if they'd thought there was a mosquito's toenail left.'

They moved all round the chamber holding up the candles or flashing the torch over the walls and ceiling. 'Beaut isn't it,' Nick said. 'Just like Fellini's dugout.'

The mottled sandstone walls were hard and clean, marked here and there with impurities that gave the usual decorative, patterned effect. It was the sort of stone that you could trust for strength. All over the fields for twenty miles or more miners relied on it with complete safety;

there was no bracing, no shoring up with timbers, no boxing of shafts or drives. Which was just as well, because there was precious little timber within miles of the place, and to have hauled it up from Port Augusta would have been far too costly. Here and there in the very big drives they might leave a pillar of sandstone standing, but the size of the dug-out rooms in the town, or some of the underground shops, or the span of the church, showed the wide stretch of roof you could have in rock like this without the slightest fear that the thing was going to come caving in on top of you.

'If you've got to be a miner I guess this is the sort of rock you want,' Nick said.

'Till you tackle it with a pick,' Ernie added feelingly. 'Then you'd sooner have cheese.'

'Can't have it both ways.' Nick ran his hands slowly over the wall.

'You know, this'd be a good spot to try our luck; nice, easy digging.'

'No good unless there's opal here.'

Nick laughed. 'You never know where it is.' He looked about. 'How far to the second shaft?'

Willie squinted and shone his torch up the tunnel leading out of the gallery. 'Not far, I reckon — up there.'

'What about the mullock?'

'That's the beauty of it,' Nick said. 'In here we've got enough room to dump a truck-load — put it in a drive in the sides, or toss it down a deep shaft.'

'What about you, Willie?' Ernie asked. 'What d'you reckon?'

Willie's smile flashed in the candle-light. 'Give it a try, maybe. When we start? Tomorrow?'

'As good a day as any,' Nick said, '—to find a fortune.'

Listening to them Ernie suddenly had an overpowering urge to tell them his secret. It had been gnawing away at

71

him all day, the thought of the double robbery still raw in his mind and the wish for revenge still fierce.

'Listen, you fellows,' he said. 'I'll tell you something.'

Nick turned and paused. 'This'll be good.'

But Willie detected something in Ernie's voice and stood watching him closely. 'What you find?'

Ernie took a packet of biscuits from his pocket and pushed them at Nick. 'Sit down and eat this.' So they sat with their backs to the wall, all three of them, the candles stuck in a heap of loose rock on the floor.

'What did I find?' Ernie said, then, looking at Willie. 'How d'you know I found anything?'

'I reckon,' Willie said laconically.

'Reckon what?'

'Opal.'

Ernie looked at him quizzically. 'My gosh, I don't know how you do it.'

'Got X-ray eyes,' Nick said, his mouth full of biscuit.

'Grandpa Yirri see you that night,' Willie said simply. 'With your pants full.'

'My pockets, you mean?'

'Yes, full up. Must be opal he reckon.'

Ernie was astonished. 'He must have eyes like search-lights. Anyway, it might've been jasper, or bits of potch.'

'Opal, I reckon.' And Willie deferentially took another biscuit from the packet.

So Ernie told them his story: his three weeks of secret digging in the other drive, his discovery of the slide of potch, his strike, and the robbery—first from the mine and then from his own dugout. And to end it, he offered to take them to the spot and show them the hole where the thief had ratted his claim. Only the fine personal details he kept to himself—the date when he'd registered the claim in the first place, the stones he'd kept back, the deal he'd made with Mr Hiramatsu, the bank balance he had. They

72

were things that no one should know but himself.

Willie glanced quickly from side to side of the tunnel as Ernie finished his story. Nick followed his gaze too. There was silence for a while, all three of them realising, it seemed, that figures could be moving through the dark drives underground at any time of the day or night without anyone knowing. And if the thief had followed Ernie before, he could do it again.

'Rotten rats,' Nick said at last in a hushed voice. 'No wonder Mike Buzenskis reckons he'll drop a stick of gelignite on top of anyone he catches poaching his claim.'

'I'd give anything to find out who the dirty weasel was,' Ernie said. 'Anything at all.'

Nick agreed. 'Just to know.'

'Leave signs?' Willie asked.

'Not a thing in the drive—only a great hole, and my water-bag tipped on its side with most of the water gone. Even lost that.'

Nick laughed. He got up slowly and rubbed his back. 'Haven't heard anything since?'

'Not likely. Spent yesterday afternoon asking everyone around our way if they'd seen some dingo heading for the dugout. But not a hope.'

'Make you mad,' Nick said.

'Anyway, keep your ear down close.' Ernie picked up the torch. 'You never know, sometimes you hear things.' He got ready to lead off. 'You too Willie?'

'Sure, Ernie.'

They filed off into the mouth of the tunnel again, crouching low as they entered.

'Can you find your way back into that cave, Ernie, when we want to start digging?' Nick asked.

'Lead you back blindfold,' Ernie boasted.

'That's what it's like now,' Nick complained. 'Hold up that torch in front.'

And so they crawled their way back through the darkness. All round them the rock lay solid and unmoving as it had done for millions of years. If gems worth a king's ransom lay locked in it within six inches of their passing shoulders, they would never know. It was part of the great game of chance. Elusive, unpredictable, shy, the opal hid where searchers least expected it. If they had had eyes that could penetrate like rays through stone and darkness alike, the boys might have seen everything and nothing. All round them, and far out under the plains and hills there might have been cliffs and layers of empty rock, dull, heavy and worthless; but, and more likely, they might have looked on treasure unimaginable—chips and fists and chunks of it, blue, green, and red, lumps like loaves, long narrow fissures of it like yard-long neon lamps shining in the rock, scattered loops and whorls like old sea shells glowing, Aladdin's caves of it burning forever and forever undiscovered even though men probed and drove and laboured within an inch of it.

For that was the way of the opal. Secret, wayward, as patient as the slow and infinite ages by which it had come to be, it waited. But though centuries passed like seconds, millenia like minutes, it burnt ever more clearly and brightly—flame frozen in rock, fire burning in the stone.

Chapter Eight

The next strange change that helped to change the whole direction of Ernie's life happened one evening a few days later. Ernie and his friends had been doing a bit of half-hearted gouging, and Ernie's father had been doing some full-hearted grumbling at Harry. It had reached a head that day with Harry throwing down a kind of challenge: 'Look, Robbie, if you want to work with me, okay, get on with it; and if you don't, then get to blazes out of it and go and look for something else.'

So Robbie Ryan had gone off in a huff to look for something else, which turned out to be another drifter called Dingo Pelt. His real name was Dick Peltz, but his nickname was so universal that no one on the fields would have been able to call him anything else. Robbie had brought Dingo home to tea to discuss business, as he said, which as usual meant a partnership without money and without much interest in hard work.

After tea Robbie and Dingo Pelt and Ernie were all sitting outside the dugout, Ernie leaning back to count the stars in the Southern Cross and Robbie and Dingo trying to make one pipe-full of tobacco last all night. They had decided that they had no capital, that the syndicates were ruining the opal fields for the little men, and that beer was far too dear. As this seemed to cover everything worth talking about they sat for some time in silence.

'By the way,' Dingo Pelt said casually out of the darkness, 'I think I saw that bloke you was asking about the other day.'

Robbie took his pipe out of his mouth in surprise. 'What bloke?'

'The fellow you was looking for.'

'When?'

'Saturday, was it? Archie Palladis told me.'

Robbie thought very deliberately about the problem. 'Saturday,' he said at last, 'I was on my way back from Kingoonya with Harry. And I wasn't looking for anyone.'

Dingo Pelt considered the point but gave up. 'Well, that's what Archie said.'

'Why should I be lookin' for a bloke when I'm not here?'

'Dunno.'

'Archie must have got a touch of the sun.'

'He reckoned this bloke would be looking for you. Or Ernie was it?'

'Bunkum!'

Ernie suddenly sat bolt upright, his face tingling with gooseflesh. 'Where . . . where did you see this bloke?'

'Up the hill back of here.'

'What was he doing?'

'Just looking. I thought maybe he was watching for somebody.'

Ernie was very excited. 'D'you know who it was?'

'Nuh. Big fellow. Thought maybe it was Bubblegut Bistro first, but it wasn't.'

Robbie snorted and laughed. 'Bubblegut! He couldn't walk up here if he tried. Need a winch to haul him up.'

Ernie was impatient of interruptions. 'What then?'

'Nothing. I went down the Flat and never saw him again.'

'You didn't get a better look?'

'Nuh.'

Ernie was bitterly disappointed. 'You didn't see his face?'

'Nuh.'

'Don't remember his clothes or anything?'

'Nuh. Overalls I think. Wouldn't be sure.'

'Hat?'

Dingo Pelt thought carefully. 'Yeaaas. Felt hat, coming to think of it.'

'What time?' Ernie was frustrated and impatient.

'When I saw him?'

'Yes, yes.'

'Early. Sevenish. Bit later, maybe.'

Robbie knocked his pipe on a stone. 'What got you up at that hour?'

Dingo Pelt seemed hurt. 'Always out early. Never miss.'

But Ernie pressed on. 'Where was he when you saw him? Exactly where?'

'Cripes, I don't know.' Dingo Pelt was starting to fidget at all the questions. 'Like I said, up the hill a bit from here.'

Robbie turned on his son. 'What's with all the cross-examining, Ernie? You Sergeant Longnose all of a sudden?'

'No, just wondering.' Ernie was quick to cover up because he knew what his father was like when once he started to get suspicious. So the subject was dropped, although Ernie sat in a ferment for the rest of the night.

The next day he met Willie on the way to the mine as arranged, but there was no sign of Nick. 'Nick sent a message,' Willie said. 'Must help home; no digging today.'

'Blow that,' Ernie said crossly. 'What are we supposed to do?'

Willie seemed ill at ease. 'Tell you what,' he said hesitatingly.

Ernie waited, 'Well?' But that only made him more bashful than ever.

'What is it, Willie?'

'You . . . you got time now? To come with me?'

'Where to?'

'See Grandpa Yirri and Uncle Winelli.'

'What do I want to see th—,' Ernie started to say, but he bit off the rest of the sentence when he saw Willie's face. It said plainly enough that he should keep his ears open and his mouth shut.

They walked across the bare stony ground towards the Reserve, but before they reached it they saw a group of Aborigines noodling on the mullock around an old cut. 'Over here,' Willie said, and led off.

As they neared the cut Ernie could see most of Willie's

relatives—aunts and uncles, cousins and second cousins, even Aunt Merna and her husband. Most of them were working together in a tight group, moving forward slowly, going over the ground methodically for pickings. Their fingers were flicking nimbly, their eyes quick to pick up a tell-tale glint or a streak of colour. Bulldozers were heaven to them because the big machines were so true to their name—bulls let loose in the opal china shop. Inevitably they crunched and smashed as they gouged, no matter how careful the driver and the watchers were. Sometimes valuable pieces were missed altogether, and only came to light years later when the heaps were weathered by wind and rain. Then the noodlers came into their own.

As the boys approached, some of the family dogs—four or five of them—were lolloping about, barking and racing. The whole thing seemed like a picnic. Ernie knew a few of the dogs and called out to them, 'Here Buck; Hullo Yera!' but they only paused for a second in their tracks and barked at him in a half-friendly, half-hostile sort of way. Still, Ernie reckoned, it showed that he wasn't an outsider.

As the crowd moved forwards on to the next set of mullock heaps Willie and Ernie fell in with them. For a minute or two Ernie was a bit self-conscious, like someone butting into a private family outing. But he soon got used to it, and Willie helped to put him at his ease. There was a lot of chatter going on, jokes and jibes and comments, cries of success, cheeky backchat and laughter, and shouts at the dogs. Ernie marvelled at it all. There was a sort of community spirit among them that you could feel very strongly, something he had never known in his father's dour scheme of things, or even among the other white groups he knew. And when someone found a piece of good opal, or a likely looking chip, it immediately belonged to everybody. Something to be shared all around, not hidden in the finder's pocket and guarded with bared teeth.

By and by Ernie noticed that Grandpa Yirri and Uncle Winelli were working on a cut a little apart from the rest of the group, like two wise old hunters discussing the chances of having roast kangaroo for tea. Willie kept looking over at them, as if receiving messages of a special sort. The rest of the Aborigines took no notice of them at all. But Ernie sensed something, and he was right. Presently Willie nudged him and started to move over to Yirri and Winelli. 'Come now,' he said.

They joined the two old Aborigines without saying a word and went on noodling as if the four of them had been doing it together for days. After a while Ernie couldn't stand it any more, so he greeted them both like a new-chum in unfamiliar territory. 'Good-day Grandpa Yirri. Good-day Uncle Winelli.'

They flashed sudden smiles at him and murmured replies, but there wasn't a break in the rhythm of their noodling. Ernie could see that Willie was worried for his sake—embarrassed in case Ernie misunderstood the silence for unfriendliness. So in the end he blurted out an opening; the look in the old men's eyes showed that they understood the impatience of youth. 'Everyone knows that Ernie was robbed.'

Uncle Winelli didn't even look up. 'Plenty fellows robbed—down the mine,' he said.

Willie persevered hesitantly. 'Ernie doesn't know who.'

'Can't catch him, that fellow.'

'Don't know who,' Ernie repeated.

'Plenty police here; much better now,' Uncle Winelli said, referring to the recent police blitz that had cleaned up the fields and got rid of the worst characters—either put them straight in jail or warned them off the fields.

So far Grandpa Yirri hadn't said a thing.

'Someone saw something, I reckon,' said Willie obtusely. 'In the dust-storm, maybe.'

Suddenly Ernie saw what Willie was doing; he was trying to lead them on. Somehow they must have given a hint that they really knew something. A pulse of excitement swept Ernie and seemed to tingle deep inside him somewhere.

'Plenty dust all right,' Uncle Winelli said, and then went off noodling phlegmatically with Grandpa Yirri on the far side of the cut. For a while they probed and picked along the slope of the mullock heap above it.

'Why won't they say?' Ernie asked Willie in a fierce whisper. 'Don't they know?'

Willie shrugged his ragged shoulders. 'Talk later, maybe.'

Ernie almost slipped down the cut in his agitation. 'I can't stand it, Willie; not this sort of talking. Don't they trust me?'

'They think you're a proper fellow, I reckon.'

'Well, ask them if they saw a big man around Bordini's some time; with overalls and a felt hat.'

'Don't talk too much,' Willie cautioned.

Ernie was exasperated. 'Talk too much! I haven't said a thing!'

They all came together again quite naturally at the crest of the knoll. Uncle Winelli was almost touching Ernie's elbow as he bent forward, and Grandpa Yirri was just as close on the other side.

'Plenty opal,' Uncle Winelli said. 'Mister Henderson, he buy; Japan man he buy.'

'And some other man, he steal,' Ernie blurted bluntly.

'Big man, I reckon,' Grandpa Yirri said quickly. 'You know one man—Dobruzza?'

It was so fast and surprising that it slipped over Ernie's head before he was aware of it. And the pronunciation was hard to grasp. To Ernie the sound was meaningless. He turned quickly to ask more questions, but Grandpa Yirri was already moving away with Uncle Winelli towards some deep new bulldozer cuts.

'What did Grandpa mean by all that?' he asked Willie. 'Does he really know something?'

'I reckon,' Willie answered.

'Well, you know him a lot better than I do.'

'Might say again later. Might start again one night.'

'After a drink or two?'

Ernie could have cut out his tongue as soon as he'd said it. He knew Willie respected Grandpa Yirri, and hated it if anyone saw him with cheap wine. Or any other Aborigines, for that matter. Willie's eyes were downcast for a minute. 'Have to see,' he said.

Ernie knew that the matter was closed for the time being. 'What we going to do now?'

Willie looked in the direction of his people. 'I . . . I better be heading home,' he said, 'with the others.'

Ernie understood Willie fairly well. The message was clear enough — he didn't quite belong, so it was time to go their own ways.

'Okay. See you tomorrow, if Nick's ready for work.'

'Be okay I reckon.'

As Ernie headed back towards the town he turned things over and over in his mind. He still felt excited in a strange frustrated sort of way; somewhere on the fields, he was certain, somebody knew who had stolen his opal. A big thief most likely. Strong. In overalls, maybe, and a felt hat. The sort of man who kept away from people, Ernie guessed. Perhaps didn't have a partner at the moment. That was a good point. Men like that were unusual. You couldn't work a claim on your own, so before long people always started asking questions. Of course you could make-do with odd-job labour — drifters, people passing through, cast-offs from other groups.

But nothing took the place of a good partner, one you

could work with, joke with, battle through the hard times with. One you could trust. That was the thing. Trust. When one man was down below and the other up on the hoist, you had to have absolute confidence in each other to share and share alike. There was no place for suspicion, the gnawing fear that if your mate down below struck colour he would fill his pockets secretly with the best pieces before coming up to tell you.

Nothing was sadder than young Mario Spangelli who had been thrown out by his brothers on such a suspicion. He mooched about the place like a lost soul. Outcast. Pariah. Ostracised. And yet he was really innocent. All he'd done was to keep back some of his proper share instead of selling it when prices were low; then, when prices went up, he'd sold. But his family accused him of hiding stuff from the mine in the first place, instead of sharing it. So out he went—for ever.

It was the sort of thing that made Ernie wonder sometimes. Men went mad for money. There was this story the teacher had told them about three men with a bag of gold: while one man went to get some food the other two plotted to kill him in order to get a bigger share. But the man poisoned the food so that he could get all the gold for himself. When he came back his two partners stabbed him to death, but then they ate the food and they died too. So in the end the bag of gold was still there just as it had been from the start, but all three men were dead.

Miners could get like that if they weren't careful. Greedy. Treacherous. You needed to keep things in a proper balance. And the best way was to have a good partner. One you could rely on. Of course, if he broke your trust and took you down, well then maybe you had a right to run him out of town. But there were plenty of decent battlers on the fields who'd done all the right things themselves, only to find that when at last they did strike it rich some hawk had swept down and stolen the lot. Without a trace, sometimes. And often with plenty of suspicion all over the town. That was when there were threats of vengeance with shotguns and long knives. Which brought it round pretty close to full circle—as it was in the teacher's story.

Ernie thought it over. Mixed up in it all somewhere there was the certainty of his own mine and his tin full of opal. And a thief. And himself.

Chapter Nine

School started again a week later and everything seemed to slow down. Ernie, Nick, and Willie had managed to gouge a handful of potch out of the Bordini mine but that, as Ernie said, wasn't worth a crumpet. Perhaps the best result was the discovery of a few more drives and another chamber as big as a room. Sitting in the heat of the wooden classroom Ernie had only one worthwhile thought for the whole day. 'All we have to do is to find a few more openings like that and we can shift the whole school down there. And boy, would that be an improvement.'

Outside, the bare schoolyard shimmered in the February sun. Loose grit, dust, bullety black pebbles and harsh stones lay like furnace waste about to be scooped off as dross or run away as molten slag. Walking over it was an agony on its own— heat and angular edges below to test soles and ankles, grit in the wind to pepper nostrils and eyes, dust to powder clothing and hair. On a bad day it even hung on nose-ridges and eyelashes like fine red flour. Whenever the wind rose, bookwork was hopeless. With the windows and doors closed they all gasped on the point of suffocation; with them open everything was blasted away as if they'd been in the slip-stream of a burning jet.

'Northerlies in summer, southerlies in winter,' the teacher used to say in geography lessons; 'but the dust travels all ways.'

Ernie was in second year secondary. The school had grown so much that it ran classes to the third year beyond the primary. It was called a Special Rural School. Ernie had no idea what the words meant, especially since he'd always thought that 'rural' had something to do with crops and grass and farmers, and he couldn't for the life of him see what was rural about gibbers and stones and hot grit.

The headmaster was Mr Martindale. He taught Ernie's class most of the time, as well as looking after six other teachers, and watching the books, and taking assemblies, and meeting visitors, and straightening things out with the Aboriginal Welfare Officer, and complaining to Adelaide about bad conditions and poor supplies, and giving first aid, and settling arguments. And in the evenings he got the electric light plant going, and organised adult classes, and checked books, and held committee meetings, and occasionally saw his wife.

Ernie formed the opinion that Mr Martindale was a very busy man, and so he liked him all the more for the fact that he still seemed to find time to arrange interesting lessons and check their work and give them a clip under the earhole if they were caught mucking about.

The secondary classes often shared the one room. This brought everyone together—Stan Henderson in the third year, one class ahead; Willie, one class behind, the same as Hoppy Schmidt who'd lost nine months' schooling when he'd taken a header down a mine-shaft and busted up his pelvis; and Nick, and Stefan Buzenskis, and Mario Ratsone whom everyone called Ratso for short.

There were others of course—a dozen or so boys he

84

didn't know so well, and a few girls: Loulla Palladis from the store, Maria Konopas and her sister, and a group of Aboriginal girls. But the numbers dwindled away quickly at the top of the school. Mothers didn't like keeping their daughters on the Fields when they started to grow up, so they packed them off to boarding school if they could afford it, or to relatives in Adelaide where they could finish high school and find a job. It was the same with a lot of the boys. So those who stayed were the ones who were too poor, or whose fathers and mothers weren't sure, or who were waiting for opal strikes, or who said they might move next year but never did, or who had found real freedom on the Fields and swore they would stay there forever.

The first week back was hard for Ernie. It wasn't just that the cookhouse of a classroom seemed worse than ever this February—though they'd been promised a new cool school for as long as he could remember—but somehow he felt lost. He'd been unsettled by the holidays and the mine. Suddenly he'd had a glimpse of the grown-up world, like a glance through a half-open door. Not just the haggling with Mr Hiramatsu or the feel of the new notes against his fingers or the thought of the money in the bank. That was part of it, yes. But there were ugly hints too, of figures in the shadows, and dangers and menaces and threats. And beyond all that was the worry of his father and the limbo of his mother, and the end of his schooldays in sight. Next year he would finish up for sure. Then what? A slushy at the store, or a drifter on the Fields with his father for a partner in a dead-end hole? No future in that. Even Robbie was saying that the small man was finished and machines were taking over.

Ernie spent a lot of time thinking about things like that. Drooping over his desk in the broiling heat, he read only the heading of the chapter on the Industrial Revolution. Out here in the Australian summer he wasn't much interested in English spinning wheels and woollen cloth. So he sat and thought about other things instead. The trouble, he decided, was that you could never find a place where men could just be men—doing things with their hands, with an axe or a pick maybe, and working with whatever there was in the raw natural world. You couldn't find a frontier any more. Not for long anyway, because machines moved in and before long the world was spoiled, and there were too many people, and restrictions had to be made, and the restless ones were up and off again to get away from it all.

But now they were running out of space. Soon there'd be nowhere else to go. The world was closing in everywhere, even here on the opal fields. Just as Ernie's own world was closing in—the boundaries of his boyhood going down, the world of adults ringing him round relentlessly. He sighed.

'Come on, Einstein! You were supposed to have finished Social Studies and started on Maths ten minutes ago.' Mr Martindale pinched his ear and moved off down the aisle.

Ernie hastily got out an exercise book and opened up at a new page. He accidentally leant forward on it while he reached for a pen and left a clear print of his forearm from wrist to elbow across the white sheet. It was like a huge fingerprint done in dirt and perspiration. He examined it with interest. It had little curly squiggles on it where the hair of his arm had disturbed the pattern. He held up his elbow to consider the phenomenon. As well as hair in secret places and a bit of down on his chin he reckoned he now had sproutings on his arms and legs.

'Well done, Ernie. Is that for Art or Mathematics?' Mr Martindale still had a twinkle in his voice, but it was a weary sort of twinkle as if he wanted to say what he was really thinking: 'What's the use! How can you teach in a camp oven?' He was the kind of man who would have built the thought into a bit of private irony. 'Layered Education Dust-cake. Pour one Industrial Revolution over each child and spread between two half-hours of opal-field grit. Use standard daily furnace heat. Carry outside when done at four o'clock and prop up to prevent sagging. Repeat next day.'

In all the vast moon-landscape around them there was one tiny patch of green. Ernie could see it out of the window. It was Mr Martindale's piece of lawn—about a foot square, near the flagpole. As often as possible he watered it with precious little remnants of water that he saved up. Ernie felt that it was a talisman, a kind of symbol that was very important to Mr Martindale. It had a message for him, like Church or the Bible, comforting him with the assurance that there were still green pastures somewhere and maybe even quiet waters where—if he ever got down South again—he would not want. Ernie sincerely hoped the Shepherd would lead Mr Martindale back that way again some day because he deserved it.

Near the Education Department's wooden school buildings rectangular slabs of concrete had been laid down as neatly as if they had been meant for a footpath in Adelaide. But the February sun got to work on them till they shimmered like hotplates, and everyone danced over them instead of walking; they really were hot bricks, even if the children weren't exactly cats. Each building had an enclosed verandah with vertical rows of glass louvres that were supposed to let the air in and keep the rain out, but they had no instructions about the dust. And so, whenever the wind rose, even if the louvres were closed, little flat fountains of dust spurted up between each pane of glass like red diphtheria powder being puffed into children's throats in the old pioneering days. And then it went on into the room in a thick cloud and settled over everything.

The inside of the school was just like the inside of a

school—wooden desks, old ones, a lot of them, and cupboards, and chalkboards, and books with covers curled up at the corners from the heat, and aids and bits of equipment. Except that, because most of the teachers were hard-working and conscientious and aware of all the special problems here, they went out of their way to arrange good programmes and activities, art displays and projects, music and ballads. But there were problems too, plenty of them: fights and resentment among some of the bigger boys—Europeans and Australians and Aborigines—curses and threats, and visits by welfare officers and even by the police.

And so Ernie was tugged all ways at once. He was naturally gentle, almost timid, and avoided trouble whenever he could. Just as his father avoided work. He guessed that he carried a part of his father around with him wherever he went. But part of his mother too, and she'd been a determined woman, quick to stand up for her rights. So when he was finally pushed to the wall perhaps he could fend for himself.

The heat went on for twenty-one days in a row with no sign of a break. The land baked and glistened in the sun, the rocks were like clinker, the sky like brass. By the time the third weekend came around most people's tempers were as raw as gravel-rash. And the nights were almost as bad as the days. The solar still and the motel were the two most popular places—the still for fresh water for washing the outside of the body, twenty gallons a week, and the motel for quenching the inside, as much as a man could drink. Which was often too much.

Soon after noon on the third Saturday there was already a press of bodies inside the motel and a crowd of others spilling along in the shade outside with cans in their hands. And Aborigines with bottles of port or muscat, arguing or laughing, always brushing at the flies.

Ernie and Willie came out of the store with two long cold bottles of lemon squash and squatted down by the wall, watching. A dozen young fellows, part-Aborigines and whites from a station somewhere, were chiacking the locals. They'd been drinking too much already, and the afternoon had hardly started.

'Look at this,' a young fellow with a long nose yelled, picking up a lump of broken brick as big as his fist and scratching it hard with his finger nail for colour. 'Pure opal.'

The others roared and clapped, but Con Andropoulos who was just going inside pushed him away. 'Grow up,' he said crossly.

Longnose turned on him quickly. 'Who are you pushing, sport?' He was still holding the piece of brick and made as if to throw it at Con, but changed his mind and just tossed it undercarm. 'Here, catch!' It struck Con on the shoulder and fell on his foot with a thump. 'Watch it!' Con paused, glaring, and all the talk suddenly stopped, gazes all going one way, air tense. For a second everything was silent, every figure stock still like set pieces in a tableau, with Con and Longnose in the centre. But Con didn't jump forward with his fists up, and slowly everybody relaxed. 'As I said, grow up!' He bent down, picked up the bit of brick, and threw it back.

Longnose felt he had been made to look a fool. 'Pure opal, and he tosses it away,' he said. 'Here, what about you, Blue?' and he threw it over to one of the Aborigines sitting by the door.

Two or three others picked up bits of stone too, and lobbed them back at Longnose. 'Catch, sport! Here, catch!' Some of the watchers joined in, or shouted encouragement. In an instant stones and pieces of brick were going all ways at once, backwards and forwards, high and low, and everyone was yelling 'Catch' or 'Look out' or

89

'Watch your eyebrows.' The distances were getting longer, the throwing harder and the stones bigger. Some of the catchers missed their holds or ducked out of the way, and the stones rolled down the road or bounced up against cars or crashed against walls.

One piece, bigger than a fist, came spinning and leaping towards Ernie and Willie. They both jumped out of the way, and then Willie picked it up and gave a great heave to hurl it back at the fellow who had thrown it. But it veered off line a bit, up, up in a long high arc like a cannon-ball over towards the line of cars and utilities parked at the side of the road.

'Look out!'

Some of the men scattered as they saw it coming. Others who had come out of the motel to see what was going on were pushing and jostling near the door. The stone gathered speed as it came down.

'Look out! Look out!'

Yells of alarm went up everywhere and there was a rush of feet in the dust. Then there was a shattering crash, the hard sharp crack of stone on glass, and the windscreen of a parked utility had a crazy maze of shatter marks all over it like thick spider's web. Then the stone bounced off the broken windscreen, left a dent in the middle of the bonnet, and rolled off towards the motel door.

At the same time there was a roar of anger nearby and a big man rushed from the crowd. He went straight for Willie. Before Ernie or anyone else knew what he was doing he had lunged at Willie with a huge open hand like a lion's paw and struck him on the side of the head. It almost lifted Willie off his feet and sent him sliding down the road on his back in the dust. Blood started running from his nose.

'Damn boong!' yelled the man.

Ernie was appalled. For a second he froze with fright;

90

then he ran forward and tried to lift Willie to his feet. Blood was pouring from his nose now, down over his lips and chin, falling into the dust like drops from a fast-dripping tap. He had Willie halfway on to his feet when the big man took another step forward and swung his hand back menacingly. 'Damn boong!' he repeated. 'You pay for it!'

Ernie cowered. From his angle of view the man towered above him like a titan. But somewhere deep down a primitive instinct leapt up in Ernie, a call to self-defence, a cry of outrage. Stones were lying scattered over the road, one quite close to his right hand. He seized it desperately.

'Back!' he cried. 'Get back!'

David defying Goliath. The man paused, irresolute.

'Back! Or I'll throw it in your face!'

It was so fierce, so tense with fury, that the man seemed momentarily nonplussed.

'You too!' he growled. 'Get the hell out of it.' And he turned and lumbered off to the vehicle to inspect the damage, pushing his way through the group of grown-up Aborigines as he did so—Aunt Merna and Uncle Winelli and a dozen or so of their friends and relatives. There was some shoving and jostling for a minute and it looked as if an ugly brawl was about to break out. If Willie's father or brother had been there it certainly would have. But some of the others calmed things down and gradually tempers cooled. The crowd broke up and some of the drinkers went back inside.

Ernie helped Willie over to the shade and held a rag to his nose until the bleeding stopped.

'Gorilla!' he said. 'Big hairy ape!'

He heard someone calling to the man, giving advice about the broken windscreen, and he half caught the name.

Dobruzza! Dosh Dobruzza!

Chapter Ten

For a while nothing happened on the Fields. Dosh Dobruzza had a new windscreen fitted, and although he swore that he would take it out of Willie's hide if he didn't get the money, nobody took much notice of him. Ernie was more interested in Dobruzza's mine. He'd heard that he didn't have a partner, so he wanted to know whether he was working his claim, whether he'd made any strikes, and especially whether he'd sold any opal.

Stan Henderson might be a help. Because his father was one of the biggest local buyers he kept his ear to the ground and usually knew when any of the big dealers were coming up from Adelaide by plane. He also knew who had parcels to sell, and what kind of prices they wanted. If Dobruzza had something to sell, Ernie was certain that Mr Henderson would know about it. He was also certain that Dobruzza answered Dingo Pelt's description of the fellow who was hanging about the dugout on the day of the opal robbery. And Dobruzza was the name old Grandpa Yirri had muttered on the mullock heap. Ernie was more than sure of that. But there was no evidence to act on, and neither Grandpa Yirri nor Uncle Winelli was willing to say anything more. So for the time being there was nothing to do but wait.

At the beginning of April the worst of the hot weather ended at last, and they had weeks of warm sunshine that made everyone feel much better. Some of the families that had fled south in December began to return, and the tourist buses started to roll again.

'Easter's next weekend,' Nick said to Ernie at school one morning. 'How's about a camp at the Breakaway?'

'That'd be beaut.'

'Con and Harvey are going bush and they reckon they can drop us there on the way.' Nick was talking about his grown-up brothers who were always prospecting and fossicking far out, looking for new ground.

'Who else is coming?'

'Hoppy I reckon, and Willie if you like.'

'How long?'

'Whole of Easter. They can drop us there Thursday night and come back Monday.'

'Wowic!' Ernie flapped his arms like a bird about to take off.

'We've got tents and bunks and gear,' Nick said.

'I'll take the water-bag.'

'We've got a ten-gallon drum.'

'What about tucker?'

'Plenty to pack . . . Mum'll do it for them and me.'

'I'll buy some tins and stuff.'

'We can do some exploring. Beaut place for that.'

Nick was right. The Breakaway was the most beautiful place in the area. It was twenty miles out, a tumbled world of cliff edges, sudden drops and crags of old rock looking down on gullies and dry creek beds. For miles the flat table-tops of the ancient peneplain plunged down to a newer plain below. The hard capping of the old rock ended as suddenly as a wall in places, and then sloped far down in screes and jumbled masses of rock to the land beyond. Out on the plain, dotted like islands here and there, were stray tent hills, last remnants of the older landscape—their flat tops level with the edges of the Breakaway, their strata standing out clearly in coloured bands, their hard crusts ending in the usual sudden drop. And running out from the Breakaway itself, snaking from the bays and inlets of torn rock, were countless dry channels, flood-time watercourses, that meandered on to the plain in crows' feet patterns. There were deeper gashes too, red and ochre and brown, winding out into the distance and growing shallow there and disappearing in vast outwash flats of stunted grass and bushes. Under a dun-coloured haze as far as the eye could see it was a wild, beautiful, lonely world.

'Can't wait,' Ernie said fervently. 'Best place I know.'

In the end Hoppy Schmidt couldn't go because his people were expecting visitors for Easter, so only the three of them— Ernie, Willie and Nick—finished up crouching and bumping about on the back of Con's utility as soon as school ended on Thursday afternoon.

'The three musketeers!' Ernie yelled exuberantly, though he didn't quite know what that meant.

There were two vehicles—Harvey's Landrover as well as the ute—because there was so much junk, according to Nick's brothers, that one couldn't possibly cope on its own. They left the utility at the Breakaway, loaded with the tent, food, water, bunks and blankets, while they went off on their own.

'See you Monday lunch-time,' they said. 'And if anything happens Nick can drive the ute back.' Nick was barely fifteen and he didn't have a licence, but in the Outback you soon learned to look after yourself.

As soon as the Landrover had clattered off into the evening the boys started on the camp.

'Tent about here, I reckon,' Nick said, pointing.

'Be better near the tree,' Ernie said.

'Call that a tree,' Nick laughed. 'Pity we can't camp in that gully down there. Look at those beauties.'

'Break your neck,' Ernie said. 'Especially lumping this tent.' So they settled for a spot near the edge of the Breakaway, in a little dip that was sheltered from the

94

wind, and started to put up the tent. It was tough work because the pegs wouldn't pierce the hard ground and the mallet was too light. In the end they had to use a combination of rocks, pegs and scrawny bits of vegetation to hold the guy ropes down.

'She looks a bit saggy,' Nick said, 'but she'll have to do.'

Willie looked as if he'd much prefer to sleep out in the open air beside the camp fire than trust himself to a canvas cage that was likely to fall down and suffocate them during the night. But he said nothing.

'No need to unload everything,' Ernie said. 'The tucker and water-drum might as well stay up in the ute. Be handier that way.'

'Right,' said Nick. 'I'll bring it up close.'

He parked the utility near the side of the tent and sat for a while looking out over the vast plains below. 'Look at that view,' he called. 'Be something to paint, wouldn't it Willie?'

'Might try,' Willie answered.

They got the fire going, lit a lamp, and cooked up a stew for tea. Slowly the darkness fell, and the same great solitude that Ernie had come to know on the fields began to hem them round. But here it was wider still. Just the three of them. And the stillness of a continent.

Ernie looked at Willie; his dark face was lit by the firelight, immobile, thoughtful. He wondered what Willie was thinking. About the past, maybe, when warriors and hunters camped here on the edge of the Breakaway, or danced a wild corroboree, or carried out secret rites that were part of the heart of his people. Ernie felt the vastness of time crowding in no less than the vastness of distance. Where were they now, Willie's people? Ancestors gone, legends and stories lost, hunting grounds rooted up by bulldozers. The last poor remnants put into a Reserve—

camping in sheds, drinking cheap wine, sleeping in motor bodies.

It was a queer thing, Ernie thought, that had brought him and Willie and Nick together—camping side by side at the end of their own long generations going back for thousands of years. And the future seemed more ominous still.

They woke up early on Friday morning — Willie first, and the others a little while later.

'What you been up to, Willie?' Nick asked as he sat up in his bunk, scratching his head. 'You've been prowling about since dark.'

'Just a look around,' Willie said. 'See how things are.'

'Well, if you're looking for Easter eggs you won't find many here.'

Listening to Nick talking like that. Ernie had a strange twinge of memory. It was the same every year at Easter and Christmas. He never received any eggs or presents now, yet he could remember quite clearly, far back in his early childhood, his mother and father bending over him with bundles and parcels and joining in his laughter and joy.

'Last out gets the breakfast,' Nick called.

They bustled about full of excitement, arguing light-heartedly over jobs and duties, their voices shrill on the clear air.

'We'll take some lunch,' Ernie said, 'and go out exploring all day. Willie can lead the way.'

'Okay,' Willie said.

'You know these parts better than anyone, I reckon.'

'Camp here plenty times,' Willie agreed.

'With your family and friends?'

'Sometimes. Walkabout maybe.'

It was a wonderful day. They ranged for miles up and down the face of the Breakaway, climbing over boulders, exploring deep niches and gullies, scrambling past trees, marvelling at the colour of the rocks, picking up specimens, startling lizards and skinks, feeling as free as eagles as they looked down over vast continents of air. By mid-afternoon they were exhausted and began climbing back to the camp.

'Whew,' Ernie said. 'I could do with a drink and a rest.'

'Good place,' Willie said, beaming. 'Can do more tomorrow.'

'Don't talk about tomorrow. I'm pooped.'

Ernie admired Willie as they sweated their way back up the cliffs of the Breakaway—the way he walked, the easy supple way he moved, the sureness of his feet on treacherous ground. Yet he looked so small and weak. This was Willie's country, Ernie decided; over long ages his people had learned to live in harmony with it, and even though they had been reduced to Reserves and the humpies on the fringes of white settlements, something of their understanding lived on even in a boy like Willie. It seemed natural, therefore, that Willie should lead them back to camp.

'Boy, am I glad to see that tent,' Ernie said as he strained up the last sharp pinch and flung himself down in the shade of the canvas. 'I'm double-pooped.'

'You're pretty poopy all round,' Nick said. 'D'you want a drink?'

'Do I want a drink?' Ernie repeated disgustedly. 'Can't you see I'm perishing?'

'You, Willie?'

'Yes, pretty thirsty too.'

Nick went round to the cabin of the utility to get some drinking mugs. The sun, shining through the windscreen, made it beautifully warm in the afternoon light. 'I've found my spot,' he said. 'You blokes can call me tomorrow.'

And as soon as they'd all had a drink he went straight back to the cabin and curled up on the seat.

For a while Ernie and Willie called out to him but he only grunted, so they gave up. Nor would he budge later on when they'd finished resting and wanted to gather wood for the fire.

'Let the bludger sleep, then,' Ernie said at last. 'We'll get the wood on our own.' And he and Willie went off scouting for sticks, shading their eyes from the sun. They had to go a long way. The country at the top of the Breakaway was windswept and mostly bare. There were acres of small black stones, sun-scorched to look at and as smooth as fire-hardened flint. And beyond that, gibbers and angular chunks of rock, and weather-worn dips and scars. Here and there a few patches of scraggy bush still lived, or spinifex grass, or a morbid tree or two, but there was little enough of wood. So they kept close to the Breakaway where the growth increased, and looked down over the edge searchingly at the trees that thrived in the gullies and waterways.

Suddenly Willie stopped and stood stock still. He nudged towards something with his head but didn't make a sound.

Ernie was slow to stop; he couldn't see a thing.

'What?' he asked in a whisper.

Instead of answering, Willie inched forward stealthily towards a crevice in the rock, pounced suddenly, and hauled out a lizard by the tail. It was thin and tapering, with light brown scales.'

'A Jewy!' yelled Ernie. 'No, a pint-sized goanna.'

'Goanna,' Willie said, nodding agreement, 'We take him back for Nick.'

Ernie screwed up his face. 'Nick won't eat goanna.'

'Needn't eat him. Just for a present.'

'Won't be too keen on that either, I reckon.'

Ernie took the armful of wood they'd gathered, and Willie carried the catch. He held it far out by the tip of its tail, arched and angry, scrabbling at the air with its splayed feet and sharp claws. Once or twice it nearly got a grip on something—the ground or a bush or Ernie's bare leg—and Willie had to jerk him free quickly and hold him up high or he would have been off as quick as a wink.

'Quiet now,' Ernie said unnecessarily as they reached the camp, because Willie was already as quiet as a shadow. 'We'll have to put him in a bag or something. That's going to be a nice lively job.' Then Ernie had a bright new thought and hugged himself with laughter. 'Take him over to the ute,' he whispered in Willie's ear, 'and pop him into the cabin.'

Willie grinned hugely. 'You open the door.'

They crept round to the passenger's side and peeped in. Nick seemed fast asleep behind the driver's wheel, with his legs stretched out towards the far corner under the dashboard somewhere. As softly as he could Ernie turned the handle and eased open the door. It gave a slight squeak but Nick didn't seem to hear. 'Now,' Ernie whispered urgently. 'In with him, quick!'

Willie's job turned out to be easy. The lizard hooked on to the seat in an instant and drew himself in. Then he sat there quite motionless, gazing about with his neck arched up and his eyes beady with alarm.

Ernie closed the door quickly. He slapped Willie on the back and they both doubled up with silent glee, leaping about outside the tent in self-congratulation.

'There'll be some fun in a second,' Ernie gloated, hugging his elbows to his chest at last. 'Wait till Nick gets a gander at his bed-mate.'

'Hope the goanna won't hurt him,' Willie said. 'Still very frightened.'

'They'll both be very frightened then, believe me,' Ernie answered, still hooting and laughing. 'Nick hates lizards. Or anything creepy, with claws and things.'

Willie laughed too. 'Won't like him then. Got pretty sharp toes.' They waited for a while, putting more wood on the fire.

'Think I'll wake him up a bit,' Ernie said. 'They're getting too matey.' And he picked up a couple of black pebbles and tossed them against the cabin. They clunked sharply—one on the bonnet and the other on the windscreen.

'Better watch the windscreen,' Willie said feelingly.

'I'm not like some blokes when it comes to smashing 'em.' Ernie had hardly finished saying it when he would have given anything to call the words back. But it was too late; Willie looked away bashfully and Ernie could see that he was hurt.

'Don't take any notice of me,' he said. 'Just shooting off as usual.' But it wasn't much of an apology and only left an awkwardness between them.

A minute or two went by and there was still no response from Nick. Ernie was about to throw another pebble when they heard him stirring and yawning. He seemed to be stretching his arms or scratching.

They waited expectantly. 'Hasn't seen him yet,' Willie whispered.

Ernie was impatient. 'Taking his time about it. Don't tell me the thing is mugging up to him.'

'Might be hiding on the floor.'

Ernie's curiosity couldn't stand it any longer. 'Think I'll go and take a look.'

But he'd only taken two steps forward when pandemonium broke loose in the cabin. They saw Nick's leg

100

with a boot on the end of it fling up against the roof, followed by a chaos of knees, feet, hands and elbows going all ways at once. At the same time there were yells of 'Phoo,' 'Arrhh,' 'Grrrrh,' and 'Get OUT!' while the whole cabin was heaving and shaking. The little goanna must have had the same thoughts about Nick as he had about it, because they could glimpse it momentarily flashing from the top of the seat to the dashboard and then back again via the steering wheel or Nick's head.

It was at the height of this commotion that Nick must have kicked off the hand-brake accidentally without even noticing it. He was probably too busy fending off the monster with one hand and searching for the door-handle with the other. Willie was the first to sense danger.

'Ernie!' he yelled. 'The ute, look! It's moving!'

Although the slope leading to the edge of the Breakaway was very gentle, Nick was banging about so much inside the ute that he'd set it moving. Once under way it gathered speed quickly. Ernie leapt forward, reaching for the door. 'Look out!' he yelled frantically. 'Nick! Quick!'

It was no more than ten or fifteen feet to the edge of the Breakaway. Realising that he had no chance of getting into the cabin in time, Ernie spun round, seized a big stone from the fireplace, and tried to fling it down in front of the back wheel. The stone was very hot and it burnt his hand badly, but he hardly felt the pain. For a second it looked as if the plan might work, but the wheel just struck the edge of the stone, tilted it up, and squeezed it out sideways like a pip.

'Jump!' Ernie roared at the top of his voice, dragging desperately at the door-handle. 'For God's sake, jump!'

It was too late. The utility gained speed astonishingly over the last few feet and Ernie had to leap aside frantically himself to avoid being carried over the edge with it. The two front wheels reached the lip of the cliff together, suddenly found nothing but air beneath them, and dipped forwards sharply. The chassis came down hard on the edge and for a second it seemed that the ute might balance there precariously like a see-saw; but then momentum carried the whole vehicle catapulting forward. With Nick still trapped in the cabin it went over almost in slow motion, turning a complete somersault and coming down with a sickening crash thirty feet below where the slope met the sheer drop of the capping rock. There it rolled over and over and over for hundreds of feet down the steep incline, slid on its side for some distance among stones and bushes, and finally came to rest in the rocky gully below.

'Oh God!' Ernie cried out. 'Oh my God!'

Willie moved with lightning speed. He raced to a break in the cliff where erosion had cut out a kind of notch, and was climbing down backwards, hands and feet, before Ernie had even moved. Then he leapt down on to the talus slope below and went bounding and sliding, leaping over rocks and ducking round trees and boulders, until he reached the utility. There he wrenched at the door to try to get it open. He managed it just as Ernie joined him, panting and heaving.

'Is he . . . Is he all right?' Ernie could hardly get the words out.

Nick was lying spreadeagled in the wrecked cabin. He seemed to be unconscious. There was a trickle of blood from a cut on his forehead, and more blood at the corners of his mouth.

'Try . . . try to get him out,' Ernie said. 'Careful!'

They lifted and pulled him as best they could, and finally had him lying on a patch of flat stony ground a few feet away. Nick groaned once as they lifted him, but they didn't know whether this was good or bad. Ernie looked up at Willie. 'He's alive.'

'Nick,' he said, bending forward and watching intently. 'It's me—Ernie.'

'Hurt pretty bad,' Willie said.

A terrible feeling of helplessness came over them now. They looked at one another miserably but neither said what both were thinking. That they were responsible. That it wouldn't have happened if they hadn't started fooling about. And that they were twenty miles from home without hope of help.

'Better get him up to the camp,' Willie said at last. 'Be night time soon.'

Ernie looked up at the scarp despairingly. 'How?' he asked.

'Make a stretcher.' Willie gazed round quickly. The gully was already in deep shadow, but the edges of the Breakaway to the left and right still flared in the sun. 'Get very cold down here. And dark too.' He stood up. 'You watch Nicky. I'll get blankets and things.'

He ran nimbly up the slope, his bare feet again moving fast and sure-footed over rocks and logs. A minute or two later Ernie saw him clamber up the last steep pinch and disappear over the edge. Ernie was still gazing up at the high beetling ledge above him when there was a groan beside him. He looked down quickly. Nick was stirring. A few moments later he groaned again and moved his feet as if in pain. Then he opened his eyes.

Ernie felt a pulse of hope and leant down over Nick. 'It's Ernie, Nick. Ernie Ryan.'

A queer look of surprise and recognition wavered in Nick's eyes. 'Hullo Ernie,' he said vaguely. His voice was blurred and he still didn't know where he was. Ernie bent so low over him that it would have been impossible for Nick's gaze to be anything but blurred. 'How you feeling, Nick?'

Nick was searching for something mentally, trying to

make sense of things. 'I...I...What's up?'

The hope in Ernie's heart began to give place to fear. But he tried to look self-possessed. 'Lie still, mate,' he said.

But Nick persisted, puckering up his brow in a puzzled sort of way. 'What...what happened?'

'You went over the edge in the ute.' Ernie decided it wasn't any good trying to hide the thing.

Nick groaned again, but then seemed to grasp Ernie's message. He made a quick move to sit up, but as he did so he caught his breath and cried out in agony.

'Lie still,' Ernie said sternly. He wiped some of the blood from Nick's mouth and face, and tried to push a smooth stone under his head. Then he remembered the wrecked utility lying nearby and ran over to find something softer for a pillow. Everything was in a shocking mess. The water-drum and the food boxes had been thrown out on the way down and were lying all over the place, scattered or smashed. Most of the water had leaked out of the drum, but he stood it upright hastily, hoping to salvage a drop or two in case they needed it. He was still scratching about when Willie came back with blankets and Nick's camp stretcher. Luckily the stretcher was one with springs underneath and round bracing rods on the sides, so all they had to do to turn it into a field stretcher was to lash sapling sticks to the sides and cut back the canvas to expose the ends as handles. Then they lifted Nick on board and wrapped him in blankets.

For a minute, as he looked up at the scarp above, Ernie quailed. But it had to be done. Nick was still conscious and seemed to have a vague notion of what was going on.

'You okay?' Ernie asked.

'Okay,' he answered feebly.

'Won't be a feather-bed ride.'

'Sorry about that.' Nick smiled wanly.

'Do the best we can.'

'She'll be right.'

Willie stepped into place at the back of the stretcher, ready to lift. 'You want to lead first?' he said to Ernie.

'That's the heavy end you've got. Want to swap?'

'Later, maybe.'

Ernie took his place and bent to get a grip. 'Ready?'

'Ready.'

'Okay, lift!'

They both moved together and the stretcher came up horizontally.

'Walk!' Ernie stepped forward uncertainly and Willie followed. And so their Easter agony began, the bearing of their cross up their own particular mountain.

For they hadn't gone five yards before they realised the monstrous task ahead of them. It wasn't just the climb, though that was bad enough. It was the uneven surface, the wild jumble of rocks and loose stones they had to cross. When Ernie stepped up on to something, even though it was only six inches higher than the rest, the stretcher immediately tilted back, throwing extra weight on to Willie. To prevent Nick from slipping Willie tried to lift his end higher so that the stretcher lay level again, but the weight bore down painfully on his wrists and shoulders. Then Ernie would step down for a yard or so and the stretcher would tilt forward until the next obstacle sent the front up again. And so it went on. Worse still, Willie couldn't see where he was going. He had a vague idea from Ernie's movements ahead of him when something was coming up but he couldn't see what it was, so half the time he blundered into it with his bare shins, barking the skin, slipping off sharp edges of stone, stumbling, falling forward and saving himself at the last minute with his knees.

They hadn't gone ten yards before they were both panting and staggering about like old men, gritting their teeth at each new pain. It was a little easier for Ernie, but the uneven pressure pushed and pulled him ruthlessly too, sometimes threatening to force him forward on to his knees, sometimes catching him off-guard and tugging back so violently that he nearly overbalanced and toppled back on the stretcher, Nick and all.

They struggled on for a few minutes longer and then Ernie called a halt. 'Put her down, Willie! Put her down!' He wondered how much longer Willie would have gone on without a word. Though his knees were bleeding and his nostrils were wide with exertion he hadn't made a sound.

'Hard,' was all he said now, resting with his hands on his knees and his chest heaving. 'Very hard.'

'Torture,' Ernie said succinctly. He stumbled round to the back of the stretcher. 'Give you a spell back here; you take the front for a bit.'

Nick tried to interpose once or twice from the stretcher, but they both told him to lie still and keep quiet. They did it so decisively and firmly that poor Nick looked forlorn and friendless.

Ernie and Willie lined up again like horses in their shafts.

'Ready?'

'Yes, ready.'

'Lift.'

And they were off again, stamping and staggering, weaving and heaving and straining, making a yard, a foot, an inch in their desperate kind of tug-of-war.

For now they were approaching the steep steely slope that led up in a sharpening angle until it joined the cliff under the base of the capping rock. The tilt of the stretcher increased and Ernie found the weight bearing back on him constantly, relentlessly, until it was too much for anyone to bear and he had to give up.

'Down!' he said breathlessly. 'Down!'

They waited again, panting more than ever, frightened in their hearts at what they knew to be ahead, aware of their growing exhaustion. And there were other problems too.

'Nick's starting to slip on the stretcher,' Ernie said. 'The slope's too steep.'

'And he'll slip more, further up.'

'Nothing to brace his feet on. And even if there was, it wouldn't be any good for him; only hurt him inside more than ever.'

'Ought to tie him down.'

'Like those cliff-rescue blokes.'

'We ought to, I reckon.'

'Yes, but with what?'

'Rope'd do.'

'What rope?' Ernie looked up at Willie, partly in impatience, partly in weariness.

'Could cut a guy rope from the tent.'

Ernie stood up in admiration. 'Willie, you're a genius.'

'I'll get it.' And Willie was off up the steep slope with the same quick movements as before.

Nick had been lying half conscious most of the time, his eyes closed and the blood still oozing slowly on to the bandage they'd tied around his head. Now and then, especially when they jerked the stretcher sharply, he moaned in pain. But now he was lying quite still at Ernie's feet, his arms at his sides and his face startlingly pale in the deepening shadow.

Willie came back with two lengths of thin rope and they set about securing Nick to the stretcher.

'Can't tie it around his chest,' Ernie said. 'Not the way he is. Might hurt him bad.'

So they brought a couple of lengths high under his armpits, passed them under the stretcher, through the metal brackets on the sides, and finally hitched them firmly around the front handles.

'Should stop him from slipping very much,' Ernie said.

'I reckon.'

'Take a piece around his knees and ankles too. Keep him firm.'

'Won't slide so much.'

'We hope.'

Ernie looked down at their handiwork. 'You'd think he was a burglar, all trussed up like that.'

'Call the police?' Willie asked with a half-smile. But it was too serious for jokes.

Ernie bent down, speaking quietly to Nick. 'It'll be better now, Nick. Ride easier.'

Nick didn't open his eyes, but he must have heard. 'She'll be right,' he said, so softly that it was barely audible.

Willie looked round at the darkening gloom in the gully. 'Better start again, I reckon.'

Ernie was inwardly conscious that he was wasting time now, just putting it off. 'All right,' he said. 'Give her another go.'

Though the steepness was cruel, the track improved a little underfoot as they rose higher. The big boulders and chunks of rock fell away behind them and only the smaller pebbles and stones that could cling to the sharp slope remained. But these were bad enough, slipping like screes as soon as the weight of the stretcher bore down on one or other of the carriers, so that it was the old story of two steps forward and one step back. Ernie's hands, especially the one he had burnt on the hot stone from the fire, had gone beyond pain now. From the armpits to the last joints of his fingers, crying out against the pressure of the handles that were trying to force them open, it was all one long fire, universal, all-pervading. Differences in feeling only came when one part of his suffering body more than another took some new blow—heel kicking heel, or elbow jolted down against stone, or stretcher handle driven cruelly into the soft flesh of his groin as the weight came back on him suddenly down the fierce incline.

'Stop here!' It was the first time Willie had taken the initiative, but Ernie was too far gone even to notice. 'Must look around for the best way.' And, despite his exhaustion, Willie went scrambling forwards to spy out the track.

Ernie lay on his stomach like a wounded soldier, his body pressed against the stretcher to prevent it from sliding back down the slope again. Behind him stretched the long bitter way of their coming, the tumultuous route from the wreck. He could make out the dull shine of the metal in the last of the daylight. It wasn't far really—seventy or eight yards perhaps—but it seemed like a Golgotha. And above them was the final cross, the last agony that might go beyond endurance.

Ernie lifted his head from his arm and strained his neck back to look up and judge the height of the cliff. It was the thickness of the capping rock, the hard crust that formed all breakaways, capped all tent hills and mesas and buttes and tabletops around the world. And the thickness of this one? Twenty or thirty feet perhaps. Not much in itself, but at the end of a haul like this? With a stretcher? Of course, where it was vertical it was impossible no matter what the thickness. Five feet would have crippled them unless they'd been a Cliff Rescue Squad with rope and block and tackle. But Willie was searching out a sloping route, the best one there was within reach of the camp. And he would know.

His return was so silent that he was squatting by Ernie's side before he knew.

'That way's best.' He beckoned up the pipe ahead where eroding flash-floods had cut out the niche they'd used to get down. 'Nothing else around here. Unless we want to go miles.'

Ernie grovelled to his feet. He wondered whether Nick was unconscious again because he hadn't made a sound or movement since the last stop. Perhaps it was just as well. How could they have coped with it if he had been writhing in agony the whole way up.

Ernie went round to the front of the stretcher. 'What d'you think?' he said softly to Willie. 'Can we make it?'

'Can try.'

'Okay then. I'll take the back again. But we'll have to make it bit by bit.'

It was the only way. They lifted, made a yard, and put down; lifted, made a foot, and put down. They were reaching the crucial point. For twenty feet the climb, even the best that Willie could find, was so steep that the stretcher sloped like a ladder against a wall. Nick almost hung there suspended by the ropes around his shoulders. And his two carriers—Willie on hands and bleeding knees above, Ernie lying forwards against the slope below — heaved like sailors in unison: 'One, two, three, heave! One, two, three, heave!' A foot, an inch, nothing. Sometimes even a slip backwards amid anguished clutching and grabbing, fingers like hooks scrabbling the rock-face blindly for a hold, toes scourging the loose scree behind. And in their minds' eyes always the fearful spectacle of the whole cavalcade, stretcher and all, falling backwards out of control, pinwheeling down head over heels in agony and destruction back towards the spot they'd started from.

'One, two, three, heave!' The gains were getting smaller and smaller each time, the effort more impossible. Ernie was vaguely aware of the sunset nearby like a vast blood-stain, spreading over the sky and the plain and the rocks of the cliff, moving into the bruises of his body, his torn fingers and lacerated arms, flowing over Willie too, and

Nick's face on the stretcher. A kind of universal suffering that covered the world—agony the colour of crimson that swallowed up his body and rolled it around like a shell in a sea of pain.

'One, two, three, heave!' It was Willie who was calling the sea-chanty now, with Ernie pushing at the capstan while someone bludgeoned him with marlin-spikes and stuck hot skewers under his finger-nails. 'One, two, three, heave!' 'One, two, three, heave!' For a minute Ernie had the strangest view of the world at eye-level, as if he was a snail or a cricket with the whole plain around him flowing up to his chin, a floor for his eye-ball. Then the stretcher seemed to take off on its own, moving forward like a sledge, and he was left on his hands and knees playing bears like a baby.

They had reached the top! Willie was dragging the stretcher forward into the tent, and Ernie was crawling along the top of the Breakaway. Everything was bathed in twilight, a strange unnatural light that seemed more of the earth than the sky. Until they all got into the tent which was dark with shadows and exhaustion. And there they lay, all three of them, silent and unmoving while the twilight drained away outside and the stars came out above them and shone down coldly on the tent, and on the twisted metal lying at the bottom of the Breakaway, and over the whole vast brooding land beyond.

Chapter Eleven

Their strength came back quickly. Willie climbed down the Breakaway perilously yet once more in the starlight and returned with an armful of food—tins of soup, stewed fruit, packets of biscuits, bread, butter in a jar, Vegemite. Then he stoked up the fire, heated some soup, and ladled some out for Ernie.

'Good stuff,' he said. 'Make you jump.'

He had some ready for Nick too, who was wide awake now, but he coughed and shook his head. There was still blood at the corners of his mouth. Ernie crawled over to him and felt his forehead. 'How you doing, Nick?'

Nick tried to smile but he looked pale and miserable.

'Don't worry sport,' Ernie said encouragingly. 'You'll be all right.'

'Yea, I'll be all right.'

'Where does it hurt?'

Nick pressed his side and winced. 'Can't breathe properly. Catches me something awful when I try to take a deep breath.'

'Don't try then.'

'And I feel woozy in the head.' He felt his forehead gingerly. 'Got a lump like an egg.'

'We're short of'em,' Ernie said. 'Need some for breakfast.'

The thought of the wreck suddenly brought fear into Nick's eyes. 'What are we going to tell Con and Harvey—about the ute? They'll kill me when they find out.'

'They'll be too glad that you're okay to worry about that.'

They were silent for a long time. 'Pain bad, Nick?' Willie asked after a while.

'Bit bad.'

'When you breathe, eh?'

'When I breathe big.'

'Don't breathe big, then.'

'I'm trying not to.'

'Some pills'd help,' Ernie said. 'For the pain. And for your head too.'

'There are some in the ute,' Nick said. 'Con always keeps 'em. In the glove box.'

'I'll go.' Willie was out of the tent in an instant, making the perilous descent for the fifth time. They didn't even hear his footfalls outside, though they were waiting silently and listening for his return. Then the tent flap opened and he was back. 'This it?' he asked. 'In a tube thing?'

'Veganin,' Ernie said. 'They'll do.'

He unscrewed the lid. 'Better have two.' So they played Doctor Ryan and Doctor Winowie at the frontier aid-post for a minute, and when they'd dosed up their patient they tucked him in with blankets and told him to go to sleep for the night. For a while they sat watching but when he dozed off Ernie turned down the lamp and he and Willie went outside.

The land lay huge and silent under the faint starlight. Ernie felt very lonely, and the little tent on the edge of the Breakaway made him feel lonelier still.

'Nicky's hurt,' Willie said quietly. 'Someone'll have to do something.'

'Yes,' Ernie said, shifting uncomfortably.

There was a pause. 'What can we do, though?'

'Can't wait till Monday,' Willie said.

Ernie knew he was right. It was still only Friday—Good

113

Friday night. And Con and Harvey wouldn't be back till Monday, maybe late at that. Too long to leave Nick lying in the tent without help.

'He's hurt inside,' Ernie said. 'Worst part, inside.'

'I reckon,' Willie agreed.

'Busted ribs, maybe.'

'Something like that.'

'There was a fellow in hospital fell down a mine,' Ernie explained, 'and broke three ribs. Couldn't breathe properly, couldn't laugh even.'

'Like Nick,' Willie said.

'Or cough neither.'

'No.'

'Expect it hurt something awful.'

'Yes.'

'When it's bad a broken rib goes into a lung,' Ernie said. 'Like a puncture. Then you cough up blood.'

'It's bad, then.'

'That's real bad.'

They were silent again, miserably aware of their isolation, their helplessness.

'It's twenty miles,' Ernie said. 'We couldn't carry him that far.'

'He might die,' Willie said. 'He might by Monday.'

Ernie felt his sore hands where the hot stone had burnt the skin. A big red patch was throbbing with pain.

'How far d'you reckon we'd get?' he asked. 'In a day, say?'

Willie paused, thinking. 'Ten mile I reckon. Resting and carrying.'

'Getting close to the outliers then. One or two new mines. Might run into a fellow.'

'Might, I reckon.'

There was silence again.

'Won't be too hot tomorrow,' Ernie said after a while.

114

'Not much. Nice day, I reckon.'

'Unless the wind comes up.'

'Could be wind.'

'Be wicked with wind; dust in your face.'

'Hope for the best.'

Ernie looked round and shuddered. He couldn't help it; the shudder seemed to come out of the air of its own accord as if someone had taken him by the shoulders and shaken him hard. 'Better start early, then.'

'Early is better.'

Ernie stumbled towards the tent. 'Tell you what,' he said. 'We'll go to bed now and get a good sleep. When we wake up, we'll go.'

'Best way, that way.'

Ernie touched his burnt hand. 'Wish I had a bit of ointment or something for this hand.'

'Hurts bad, eh?'

'Hurts something terrible. Burns always hurt like that.'

'Burns are bad.'

They crept in beside Nick and lay down in their clothes as they were. And in spite of the pain and anxiety and exhaustion they slowly dozed off. Outside, the night ringed them round; three boys, three lives in the tent like sparks in the darkness. And beyond them endlessly the starlit horizon rising and dipping, and the vast plains flowing away into distance. It was as if the land was waiting. Waiting for something in the universal cycle; a message perhaps. Something to measure man by.

It was still dark when Ernie and Willie set out next morning. The night breeze was cold and they shivered as they rubbed the gooseflesh on their bare arms and legs. They wrapped a few things in a towel and put the parcel on the stretcher beside Nick. Ernie took the water-bag down from the ridgepole of the tent and hooked it on to the stretcher handle. Then they bent, Willie in front, Ernie behind.

'Okay?'

'Okay.'

'Lift!'

At first it seemed easy going. Their memories were still raw from yesterday's agonising climb up the Breakaway, and so the straightforward carry on the level track almost came as a pleasant surprise.

'Not bad, is it?' Ernie said.

'Not bad.'

'Reckon we can keep this up for a while.'

'Reckon.'

They plodded on in silence for a while.

'Not a bad day, d'you reckon, Willie?'

'Not bad.'

'Stay like this?'

'Might stay. Wind later, maybe.'

'Hope not. Hate wind.'

The track wound vaguely through the stones and gibbers in the half light of dawn. It was firm underfoot with a few angular bits of rock lying here and there to turn their ankles painfully if they happened to tread on them unaware. But otherwise it was easy enough. They walked with a good swing after a while, the stretcher rising and falling slightly with the rhythm of their movement. The ache in their arms came on slowly, dragging down at their armpits, nagging at their muscles and wrists, but it had the distant quality of a mild toothache at first so they carried on. It was something you were aware of without being able to do anything about.

In addition to the ache in his shoulders Ernie had to contend with the burn on his hand. He'd wrapped an old rag around it before they'd set out, but the pressure of the stretcher handle came through the cloth and rubbed cruelly against the inflamed patch on the ball of his palm.

116

'Want a change?' Ernie asked at last.

'If you like.'

'Okay. Put her down.'

Neither of them admitted how grateful he was to stand up free and light without that dragging weight. Ernie swung his arms and reached high at the air to stretch his shoulders. 'Whew,' he said. 'Makes you feel you've got a lump in your back.'

'Hurts your hands,' said Willie.

'Hurts everything.'

Willie looked back across the brown jumble of stones, the track wavering and losing itself among them. The edge of the Breakaway stood out clearly like a dark line where it dipped away or changed direction. It seemed a long way off and they were pleased at what they'd managed at the first carry, but when they turned to the front again and saw the distant horizon with the endless plain ahead, their confidence drained away.

'Ready for another go?'

'Ready.'

'Okay. Lift!'

The day was coming in quickly now, sweeping from the east over the low hills and the undulations of the plains, brightening around them minute by minute. The landscape ahead began to stand out bold and clear, the track before them winding and dipping, losing itself and reappearing far off like a faint line on a map. It was the way of their agony.

They didn't go so far this time, a few hundred yards perhaps, before Ernie asked for a halt. The handles of the stretcher were chafing badly now, especially against the burnt skin, and the pain was getting unbearable.

'I've got to wrap something thicker around my hand,' he said. 'Wish I had a padded glove.' Willie fossicked but there was nothing.

'Haven't got anything.'

'Got to find something. Go mad otherwise.'

In the end they tore a strip off the towel they'd wrapped their provisions in and wound it around the handle.

'Okay. Give it another try.'

'Change ends again?'

'If you like.'

Willie took the front once more, and Ernie the back.

'Ready?'

'Okay.'

'Lift!'

From his position at the back Ernie couldn't help looking down at Nick lying on the stretcher in front of him. It was hard to hide his fear from himself. Nick was flushed and feverish and he kept tossing his head from side to side on the pillow. His eyes were open most of the time but they seemed to be staring hard and unnaturally, and his talk, when he spoke to them, was broken and queer.

The sun came up like a blast of trumpets just then. The first rays shot across the plain quite suddenly in long, low shafts of red and gold that caught them in the eyes. Colour leapt out of the land—yellow and brown and ochre—and the air quivered with light. The cold seemed to drain out of the breeze and the bare flesh on their faces, arms and legs seemed suddenly touched with warmth.

'Sun's nice,' Ernie said.

'Nice now.'

'Long as it doesn't get too hot.'

'Hope it doesn't.'

They plodded on, the pain in their backs and arms rising steadily like a beaker filling, till they couldn't stand it any more.

'Put her down, Willie.'

'Right.'

'Whew!'

This time they sat down beside the stretcher, their elbows on their knees, heads hanging forward. It was beginning to be the nightmare they'd always known it would be.

'How far d'you reckon we've come?'

'Done a fair bit. Mile maybe.'

'D'you reckon a mile?'

'Pretty close to a mile.'

Willie looked up from under his lashes at the immensity ahead.

'Long way yet.'

'Say that again.'

'Better start maybe.'

Ernie got wearily to his feet. 'I guess.' He bent over Nick and spoke quietly. 'How you feeling, mate?'

Nick rolled his head on the pillow and opened his eyes. 'Had an accident,' he said thickly. 'Went over the cliff.'

Ernie caught a glimpse of Willie's face, bent down low over Nick beside his own. There was anguish in his look. With a rush Ernie was aware of something: Willie was afraid and self-condemned. He was blaming himself for everything, for catching the goanna in the first place and for putting it in the cabin. If it hadn't been for him the whole thing would never have happened—utility over the cliff, smashed to pieces, Nick badly hurt, dying maybe, and now this impossible journey. Ernie felt a sudden companionship for Willie.

'Don't worry,' he said quietly. 'Nick'll be all right.'

Willie looked at him miserably. 'He's hurt bad.'

'All my fault,' Ernie said. 'My idea to put the thing into the cabin in the first place.'

'I caught him,' Willie said simply.

'And I egged you on. If it hadn't been for me the ute'd still be okay. And Nick too.'

Willie went round to the front of the stretcher. 'Better start,' he said.

A strange bond was starting to form between them. Born out of self-blame and fear and a desperate need for hope and reassurance, it began to bind their lives in common suffering. Willie, full-blood and black, born in the barren squalor that had been thrust on his people by greed and inhumanity; Ernie, strange white mixture, victim of his parents' selfishness, failing son of a failure, drifting towards drift. Both brought together in a shared calamity and the pain of their common burden. The stretcher was like a penance that yoked them together—from Willie's aching arms to Ernie's, hands to handles and handles to hands. With Nick's life in between.

'Put her down! Put her down!'

Ernie stood up again, wringing his burnt hand. Blisters were forming there now, in spite of the towel, and the burnt skin was raw. They had covered another stretch, a couple of hundred yards perhaps, but their strength was going.

'Don't know how long we can keep this up.'

'Hard now.'

'Getting worse each time.'

The breeze was freshening a little from the southeast—not hot, not uncomfortable in itself, but it was beginning to be strong enough to raise little puffs and skirls of dust about their legs, and sometimes even into their faces.

'Blasted wind,' Ernie said. 'Doesn't want to get much stronger.'

'Getting stronger, I reckon.'

'At that rate we'll be picking gibbers out of our eyes.'

'Hope not.'

'Always blowing up here. Don't know why.'

'Better start again,' Willie said. 'Long way to go.'

'Better, I guess.'

'I'll take this end.'

'Okay.'

'Ready?'

'Ready.'

'Lift!'

Pitiful little cavalcade trooping along on the vastness of the plain. Flies on a continent. Ernie and Willie were sinking into a kind of torpor now, a mechanical motion, foot before foot, step after step, dogged, persevering, relentless, unending. The rest between each carry was like a reward, a moment of peace between pain, a beacon to struggle on to and reach. After an hour or so, Ernie made it an organised goal.

'We'll go as far as that washaway,' he said, indicating a channel across the track a few hundred yards further on. 'And then we'll have a rest.'

'Fair way,' Willie said.

'Got to do it, though. Can't give up till we get there.'

It was a long hard haul, like steps up a mountain. By the time they reached the goal Ernie's muscles were raging and his hand was on fire. But he couldn't back down, no matter how much he wanted to suggest it; it would have been like breaking a promise, letting themselves down.

Willie now began to emerge as the stronger of the two. Not physically, but in spirit. He never complained, never wanted to cut a carry short. If Ernie dawdled over a reststop or fiddled with a handle, or wanted to empty grit from his boots or tie up his laces, Willie was first to suggest moving again.

'Better start now. Still a long way yet.'

They set themselves shorter stints now, a hundred yards perhaps, to a rock, a bush, a stick. But even then it was hard enough, each step getting slower and slower, sixty-seven, sixty-eight, sixty-nine, and still a long way to go to the rest-stop, their hands burning and their arms pulling out of their sockets. The sun was rolling around the sky and moving in and out of their heads like a red ball, until they blinked hard and steadied it down in its place again. Their knees were starting to sag too, and the track they made wasn't straight any more, but wandered from side to side, sometimes jerkily, sometimes in a big sweep sideways. And then they only had ten yards to go, five yards, and they forced their feet on doggedly over every one of them till they both said, 'Down!' and lowered the stretcher so fast that it bumped hard on the ground and Nick groaned as it jarred his body.

'But the stop was so short, a second or two it seemed; then Willie was saying, 'Better start now, it's a long way yet,' and so they stood in the shafts again like horses waiting for the driver to say, 'Get up.'

'Ready?'

'Okay.'

'Lift.'

When they'd gone three or four miles—they couldn't guess which—they called a long halt and had biscuits and water.

'What time d'you reckon it is?' Ernie asked, sitting with his head down and his torn hands drooping from his knees.

Willie looked at the sun and rolled his gaze round the far still plain. 'Nine o'clock maybe.'

Ernie was beginning to fear the rest of the day. He had doubts in himself, in his hands and feet, in his body's strength to carry. 'D'you reckon we can do it?'

'Can try,' said Willie. 'Better be making a start.'

The struggle to reach noon grew harder and the climb up the thousand-step mountain grew steeper and steeper. Out of their stupor things came and went, breaks they welcomed, even mishaps to stop the torture for a minute and give them a rest without breaking a promise to themselves—the water-bag tangling up their staggering legs, or food coming unwrapped, or the blankets slipping off from the stretcher. Once Ernie's foot blundered into a hole and the sudden strain on the stretcher cracked the wood on the sides. For a while it looked as if Nick would be bent in a bow, doubled up in agony for the rest of the trip, but Willie found a bit of bush and lashed it up tight like a splint and they were ready for marching again.

Ernie almost regretted Willie's first aid. If he hadn't succeeded they could have given up in good faith and rested all day. Nick, on the stretcher, had phases that came and went, good patches and bad. Sometimes he was sweaty and feverish, sometimes cool and clear when he talked sense and apologised for all the bother and trouble. 'Sorry,' he'd say. 'Why don't you take a rest?' And Ernie, toiling hopelessly up the foothills of the next mountain, ground his teeth to stop himself from calling to Willie to listen to what Nick wanted.

Once a cloud of dust moved along the horizon—a streaming yellow patch the size of a fist—and they both stopped agog, mouths open like the Ancient Mariner looking at the ghost ship before he bit his arm and sucked the blood to get his voice working. But whatever it was—a truck or a utility in a hurry—it kept going away from them until the cloud slowly disappeared. Men with business of their own, no doubt, and no ideas about two boys carrying a cross far out on the plain.

And twice they saw willy-willies like decoys far to the east—tall, brown columns spiralling up, spun pillars of visible air as graceful as gossamer. But they had nothing to do with humans. There was no help there, any more than there was water in the lakes of mirage that were starting to shimmer and dance to the left and right, and down in the hollow ahead—miles of clear rippling water to run into and bathe in, to plunge over their faces and blistered hands and cool the burning of their arms and feet. It was all real, for their eyes to see, but as empty as a dream.

After another hour or two Ernie was getting ready to tell Willie that he couldn't go on. It wouldn't be so bad, he said to himself, because Willie would know about the burn on his hand, and the blisters. And he would understand why they had to stop here for the rest of the day. He had lost count of the steps up the mountain. But just then they came up to the next marker-rock without Ernie even knowing, and Willie called, 'Down.' And they dropped the stretcher and fell down beside it in the dust.

After a while they took some bread and puddled it thick with dollops of jam, and washed it down with water from the snout of the water-bag. So that, after the rest, Ernie didn't think he should tell Willie about giving up, at least not for a little while. So when Willie called he went over to the shafts as usual like a good old horse.

'Ready?'

'Okay.'

'Lift!'

And on they staggered up the next impossible mountain and down the slope of the afternoon. Before long Ernie was doing sums in his head and leaving the landmarks to Willie. His sums were about distance and time: how many steps in a chain or a mile, how many seconds to a yard, how many miles in an hour. But the units kept slipping away and getting mixed up with one another, so the answers were nonsense. He was really trying to find out how far they'd gone—eight miles, nine miles, ten miles—so that he could tell Willie when he asked him to give up. He also had something to say about how they would have to camp for the night, because they hadn't brought the tent, or the lamp, or any of their other things. Not even any matches, not that they'd find wood out here for a fire. So it

124

was going to be a hard night ahead if they didn't sit down soon to work it out—sleeping on the stony ground without blankets or campfire. Unless Nick died and they used his blanket instead.

'Down,' said Willie, because they'd reached the next goal. And they dropped the stretcher and crawled down beside it on their knees.

It was on the next lap that Ernie was going to talk to Willie about giving up. His own legs weren't walking straight any more, and neither were Willie's. He could see that because he was at the back this time and Willie was leading all over the place in front, staggering about like his Aunt Merna when she was drunk. His head was down too, his eyes staring at the ground in front of him instead of looking ahead to see where he was going. Ernie had a very clear thought for a second. 'Willie's cooked,' he said to himself. 'He's cooked all over, but he won't give up.' Ernie wondered how a small fellow like Willie could keep going like that; it must have been a penance, a punishment of himself for having hurt Nick.

But in the middle of this idea there was a roaring noise which Ernie first thought must be in his head, but it was really in a cloud of dust beside them. And he heard Willie saying, 'Down! Down, Ernie!' and he thought to himself, Willie's given up at last. So he put the stretcher down and was amazed to find big Kurt Muller there, a miner from the Eight Mile, and one of his partners in a shirt with checked patterns on it.

'Vot's zis? Vot's going on here?' Kurt was saying.

'Vos dere a accident, den?' his partner asked.

'So ho? Ve better be getting dem back to d'hospital.'

And in a maze of dust and noise and utter exhaustion Ernie was being bundled about in the back of a ute, with Nick on the stretcher beside him, and Willie sitting by the tail-gate holding the blankets down.

Then the sisters from the hospital were suddenly there, coming out of the door and telling the men to carry Nick carefully. They took Ernie and Willie in too, and bathed their hands and put bandages around them, and then made both of them lie down in the cool and rest. There were voices about, and radio messages: orders from the Flying Doctor, and words like 'concussion' and 'haemorrhage,' 'exposure' and 'exhaustion'.

And finally, as his strength and his senses started to come back again, Ernie heard words of praise from the sisters for what he and Willie had done, and sobs from Nick's mother, and looks of amazement from his father and all the men.

'Nick's father even seemed to forgive them for wrecking the ute. 'Ten miles,' he said. 'Would you believe that?'

'Ten miles,' the sister echoed.

'Robbie Ryan's lad.'

'Well he's got guts.'

'And that Aboriginal boy. Young Willie.'

'Nothing to him; skinny as a whip-stick.'

'Wouldn't think he had it in him.'

But when Ernie looked round, Willie had gone off home. To the Reserve. To sleep on the floor.

Ernie got up to go too. 'I'm all right,' he told the sister. 'I'll have a sleep.'

As he went out he was glad he hadn't asked Willie to give up, hadn't asked him to break a promise he'd given to himself. But he had been so close to asking it; so close. He wondered whether Willie had really been close to asking it too.

Chapter Twelve

Nick was back at school after three or four weeks. He'd had concussion, two broken ribs, a cut on his head, and lacerations inside his mouth, probably from his own teeth. The story of Willie's and Ernie's marathon march with the improvised stretcher was published in the papers down South and reported on the radio news. Robbie Ryan was overjoyed at his son's sudden importance, not least because it brought him a dozen or more free drinks from well-wishers who slapped him on the back and toasted him 'for having such a fine lad'.

But all this only made Ernie more restless. The Easter accident had shaken him deeply—not just the destruction of the utility, though that had frightened him half to death, and not the injuries to Nick, though these at first had filled him with terror. It was the glimpse he had had of something beyond himself. Strange insights were stirring in him, especially about Willie: the links between his own life and Willie's, the nature of his father's place on the one hand and of Willie's father's on the other, and the whole vast confused future for all of them.

For while people toasted Robbie Ryan on the strength of his son's exploit, nobody mentioned Willie—nobody except Mr Martindale who called a school assembly after the Easter break and spoke briefly about the incident. It was a double-edged comment: about foresight and carelessness, presence of mind and panic, weakness and courage. But at the end he praised Willie Winowie and Ernie Ryan for their tremendous endurance. 'There must have been lots of times when they felt they had to give up,' he said, looking at them curiously, 'but they didn't. And that's something worthwhile. It helps you to look at yourself without being ashamed of what you see.'

Ernie wanted to go out to Mr Martindale there and then and tell him that *he* had wanted to give up, but that Willie hadn't. But Mr Martindale was dismissing the assembly by then and the moment was lost. Still, it nagged him to see Willie forgotten, to see him going off on his own after school, back to the Reserve, to the tin shed without a chimney. And he wondered what he and Willie would be doing at this time next year.

Nick had only been back a week or two when the May holidays started. 'What are you doin' next week?' Ernie asked as they all jostled out of the schoolyard gate on the last day.

'Dunno,' Nick said.

Ernie looked sideways at him. 'What about a camp out at . . .'

'Not on your Nellie.' Nick cut him short even before he'd finished. They walked on in silence. 'What about you?' Nick asked.

'Nothing much. Noodling maybe.'

They walked across the apron of small angular stones that lay over the ground like a scree between the school and the motel. A tourist bus came roaring down the Alice Springs road towards them, pouring out a dustcloud like a crop-duster.

'Indians,' said Nick.

'Mobs of 'em.'

The bus roared across the flat stretch towards the town and slowed down as it approached the motel corner. As it passed them the passengers stared from behind the glass windows with big flat eyes. They looked tired and dried-out, like packed kippers.

'Come and watch 'em,' Nick said. 'Be good for a laugh.'

They ran across the road and turned the corner just as the bus pulled up in front of the motel. Two other buses that had come in earlier in the day from Adelaide were standing nearby.

'Invasion,' Ernie said.

'Be the same all this month—school holidays and that.' Nick flicked the flies from his face. 'They're pooped, this lot.'

The driver had opened the door and the passengers were disembarking slowly. The seemed to carry the whole five hundred bone-shaking miles from Alice Springs with them as they stepped down on to the dusty street. Some of the older ones had trouble straightening themselves up and waddled about on bent knees.

Willie came out of the store just as Ernie and Nick walked up, and all three of them stood watching the tourists milling about at the motel entrance. Ever since the stretcher incident at Easter there had been a quiet bond between the three of them—something they felt but had no need to mention. They were so busy watching the unloading that they didn't notice another group of tourists from a previous bus come up behind them, until a woman in a ridiculous floppy hat suddenly popped herself in front of them with a camera. 'You three boys,' she said fussily, 'just stand right there while I get a picture.'

She squinted at them through the view-finder.

'Come in a bit closer together,' she said, still squinting. 'The one on the right, turn sideways towards the others.'

'Yuk to this lot,' Nick said under his breath. 'Who does she reckon she is?'

The woman lowered her camera and bustled forward. 'I know what's wrong, it's the balance,' she said. 'The black one should be in the middle.' She pointed at Willie and Ernie. 'Change places you two.' She stepped back again and squinted. 'That's better. Hold it now. Smile.' The shutter clicked. 'One more now. Don't slouch; stand up straight.'

A man standing nearby in a khaki safari suit, a Tyrolean hat and huge sunglasses laughed approvingly. 'You're a real photographer now, Verna,' he said. 'But you'd better watch out that they don't charge you twenty cents each. Especially the Aboriginal.'

The Floppy Hat clicked her tongue as well as the shutter. 'Not down here,' she said, 'they're civilised.' She squinted and clicked again. 'This'll be a good slide,' she added without drawing breath. 'I'll use it to show assimilation.' She walked forward, the man tagging behind. 'Now, you boys, I'd like to get a few details about you,' she said. 'Your ages, names, where you live, how long you . . .'

But it was too much for Nick who'd been fidgeting uncomfortably ever since she'd started. 'Ahr, belt up,' he blurted out. Then, turning sharply, he muttered, 'Come on, let's get out of this,' to the others and strode off.

The woman wobbled her wattles and glared after them in anger and disgust. 'Well!' she said, outraged. 'If that's the way children behave up here I wonder what the schoolteachers are doing. And the parents too; they ought to be washing out their mouths with soap and water.'

Nick was striding ahead angrily with the others at his heels. 'Crazy old packet,' he said. 'Ought to keep her locked up.' They were approaching the chapel when Nick suddenly paused. 'Blazes, here's another lot.'

A small crowd was gathered near the entrance to Mosha Manton's jewellery workshop. Mosha had come out into the open because he couldn't accommodate everyone underground and, sensing some good sales, was busily demonstrating how to make a doublet or triplet. 'See,' he said eagerly, 'I take a dop-stick with a thin piece of opal cemented to it. The opal is of high quality but it is very thin — so thin that it might break or crack if I used it for a brooch or an ear-ring. So I polish it on the revolving wheel or lap.' He paused to let the name sink in. 'That's why I'm a lapidary.'

There was a murmur among the crowd as some of them recognised the word. Mosha cracked his next weak joke on schedule. 'I tarry with a lap,' he said. 'I always have my lap close to my lap.' The crowd tittered obligingly. He held up and tilted a piece of opal that shone and shot its colour at them in the afternoon light. 'Now, I take a beautiful piece like this which might otherwise be lost, and I cement it on to a stronger background, like this.' He worked skilfully to demonstrate the point.

'What's the background made of?' asked a voice.

'Dark potch, or inferior opal. Even black glass if you like. It doesn't matter much because the opal is the only part you see.'

'So the doublet is inferior?'

'The *opal* isn't inferior. It's a hundred per cent pure gemstone. Only the backing is inferior. And that doesn't matter.'

Mosha was a good craftsman, and an even better salesman. He held up a doublet. 'There you are. A beautiful doublet. A sandwich, with potch below, cement in the middle, and lovely gem opal on top. Anyone would be proud to wear it to Government House.' He gathered up his things. 'Now, if any of you would like to come inside I can show you various lines for sale.'

'What's a triplet?' asked the voice again.

'Ask the matron at the maternity hospital,' called a smart Alec.

'Same idea, but with a dome of clear crystal or quartz above the opal layer. Gives protection and improves the appearance.'

'An opal hamburger,' said the smart Alec.

Mosha shuffled ahead among the jostling group. 'This way.' They looked like sheep being yarded into the funnel of a race.

'Who'll buy my pretty flowers,' said a cynical old traveller at the back, turning away. He saw the three boys watching curiously and approached them.

'Good day,' he said. 'Watching the tourists?'

Ernie shuffled slightly. 'Just going past.'

'What d'you think of'em, eh?'

The boys wondered what to make of him. He didn't seem to fit in with the others.

'There are a lot coming through now,' Nick said noncommittally.

'Mobs of'em,' the stranger agreed. 'Mobs and mobs of'em.' He took out a pipe with a long straight stem as stiff as a spike. 'And I'll tell you something,' he said, filling the pipe with tobacco, 'it's only the beginning. It's a trickle. But the flood's coming.' He searched his pockets for matches. 'Three buses here today, twenty-three tomorrow.'

'It's good for the town, I guess,' said Ernie.

The stranger got his pipe going and looked at Ernie sharply. 'You think so?'

'They reckon.'

'Who reckon?'

'Everybody, just about.'

'Well, I'll tell you something, then. It's bad for the town. Very bad. Horrible.'

Ernie was sorry that he'd said the wrong thing. He always liked to be pleasant and agreeable, and since the visitor felt so strongly about it he would have been quite happy to reverse his own opinion and say that he agreed with him. But it was too late for that.

'They'll ruin your town,' the stranger said. 'Thousands of 'em. Tens of thousands of 'em. In buses and cars and planes and dune buggies and caravans and junky old bombs. Tearing through the place without really giving a damn. With full bellies and empty heads. Throwing out rubbish, littering the place with tins and bottles, chopping down any last tree they can find and shooting any last kangaroo, painting their names on the rocks, kicking up hell's delight.'

He pulled at his pipe vigorously to get it drawing.

'And as for you,' he said, pointing at Willie with the stem, 'keep away from 'em every minute you can. Because they'll treat you like dirt, or coddle you like a poodle, or line you up for pictures like a bear in a circus. And they'll kill your self-respect. Just as their fathers and grandfathers have for a hundred years.'

Nick and Ernie were still puzzled. 'You don't like tourists much,' Nick said quizzically. 'But they bring money in, especially when it's winter down South.'

'What a price to pay,' said the stranger. 'Have you been to Ayers Rock lately?' he asked suddenly, 'or Alice Springs or Chambers Gorge or any other place up that way?'

'Been to Alice Springs and that,' Ernie answered. 'But not to Ayers Rock.'

'Don't go,' said the stranger vehemently. 'Don't go.' Then he smoked sadly for a while as if observing a minute's silence. 'That beautiful, lonely, sacred place,' he said at last. 'Desecrated for ever. Destroyed. With motels and signs and oil drums and empty beer cans. Soon they'll have neon lights and juke boxes.'

Ernie was beginning to understand the bee their queer visitor had in his bonnet.

'They even wanted to put a chair-lift up Ayers Rock.' He looked at the three of them incredulously. 'Can you understand the mentality of a man who would want to do a thing like that?' He puffed at his pipe again. 'They ought to ban all tourists and put a bomb under every tourist

133

bureau. Because you can guarantee that if there is a beautiful, natural, wonderful thing somewhere, then someone will want to make money out of it.'

'You sure don't like tourists.' Nick felt he had to say something.

'Up at Chambers Gorge,' the stranger continued, 'they behave like animals. Jostling and elbowing to see the sun for a couple of minutes. Made me sick to watch.'

He searched about for more matches. 'Same in every place. Hopping in and out of their buses like jack-in-the-boxes. Click, click, click with cameras, and that's that. Back on board again; let's get rolling, driver. Don't see a thing. Look at it, maybe, but don't see it. No understanding, no hearts or minds. Just mass-produced elephants, trampling over everything.'

He struck a match and puffed again. 'Places like that should be protected from people.' His pipe was going nicely now. 'Real trouble is that there are a damn sight too many people in the world. Too much breeding. They're pouring everywhere like a flood—even up here. And there's always some Charlie who wants to make money; more and more money, faster and faster. So he brings in more people to work for him, and machines and what not. Till the heart's torn out of the place and everything's ruined.'

Ernie had at last formed the question he'd been wanting to ask for a long time. 'But aren't you a tourist yourself?'

The stranger looked at him cunningly and laughed. 'I'm a special kind of tourist,' he said. 'I'm travelling all over Australia with tourists on purpose. Been doing it for more than a year.'

'Why?'

'So that I can write a book about it.'

'Write a book?'

'Yes. Showing the damage and destruction they do. And

boy, have I got some material.'

There was a commotion at the front door of the dugout as some of the crowd began to emerge. 'Here they come,' he said. 'I'd better admire the treasures they've bought.' And still sucking his pipe he went off to join his fellow travellers. After a few steps he turned and called back in a loud whisper: 'Looks like thunder. Hope we all get bogged to our bottoms.'

'Queer nut,' Nick said. 'Halfway round the bend, I reckon.'

'Always crazy coots about somewhere,' Ernie said.

'Might be sense,' Willie said suddenly, 'something he's saying.'

They both looked at him strangely. 'Sure,' said Ernie.

Nick kicked up the dust deliberately as they moved on. 'Might be something in what he says.'

The tourists had all left the dugout and were straggling up the slope back to the motel.

'What we going to do now?' Nick asked.

'I better go, I think,' Willie said. And he set off towards the Reserve as simply as if he was going home to the suburbs to watch television after school.

Nick and Ernie watched him go. They were aware of something they couldn't express. Even for them Willie's world was different. They stood uncertainly for a minute.

'Where you heading now?' Nick asked.

'Dunno. Home I guess.'

'Father home?'

'No. He's camping out at the Ten Mile for a few days.'

'What you going to do, then?'

'Nothing.'

'Why don't you come home with us? Mum says you can stay the night any time.'

'Be all right, d'you reckon?'

''Course it's all right.'

'If you say.'

'There's a barbecue on at Hendersons tonight; we're all going, so you can come too.'

'You sure?'

'Sure I'm sure. Come on.'

Mrs Andropoulos welcomed Ernie as Nick had said she would. She also sent a message over to Mrs Henderson's to say that he would be coming to the barbecue with them, but not to worry because they would be bringing extra meat.

The barbecue was a birthday party for Mr Henderson. Ernie's eyes goggled at the preparations when Stan took him through the dugout with Nick: mountains of meat, loaves of bread built up into a small haystack, flagons of sauce, cheese, nuts, cake and coffee. To say nothing of a brewery of beer and seas of savouries.

'Some party, looks like,' Nick said to Stan Henderson. 'How many coming?'

'A hundred or so.'

'Moses.'

It was the first time Ernie had really seen the inside of the Henderson dugout. He was open-mouthed. Tiles and carpets on the floors, electric light from a private generating plant, two huge refrigerators, stereo-players, luxurious bedrooms, expensive furniture, even a bathroom and stainless kitchen sink—although the waste water from both had to be caught and pumped out.

'Some place,' Ernie said to Nick on the side. 'Underground palace.'

Nick rolled his eyes. His own home was neat and pleasant enough, but it looked like a shack compared with this. 'Shows what happens when you hit the jackpot. Opal does it.'

The guests began to arrive and the noise of laughter and greeting grew. Lights had been strung up outside and tres-

136

tles and benches stood ready by the barbecue. It was a
calm night with a heavily overcast sky. 'Good weather for a
barbecue,' said Harry Driscoll from the Miners Store. 'No
wind, and nice and cool.'

'Might rain,' George Andropoulos answered, laughing.

'Rain! Only rains on the 29th of February—every second leap year.'

Before long the chops and sausages were sizzling might-
ily. The huge supplies of meat, bread, sauce and salt were
ferried out from the kitchen, and the beer was let loose in a
frothing torrent. Soon people were milling about the barbecue like animals at a feed trough, holding out slabs of
buttered bread, licking fatty thumbs and burnt fingers,
holding up glasses of beer, and singing 'Happy Birthday,'
or 'For he's a jolly good fellow.' A hundred voices were
talking, all at once, laughing and shouting to friends
twenty yards away; and a hundred people were brandish-
ing bottles, rushing at dogs that threatened to make off
with the sausages, and spilling beer, tomato sauce, butter
or chops down their shirt-fronts. Stan led Nick and Ernie
in and out among the revellers, munching as they went,
helping themselves whenever they darted past the tables.

Yet with all this excitement and good food Ernie was far
from happy. There were too many people for one thing,
and there was far too much noise. He remembered the
strange tourist and his warning about numbers. Once,
when he walked far beyond the circle of light and left the
enormous dancing shadows of the revellers behind him, he
couldn't help looking out over the dark crouching landscape towards the Reserve where he knew Willie would be
lying down on the ground with a dirty blanket around his
shoulders and most likely an empty stomach too. He heard
the sound of coughing and retching nearby where someone
who had eaten too much and drunk too fast was doubled
up excruciatingly for his folly. The noise and the smell

offended Ernie and he moved away by himself again. It was a crazy world where some people had so much that they killed themselves with over-eating, and others died from having nothing.

'Lightning!' he heard a woman's voice say above the din of the party. A distant stab of light ran like a silver-red slit down a foot of the distant sky and was swallowed up in an instant.

'Where?'

'Over there.'

'Imagination.'

'No it wasn't. You just watch.'

They waited for a moment or two, watching carefully.

'There it is again.'

'So it is.'

'And another. They're getting angrier.'

'Storm coming, maybe.'

A rumble of thunder reached them, like distant gunfire. Most of the celebrators stopped their antics to watch the lightning. 'Ooh, look at that.' A flash like a dragon's tongue a mile long blazed down the western sky. It was gone instantly, but the night was now so dark that the flash seemed to be printed on it in front of everyone's eyes.

'Coming up fast,' said George. 'Maybe it *is* going to rain.'

'Be a dry storm,' Hugh Driscoll said portentously as if he had a personal hot line to Jupiter Pluvius.

'As long as *you're* not dry,' someone shouted. 'Have another beer.'

The revellers resumed their eating and drinking, and the din of laughter rose again. But not for long. A few minutes later Hugh went to lift a bottle from the table but dropped it with a yell as a tremendous bolt of lightning came straight down from above and struck the ground nearby with a shattering thunderclap. White fire seemed to fizz about their feet, and for a second they were blinded and deafened.

'Donner und Blitzen!' said Kurt Muller shakily.

'Hughie's in a temper,' a voice yelled.

'Not me,' answered Hugh Driscoll. 'I'll go quietly.'

'Better hurry up,' Mrs Henderson called. 'Finish those chops, somebody, or they'll all be . . .'

Another tremendous flash, as white as naphtha, printed out everyone's figure like a photographic negative, and simultaneously the roar of the thunderclap went echoing around Post Office Hill. Ernie had been about to grab another chop as Mrs Henderson had suggested. He jumped like a colt and collided with Nick who was blinking and thumping his ears. 'Let's get out of this,' Nick yelled, still deafened temporarily. 'Come down to Stan's room.'

A woman's high-pitched voice cut him off shrilly. 'Rain! I felt a drop of rain.'

Everyone paused. 'Listen.'

They were like animals, like horses poised for alarm, heads held high, ears cocked, nostrils wide. They sensed something, a rare phenomenon abroad in the night. The darkness bristled.

'Listen!'

'What's that noise?'

'It's rain! It's a rainstorm!' Hugh Driscoll's voice roared his disbelief, as if his landline to the heavens had just come tumbling down. But the others were still transfixed, women with faces up and eyes big like startled kangaroos.

It was a fast rushing sound, a sound of big wings in the air.

'Go for your lives,' Hugh yelled. 'Get these things inside.' Ernie and Nick ran to help Stan shift cakes and savouries, but it was too late. The rain-storm struck like a wall of water.

Nobody on the opal fields would have seen anything like it in twenty years—not even those who had lived in the South. One or two, perhaps, who had come from Darwin and seen a real monsoon on the rampage might have run through a downpour such as this. It left everybody helpless. Some scattered off left and right towards their own dugouts, one or two ran to utilities or cars, and many stampeded down into the Hendersons' porch.

Within minutes the fields were awash. Water started streaming off the knolls and slopes, tumbling into bulldozer cuts and trenches, flooding the flats, turning dust into sludge. Instant mud. The fleeing celebrators had barely reached the shelter of the dugout when Mrs Henderson was already crying out to her husband.

'The shovel! Get the shovel, quick! It's starting to come inside.' The entrance had been excavated like a small cutting which sloped back towards the door, and now the water was charging down the slope like a mill-race.

'Quick! Quick!' Mrs Henderson shrieked. 'It'll get inside and ruin the carpets.'

She might as well have shouted to the mountains. Amid cries of panic from the refugees who were busy taking off their shoes and puddling about in bare feet, the water swirled muddily across the sitting-room floor and started pouring into the kitchen and bedrooms in an irresistible tide.

'We'll all be drowned down here,' said George Andropoulos. 'The dugout'll fill up and we'll be snuffed out.'

'Don't say that!' Mrs Henderson was almost hysterical.

Outside, the cloud-burst continued to roar, plunging down thousands of tons of water, pummelling the plains like someone flailing the land with knouts and truncheons.

'Lift up the rugs and bedspreads,' wailed Mrs Henderson. 'And the fridge, and the stereogram and everything

140

else on the floor.' Men and women rushed about frantically, but it was already too late; everything was in a fearful mess by now—lapped by dirty water, streaked with mud from the hands of the helpful. Mrs Henderson was distraught. 'It's awful! It's awful! What are we going to do?'

At last the deluge began to ease off and the furious cataract at the front door died away slowly to a red-brown trickle. But the damage was done forever. There was a foot of water throughout the dugout and the carpets were utterly ruined. Years later visitors were to wonder why all the walls were eaten out like a recessed frieze for a foot or more above the floor, and were to laugh politely every time Mr Henderson answered 'Rain—it's worse than bush-rats or bandicoots. Loves to get its teeth into the walls.'

As soon as the rain had stopped, most of the revellers rushed back to their own places. The barbecue outside the Hendersons' was a shambles—everything drenched or washed away except for a few forlorn sausages curled up ridiculously on the hot-plate. Even the dogs had fled before the flood.

Nick's parents hurried off too, making sympathetic clicking noises as they left, and calling Ernie. They had a torrid time of it on the way home, stumbling about in the dark, slipping in the mud and falling headlong into unsuspected lakes, but they reached their front door at last and ran inside. All was well. Their entrance sloped uphill and the water had dashed past, all except a puddle that had found its way under the cowling on the ventilation shaft and dribbled down from the ceiling of the sitting-room.

Ernie spent the night in Nick's room, but the following morning he excused himself as soon as he could and set out for his own miserable cave in the hillside. All around him the fields were emerging again: people working like disturbed ants, digging and shovelling at their entrances, hanging out sodden articles, pushing out bogged vehicles.

Rain was a rare surprise at any time, but a flood happened once in a lifetime.

There was a sense of outrage abroad, of unfair play. The water had come secretively into many dugouts when the inmates were already asleep, like a burglar on tip-toe. The first inkling they'd had 'was a sudden chilling of the buttocks as the water reached the bottom of the bunk, or a kind of electric shock when they'd accidentally drooped a hand over the side in their sleep. Ernie could feel the sense of upset as he hurried along.

There were unexpected swimming pools everywhere, and he hoped for a few warm days while they were still deep enough to use. As he neared his own dugout he started to worry more and more about it — his spare clothes, school books, food that could have been ruined. He leant forward as he pressed up the last incline and was panting hard when he finally reached the entrance. He was about to brush aside the wet hessian screen when it suddenly parted and a man almost collided with him. It was his father.

'Dad!'

'Where the devil have *you* been?'

'When?'

'Last night.'

'At Nick's place.'

His father seemed relieved. 'Nick's place? Then why the blazes didn't you let me know? Had me half dying of fright.'

'How could I let you know?'

His father seemed utterly unreasonable all of a sudden. 'You could've left a note.'

'But you've never worried before. I've been a week, two weeks even, all on my own. I could've been dead and you wouldn't have known.'

Ernie seemed to have hit home, but it only made his

father angrier. 'That's just it,' he said. 'What *have* you been up to, I'd like to know?'

'When?'

'When I've been away.'

Ernie was uneasy and mistrustful. 'Nothing. Why?'

'Oho!' his father crowed. 'Nothing you reckon.' He seized Ernie roughly by the nape of the neck and pushed him through the curtains into the body of the dugout. 'Then what's this?' He snatched up something and flourished it in front of Ernie's nose. 'What's this, I'd like to know.'

Ernie's eyes were still trying to adjust to the gloom and he peered in puzzlement.

'Well?'

With a leap of the heart he saw what it was. A bank pass-book. *His* pass-book.

'Dad, that's mine! Give it back, dad!'

His father was coldly furious. 'Not on your bloody life!'

He grabbed Ernie by the arm so hard that the pain made him wince. 'Where'd you get it?'

Silence.

'Come on, lad. Where'd you get it?'

Still silence.

A great roar from his father then, a shouting voice loud enough to carry halfway down to the Flat. 'There's over a thousand dollars in this here pass-book, and I want to know how it got there.'

Ernie's lips twitched, half from the pain in his arm, half from fear and anger that his secret had been discovered. But still he said nothing.

'Look, boy, I'll break your arm. I'll take you to the police, straight to Sergeant Brogan.'

Ernie was standing like a cowed dog, like an animal being beaten, with his shoulders stooped and knees bent. Only his eyes moved. He could see what had happened—

143

junk shifted about, beds moved from the walls. The flood had made everything damp and his father had started cleaning up. And found the pass-book.

'If you don't tell me how you got this money in ten seconds I'll belt the living daylights out of you.'

Still silence.

'You didn't steal it, did you? You're not ratting other people's claims?'

The accusation was like the jab of a pin, a needle under the nail.

'No! No!'

'How then?'

'It's mine.' Ernie was close to tears with the pain and the torture of the questioning. 'It's mine I tell you.' He finally gave way in a rush of words. 'It's mine. I mined it. In a proper lease. I found a good pocket. Gem opal it was. Thousands of dollars' worth. Ten thousand even. But someone ratted the claim during the night, and then stole my whole packet from here too, out of the dugout. Except that lot. And that's the truth.'

His father released his arm and stared incredulously from Ernie to the bank book. 'You *mined* it? You struck colour? A thousand dollars' worth?'

'Ten thousand.'

His father gaped. 'Ten . . . ten . . .'

'And I reckon I know who stole it.'

The thought of the theft of so much money momentarily infuriated Robbie Ryan in a different direction. 'Blazes, what couldn't I have done with that.'

They both stood silent. 'Pinched it out of here—out of this dugout?' his father repeated.

'Yes. One morning.'

'In *daylight*?'

The enormity of the whole thing, the extent of the loss, was sweeping his father; frustration at the thoughts of such

144

riches snatched narrowly from his grip. He turned on Ernie again.

'Why didn't you tell me, boy? Why the devil didn't you tell me?'

'Because you weren't here!' There was spirit in Ernie's reply.

'After I came back, then?'

'It was too late then.'

His father made an angry movement and for a terrifying second Ernie thought he was going to beat him about the head with his fist. But he checked himself and turned away.

'Well, a thousand dollars is better than nothing,' he said. 'It'll just pay the debts at the store.'

Ernie looked at him aghast and gave a great cry. 'No! No, dad!'

His father pushed him aside. 'Don't be stupid. What sense is there having all this lying in the bank when we've got a thousand dollars owing at the store.'

'But it's *mine*, dad! It's *mine*! I found it. Please, dad, don't take it.' He flung himself at his father, clutching him around the legs, weeping and shouting. 'Please, dad! Oh, please! Don't take my money!'

His father kicked him off cruelly. 'Get away!' He stepped back a yard. 'You're still a kid. What d'you want with a thousand dollars! To hoard it up? Is that it? You're just like your mother.'

Ernie was lying half-raised on one elbow, sobbing and yelling. 'But it's mine, dad! It's ... it's my money. You ... you can't take my money.'

'Oh, can't I!'

'I won't sign! I won't sign!'

'Don't worry about that! I'll get it. You're just a kid.'

'No.... No, dad! You mustn't take it. It's not yours! It's my money.'

His father turned away impatiently.

'Please! Please dad!'

'Stop your snivelling! Get up! Go on, get up!'

Ernie got slowly to his feet, wiping his eyes with the ball of his hand. His chest was still heaving with sobs. And then suddenly a great fury surged over him, something more intense than he had ever felt before.

'Give it to me!' he yelled, leaping at his father and snatching at the pass-book. 'Give it to me! You *thief*!'

He got his fingers on the book and lunged back so violently that he wrenched it out of his father's hand. Then he leapt for the doorway. But before he could escape, his father recovered enough to thrust out one foot, tripping him up and sending him sprawling on his stomach. He tried to get up again but he was too slow; the pass-book was torn from his grasp and he was flung down again like a stick-figure, with one hand pinned fast.

'Try that, would you!'

'Let me go!' Ernie sobbed in misery and defeat. 'Let me go!'

His father yanked him to his feet. 'I don't know what's got into you. Sitting on all that money, knowing there was a thousand dollars owing at the store. Smart Alecs always making wise-cracks and asking when I was going to strike it rich and pay up.' He put the pass-book into his pocket. 'Well, I'll show 'em. Tomorrow!'

Ernie wrenched himself free. 'It's *mine*! It's *my* money!' he shouted, fleeing through the door and racing away down the slope. His father ran a few steps after him but gave up and stood watching from the entrance. Ernie didn't slow down until he was half a mile away. Then he stopped and looked back. He had a queer light-headed feeling as if he was going to faint. A kind of shock. He wondered whether he was running away from home.

Chapter Thirteen

There was a ferment on the fields. Excitement and rumours ran up and down, each story more mouth-opening than the last. There had been strikes at the Three Mile and the Ten Mile, and whispers of strikes at a dozen other places. But most sensational of all was the story of the Odinsky brothers — three Polish new chums who had put down their first shaft near an old bulldozer cut less than a mile out and bottomed on a bonanza. They'd taken out a fortune already — a twenty-gallon bucket full of gemstone so everyone said — and it was still coming. They had moved their beds to the head of the shaft and kept watch night and day, with a loaded rifle ready.

It was the second week of the school holidays and Ernie and Nick were sitting on a mullock heap near 'Ryan's Riches' — the old Bordini Mine that Ernie still regarded as his own.

'A million dollars' worth,' Nick said sensationally. 'That's what they reckon the Odinsky boys have taken out.'

'How'd you be!' Ernie answered tonelessly. He was actually thinking about other, more important, things. What was to become of himself, for instance. Because his father had gone. After staying away all day following their clash in the dugout Ernie had gone back warily that night to make it up. His father had forced him to sign a withdrawal slip and then left. He heard later that Robbie Ryan had bought a lot of provisions at the store and gone out North-West prospecting somewhere. He seemed to have

147

come into a bit of money at last.

So Ernie would have to fend for himself — without money and without much food in the dugout. And he'd have to leave school, even though he was still only fourteen.

'And more to come,' Nick said.

'How'd you be.' Ernie had hardly heard him. He supposed he could live like the Aborigines, with a bit of noodling to keep going. But they wouldn't have him around the place if he tried to live with them, and neither would Aboriginal Affairs.

'More than a million. Biggest find in history,' Nick said.

'How'd you be.'

Nick turned on him sharply. 'Can't you say anything except 'How'd you be' all the time, Ernie. Drive a bloke nuts.'

'Sorry.' Ernie came back from the future to the present.

'What'd you say?'

'Pull your ears on,' Nick said. 'I was talking about the Odinskys.'

'Half their luck.'

'They reckon there was one piece, the *Odinsky Queen* they're calling it, was nearly a foot long and six inches thick.'

'Bit way on,' Ernie said. 'You couldn't lift the thing.'

Nick hugged himself with delight. 'How'd you like to be wearing it on your middle finger?'

'You could use it as a wheel-chock for semi-trailers.'

'Gor!'

A dark figure emerged from behind a mullock heap nearby and came silently towards them. It was Willie.

'G'day, Willie,' Ernie said.

'G'day.'

'G'day, Willie.'

They watched him as he came forward. It was strange

148

the way he could meet them like this without making arrangements beforehand. Almost as if he knew where they were, coming and going without words or signs.

'You going noodling?' Nick asked.

'No need just now,' Willie said. 'Later maybe.' Which simply meant that for the moment he and his family had all they needed, so there was no need to go rushing about trying to make money unnecessarily. Not like white men who went into a frenzy, and stole, and killed one another just to build up a pile of it.

'We were talking about the Odinskys,' Nick said. 'Their big opal.'

'Plenty of talk about that one,' Willie said. He turned and looked towards the airstrip. 'Plane leaving. Taking buyer back.'

'Came up yesterday,' Nick said.

'They're coming up all the time.'

Like flies since the big strikes.'

'They need big buyers for that sort,' Ernie said. He was thinking of his meeting with Mr Hiramatsu in the motel room. It seemed such a long time ago.

'Especially when they have to pay cash.'

'They always have to pay cash. Blokes wouldn't sell otherwise; beat income tax and that.'

'They have to know their business, doing that,' Nick said. 'The buyers?'

'Yes. Stan Henderson knows two blokes who went broke by buying too late in the afternoon. Colours looked better than they really were.'

'In the afternoon light?'

'Yes. Paid too much and went broke.'

'How'd you be.'

'Plane starting up now,' Willie said suddenly.

Nick and Ernie paused, listening. 'Can't hear a thi . . . Ah, yes I can.' Nick cocked his ear towards the airstrip. 'Which one is he, d'you know?'

'The buyer?' Ernie asked.

'Not the Japanese,' Nick said. 'He was here last week.'

'German one,' Willie said. 'Can fly his own plane.'

'I know him,' Nick said. 'Big bloke. Fair hair, cut short.'

'So do I,' Ernie said. 'Always flies up on his own.'

'In the motel last night,' Willie went on. 'People say he got two suitcases nearly filled with opal.'

'Flying 'em down to Adelaide today then,' Nick said.

They heard the plane's engine roar and fade and then rise loudly as it started its take-off run. A minute later they saw it lift and bank slowly as it climbed. There was a stiff cross-breeze and a good bit of intermittent dust. Ernie stood up and went to join Willie. 'What say we go over to the Filipi cuts,' he said. 'There's good picking at the ends.'

Nick followed more slowly. 'D'you reckon?'

Suddenly Willie spun round and pointed upwards excitedly. 'Hey! The plane! The plane!'

Ernie looked up and almost flung himself down on the ground with fright. The plane was coming straight at them, flying low and erratically, the engine cutting in and out and the propeller spinning fast and slow in fits and starts.

'Engine trouble,' yelled Nick.

Willie's eyes were like marbles. 'Look out!'

'Duck!' Ernie shouted. 'Duck your heads!'

They felt the rush of air as the plane swept over them and went wavering away a few feet above ground, the engine coughing and shuddering, wings tilting perilously from side to side.

'He's heading back to the airstrip,' Nick said, scrabbling hastily up the mullock heap to get a better view. Ernie and Willie scrambled after him. 'He won't make it,' Ernie yelled. 'He's too low.'

'Crash, I reckon,' Willie said.

'Can't get height.'

'He's down!'

'Quick!'

Less than a mile from them the plane dipped and touched ground. At that distance they couldn't tell whether the pilot had tried to make a forced landing or whether the plane had just flopped down from lack of air speed. For a second or two it seemed to taxi and jolt across the rough ground fairly well; then one wing tilted and touched, the engine drove nose down into the dirt, and the whole plane somersaulted. A gigantic cloud of dust went up and they caught glimpses of the tail and wing members flailing about wildly as the whole thing broke up and went skidding along through the dust, gibbers and bits of bush. The nose-wheel flung itself loose and leaped out of the dust-cloud like a startled wallaby, bouncing high into the air and racing off beyond the mounds of a bulldozer cut.

'Crash!' said Willie, awestruck. 'Real bad crash.'

'Quick!' Ernie darted off and headed for the wreck at full speed, even leading Willie who was one of the fastest runners in the school. Nick leaped down from the mullock heap and followed. It wasn't long before Willie drew level with Ernie, his thin sinewy legs leaping and dodging as they raced over stones and old heaps from test drives and fossickers.

Suddenly Willie checked Ernie with his hand. 'Look! Fire!'

A cloud of smoke with strangely intermingling plumes of black and white swirled up through the dust from the wreck. Ernie stopped momentarily. 'Gosh! Oh my gosh!' It was a terrifying sight.

'The pilot!'

Nick caught up with them, shouting. 'The plane's

caught fire. We'll never make it in time.'

Just as they were about to race on Willie caught a glimpse of a figure through the dust and smoke. 'Look!' he yelled. Ernie glimpsed it too, just for an instant. 'He's safe!'

'How lucky can you be.'

'Come on.'

All three of them ran on together. They were down in a slight hollow now, out of sight of the crash, although the column of smoke was clear enough, rising in a high angry spiral. There was still a quarter of a mile to go, and Ernie and Nick were beginning to run out of puff. 'I'm just about pooped,' Nick called.

'Me too,' Ernie panted. 'You go on, Willie. See if he's okay.'

As they came back into sight of the wreck, the whole plane seemed to be blazing furiously.

'Struth, look at it,' Nick panted. 'He'd have no hope in there.'

They were strung out in a row now, Willie in front and Ernie in the middle, but they were getting close to the crash and could see bits of detail through the smoke. Once Willie checked his run and half raised his hand as if to point out something, but he seemed to change his mind and went on. He slowed down as he neared the wreck and the others caught up.

'Can't get too close,' Nick said. 'Feel the heat!'

They came round in an arc on to the windward side and stopped when they'd approached as close as they dared. The fuselage was burning fiercely. All the fuel from the tanks had poured out when the plane somersaulted and broke up—hundreds of gallons of it dousing everything before the engine ignited it. A stiff breeze was whipping the flames and swirling the smoke violently. Scurries of dust were being flung up from the plain nearby and driven intermittently in low sheets, mingling with the flames and smoke.

Ernie moved around towards the leeward side where the smoke was sweeping away low before the wind. It lifted for a second and he glimpsed something lying on the ground a little distance from the wreckage. 'Hey!' he yelled. 'Look! Look!'

Then he dashed forward through the smoke, calling to the others. 'Quick! Quick, help!'

It was a man. Ernie didn't know whether he was dead or not; there was blood all over his face, but there didn't seem to be any burns. His clothing was unharmed.

Nick and Willie ran up, goggling. 'It's the pilot!' Willie was the first to recognise him.

'The pilot!'

'That's him all right.'

'The German one. The buyer.'

Although they were a little distance from the fire, the heat was still intense and the smoke, when it billowed down in wind lulls, was thick and choking.

'Quick, get him out of here.' Ernie gestured to the other two. 'I'll lift his shoulders. You take his legs.'

They half lifted, half dragged the man clear and stood wheezing and coughing.

'Hope we didn't hurt him,' Nick said. 'Might have broken bones and that.' He was thinking of his own experience at the Breakaway.

'Had to get him out of there, though,' Ernie answered.

Nick nodded. 'Wonder if he's still alive?'

'Still breathing,' Willie said. His eyes always seemed to be keener than anyone else's.

'Unconscious, then,' said Nick.

'Big cut on his head.' Ernie started feeling about for a bandage.

'You got a rag or something, Nick?'

'No.'

'Or a hankie?'

'No.'

'Got to get something.' Ernie stood up. 'Better tear the sleeve off my shirt.'

'Don't tear it up, you nong,' Nick said. 'Use the whole shirt; then it'll be okay again later.'

'Better be. I've only got two.'

Ernie stripped off his shirt and used it to wipe as much of the blood from the man's face as he could. There was a long cut across the side of his head where the blood was welling out steadily and running down his cheek and neck. 'Gosh, look at the blood.' Ernie tied the shirt as tightly as he could around the man's head to try to staunch some of the bleeding. There were other cuts and bruises on his face and hands, and Ernie guessed that some of his bones were probably broken too.

'Better not move him any more till someone gets here,' he said.

'People coming now,' Willie said. 'Cars and a ute.'

'Might be saved yet.' Nick looked at the white face of the pilot. 'Might be lucky.'

'Might not be too. Might be smashed up inside.'

Nick looked back at the wreck still blazing behind them. 'Better than being fried up in there though.'

Ernie looked at the inferno. 'He must've just had enough strength to climb out of the cabin and crawl a few yards.'

'Only just far enough. Bit closer and he would still have been cooked.'

'Andy Bell's coming,' Willie said, looking at the vehicles approaching. 'And Sister from the hospital.'

'They must've seen the crash.'

'Lots of people would've. Especially the fire.'

The vehicles pulled up nearby and five or six people

came running over. Sister Richards was among them. She knelt down beside the pilot and examined him quickly, then turned to one of the men.

'Andy, drive back as fast as you can and get a message through to the Flying Doctor. Tell them what happened and say it's serious. Head injuries, loss of blood, probably fractured bones.' She turned to the others. 'Fetch the stretcher from the ute— and the blankets I brought.'

While they were waiting she turned to the boys. 'Did you see it happen?'

'More or less,' said Ernie.

'Engine packed up,' Nick interrupted. 'He tried to nurse her back to the strip. Didn't quite make it.'

'A forced landing?'

'Tried to, I think. Flipped over and went somersaulting all over the place.'

The stretcher arrived and they tried to bed down the unconscious pilot as well as they could. They then lumped him across to the ute and slid the stretcher on to the tray. It was all pretty rough and primitive, but they didn't expect frills on the opal fields—not even medical ones.

It wasn't until the vehicle had moved off that Ernie suddenly thought of something. 'Hey,' he said, 'are you sure that bloke was the German buyer?'

'It's him all right,' Willie said emphatically. 'For sure.' Willie went over and stood beside Ernie who was as close to the wreck as he could get, peering this way and that at the burning fuselage.

'Then there ought to be opal on board,' Ernie said. 'Lots of it.' Willie had already thought of it, but Nick's face lit with astonishment. 'That's right.'

'In bags,' said Willie. 'And the bags in two suitcases.'

'Strong ones,' Nick added. 'Real strong ones.'

'Did you ever see 'em?' Ernie asked.

155

'We did, Grandpa Yirri and me,' Willie answered. 'At the motel.'

'Then they ought to be in there,' Ernie said, nodding at the wreck.

'What's left of 'em,' said Nick.

'Can't see anything.' Ernie turned to Willie. 'Can you?'

'Not yet. Might later on.'

'The suitcases would go, but not the opals.' Nick was peering too.

'They'd be all blackened I s'pose; on the outside.'

'Wouldn't burn though.'

'Might crack in the heat, d'you reckon?'

'You'd think we'd see something.'

The fire was subsiding as it burnt itself out, but the fuselage was still red hot and glistening. 'Have to wait a long time before it's cool enough to make sure.'

Ernie looked around at the bits of wreckage scattered everywhere. 'They could've been flung out in the crash.'

'They'd be pretty heavy.'

'Very heavy,' Willie said.

'Could've broken free—when she somersaulted.'

'Look everywhere, then—way out, all around.'

They scattered out in a wide circle but it was a fruitless exercise. The ground was bare enough, apart from stones and a few mullock heaps; anything as big as a suitcase would have stood out clearly.

'Nothing here,' Nick called after a while.

'Not thrown out then,' Ernie said as they walked back to the smouldering wreck. 'So they must be in there.'

'Not in there either, I don't reckon,' Willie said.

Nick and Ernie both stopped and looked at him. 'Why not?'

'Can't see 'em.'

'Must be. Where else can they be?'

Nick started walking slowly around the wreck. 'He

156

wouldn't have been going back to Adelaide without 'em, that's for sure.'

'They must be in there—scattered and blackened by the fire.'

Willie wasn't one to argue. 'Maybe.' But they could see that he wasn't convinced.

'Tell you what,' Nick said. 'We'll get something to poke around a bit.'

They searched and in the end found an aerial rod that had broken off when the plane somersaulted and broke up. It was only three or four feet long and the heat was still intense, so they couldn't do much more than prod at the edges.

'You fellows looking for something?'

It was a deep voice with an accusing tone in it. They all wheeled round guiltily. Sergeant Brogan was standing immediately behind them, watching sternly. 'What're you up to?'

'Nothing Sarge!' Nick always overdid his innocence.

'You realise you could be arrested?' the sergeant said unsmilingly.

'Everything has to be left untouched until Civil Aviation gets here. The Accident Investigation Squad.'

Ernie was defensive. 'We were only helping. The pilot was hurt. We helped him till the Sister got here.'

'I know.'

'Oh.'

The sergeant started to take notes. 'You fellows see the crash?'

'Yes.'

'All of you?'

'Yes.'

'Were you the first to get here?'

'Yes.'

'You pulled the pilot out?'

'No, he was lying over there—away from the plane.'

'How'd he get there?'

'Crawled, I s'pose.' Nick looked pityingly at the sergeant as if ready to forgive him for asking such a lot of stupid questions.

'Even when he was badly hurt?'

Nick opened his mouth to say something smart like 'perhaps the fairies helped him' but changed his mind when he saw how stern Sergeant Brogan looked.

'Must've managed a few yards and then flaked out,' Ernie said.

'Did the fire start straight away?'

'No, a bit later.'

'How much later?'

'A few minutes.' Ernie turned to Willie. 'What d'you reckon, Willie?'

'About that.'

'We started off as soon as she crashed,' Nick said, 'and we'd been running for a good while before she went up.'

'But you were still some distance away?'

'A heck of a long way.'

'Couldn't see anything for smoke anyway—not once it started,' Ernie said.

'And the pilot was lying on the ground when you got here?'

'Didn't even see him for a while; not till we got around to this side.'

The sergeant wrote in silence for a while. 'What things did you pick up?' he asked suddenly.

'Nothing,' said Nick in a flat, offended voice. 'We didn't touch nothing.'

'Would've been too hot anyway,' Ernie added. 'Still is.'

'What about this prodding and poking then?'

'Oh, that!'

'Looking for something, were you?'

158

'No, not really. Well . . . that is, yes.' The three of them tried to cover up and only succeeded in sounding guilty. So Ernie decided to front up honestly.

'Well, you know what she was probably carrying, Sarge,' he said; 'we were just wondering if it was there.'

'And was it?' The sergeant's voice had that funny ring about it that always made Ernie feel uncomfortable.

'Well, we don't know. Only just started looking when you came.'

'Looking,' said Sergeant Brogan, 'can carry heavy penalties.'

'Ah, come off it, Sarge,' Nick said angrily. 'We were only trying to find out. We weren't going to *take* anything.'

'Sure,' said the sergeant.

He seemed to have finished writing in his notebook for the time being. A number of other vehicles were driving out from the town towards them, throwing up wakes of dust.

'All the same,' he said, 'I don't want any of you within twenty-five yards of the wreck from now on, right?' He put his book and pencil into his breast pocket and buttoned the flap. 'But I don't want you to go away either. Might need you for questioning again later.'

He moved off to direct the approaching vehicles. 'There were two hundred thousand dollars' worth of opal on board that plane—or there should have been. And until it's found you're under suspicion.'

Chapter Fourteen

By midday the fields were buzzing with stories. As more and more people came to see the wreckage of the burnt out plane they brought fresh news with them so that Willie, Nick and Ernie knew everything that was going on even though they'd been forbidden to leave the scene of the crash.

Reports on the pilot's condition varied between 'minor injuries' and 'burnt to death', until the Flying Doctor plane took him aboard as a stretcher case just before noon and set off for Adelaide. It was then agreed fairly generally that he had two broken legs, a broken pelvis, a fractured wrist, internal injuries and concussion, but that he would live.

'Gor,' Nick said in an unbelieving voice, 'and we lugged him about like a bag of mullock.'

'Couldn't be helped,' Ernie murmured. 'He had to be shifted from the fire.'

'Been shifted before that anyway, I reckon,' Willie said quietly. The other two stopped short in their thinking and looked at Willie as if he was either mad or magical.

'What d'you mean?'

They were sitting on a little mullock heap sixty or seventy yards from the wreck where a group of men were still slowly sifting through the remnants.

'Couldn't walk, the pilot. Not with two legs broken.'

'No-o,' Ernie said thoughtfully. 'Could've crawled, though.'

'But there was a man standing up,' Willie said in a

matter-of-fact tone as if it was the simplest statement in the world. 'I saw him in the smoke.'

A light seemed to switch itself on inside Ernie's head. 'By the Lord Harry,' he said softly, using one of his father's long-forgotten expressions. 'There *was* a man standing up. I saw him too—just for a second.'

Nick had also been considering the revelation, looking sidelong at Willie. 'You . . . you reckon it was someone else?' he asked a little disbelievingly.

Ernie cut in impatiently. 'Well it couldn't have been the pilot if he had two broken legs—that's just what we're saying.'

Nick was pragmatic. 'Who, then?'

There was silence. The other two looked hard at Willie who turned his eyes to the ground and fidgeted with a bit of stone as he always did when he was uneasy or embarrassed.

'Well?' asked Nick again after a long time.

'We don't know who,' Ernie interposed, trying to protect Willie.

More silence. They could almost hear Nick's mind working.

'D . . . D'you reckon he knocked off the opal too?'

'There was a man,' Willie said with sudden conviction, 'and he was carrying something.'

The other two were electrified.

'Bags?'

'Suitcases?'

'Bundles?'

Willie looked far away as if trying to conjure up the answer from the horizon. 'Maybe cases, I reckon.'

Nick was now more excited than Ernie. 'Suitcases?'

'Maybe suitcases.'

'When was he?'

'When I was ahead.' Willie's modesty prevented him

161

from pushing the statement further.

'You reckon he nicked 'em and went?'

'And dragged out the pilot,' Ernie added. 'He must've saved the pilot.'

'A bloke like that wouldn't worry about saving pilots,' Nick said.

'Probably in his way. Probably had to drag him out to get at the stuff.'

'Before the plane blew up.'

'Blew up?' Nick said doubtingly. 'Probably set fire to it on purpose to cover his tracks.'

The flight of Nick's imagination having run itself out, he turned to Willie again. 'You sure you saw something?'

'Saw a man carrying things; something in each hand,' Willie answered doggedly.

'If he says he saw it, he saw it. He's got eyes like lasers,' Ernie said irritably.

But Nick was still in a cross-examining mood. 'Why didn't you tell the police, then?' he said to Willie. 'You're supposed to tell everything to the police.'

'Hell's teeth!' Ernie exploded angrily, 'why didn't *you*?'

'Don't want to talk to the police,' Willie said. 'Don't want all those questions.'

A long knowledge of trouble ranging from the frequent arrest of Aunt Merna for drunkenness to a shooting affray at the Reserve had made Willie silent and shy where the police were concerned.

'If it was a man . . . ,' Nick began again.

'It *was* a man,' Ernie said sharply. 'Saw him myself.'

Nick tried again. 'Well, if it was a man and he nicked all the opal, where'd he go and what's he done with it?'

'Went up there, I reckon, and then around behind.' Willie pointed to a small washaway on the right and brought his arm round in an arc behind them.

'Could've,' Ernie agreed. 'Could've at that. The smoke

162

was blowing that way, and it was so thick you couldn't see a thing. A man could've run behind the smoke and up the channel.'

'It's only a foot or two lower than the rest of the land,' Nick said scoffingly. 'He'd need to be a lizard.'

'No he wouldn't. Just have to bend low; there's a bush or two, and a few mullock heaps. We were the only ones around, and all three of us were watching the burning plane. And for quite a while we couldn't even see the thing at all.'

Nick was slow to be convinced. 'And where then?'

'Doubled round behind us—like Willie says.'

'And then I s'pose he walked back to the motel carrying the suitcases and singing out, 'I'm a tourist! I'm a tourist!'" Nick laughed disparagingly. 'Where on earth could he hide the stuff?'

'Down a mine.' Willie's voice was always so matter-of-fact that it startled Nick.

Ernie was suddenly agog. 'By Gosh, yes! In the mine. In the Bordini Mine!'

'The Bordini Mine!'

'Course! It's right there—where we were sitting almost. And it's big; got drives everywhere.'

'Ryan's Riches.'

'Be Ryan's Riches all right if that lot's down there.' Nick blew through his teeth. 'Quarter of a million dollars, nearly.'

The more Ernie thought about it, the more certain he felt that Willie was right. And if that were so, then the thief must still be down in the mine now, waiting for it to get dark. He wouldn't risk coming out in daylight.

The thought was enough to set Ernie trembling. 'Come close over here,' he said to Willie and Nick, his voice barely above a whisper. 'I've got an idea.'

Five minutes later Ernie walked over to Sergeant

Brogan. 'Hey, Sarge!' he said boldly, 'it's after lunchtime and we're dying for something to eat and drink.'

The sergeant looked at his watch. 'All right, you can go now,' he said. 'But stay around the town. We might want you again later.'

'Nick'll go and fetch something. We'll stay here, Willie and me.'

'As you like.'

So Ernie and Willie stayed behind while Nick set off for home at a trot. 'Don't be too long,' Ernie yelled after him. 'We're starving.'

'No worries,' Nick called. 'As soon as I've had a decent lunch I'll be back to tell you about it.'

It was pleasant enough, waiting. The day was mild and sunny, and although the wind was still gusty they found a bit of shelter in a shallow cut and lay on their elbows, talking. Ernie was certain that if there really was a thief who had gone below, then he would stay out of sight until nightfall. And if he did venture up to the surface during the afternoon, Willie would pick him up the moment he showed an eyebrow above ground.

So there was nothing to do but wait. He liked Willie as a companion; quite apart from the things he could do—his quick eyes and ears, and his fast legs—he was so quiet. No nattering on and on like some people till he felt like screaming. Just a word or two now and again, enough to say what had to be said, but no more.

'Plane coming.' Willie turned on his side and stretched his neck, gazing at the southern sky.

'Another one? That's three already.' Ernie gazed too. 'Beats me how you know, Willie. I can't hear a thing.'

'See him in a minute,' Willie said, as if to buck him up.

'Ah, yes. Now I can hear it.'

'Over there.' Willie stood up, pointing, but it was still some time before Ernie could pick it up.

'I've got it,' he said at last. 'Twin-engined Cessna.'

'Two,' said Willie, mildly excited.

'Yes, two engines.'

'No, two aeroplanes.' Willie was scanning the sky like a coast watcher. 'Two planes coming.'

'Two?'

'Two. I can see them.'

'Cripes.'

They climbed on to the biggest mullock heap in the area and stood peering intently, hands shielding their eyes. As usual Willie was right. The two planes made a low pass over them, probably taking in the scene of the crash, and then landed in quick succession.

Nick returned shortly afterwards with an old sugar bag stuffed full of supplies, and a tongue full of news.

'Everybody's got eyes like organ stops,' he said. 'Two planes just came in, did you see 'em?'

'Yes. Willie picked 'em up over Port Augusta,' Ernie said laconically.

'Detectives from Adelaide, insurance blokes, more Civil Aviation investigators, couple of German fellows.'

'From the buying company, I guess.'

'Be out here in a minute. The motel's like a cattle muster inside.'

'Big fuss on,' Willie observed dryly.

'Biggest turn in years.' Nick started to unpack some of the treasures from his swag. 'Here, have some bread and camp-pie. Bit of margarine and Vegemite there too.' He fished deeper and dropped his voice to a murmur. 'Couple of old jumpers for you fellows—it'll get cold as soon as the sun goes down.'

Ernie crowded in close to Nick. 'Keep 'em out of sight. We don't want old Hornbill Brogan poking his long nose in here now. Nice lot of questions there'd be.'

'He's all right,' Nick said. 'Too far away.'

'Not Brogan. He's got radar in his ear-holes.' Ernie crouched beside the swag. 'D'you get torches, candles and matches?'

'Plenty. We could explore King Solomon's Mines with this lot.'

'Might need to,' Ernie said enigmatically, 'before it's all over.'

They sat down in the lee of the big mullock heap and ate steadily for a while. 'This'll have to be lunch and tea,' Nick said, 'so better make the most of it.'

'Big crowd coming,' Willie, as usual, was the sentry.

'It'll be the detectives and insurance blokes,' Nick said.

Ernie was instantly alert and interested. 'Come on over,' he said, hastily bolting down the last of his bread. 'We want to find out what they've got to say.'

For two or three hours they watched and listened and answered questions while the whole accident was probed and ticketed and reconstructed. And by the end of it they felt they knew more about the whole thing than anyone else. At any rate they knew for certain that the plane had carried a fortune in opals, that these were now missing, and that the insurance company was going to offer a reward of ten thousand dollars for them.

And they sensed that there were probably all kinds of other moves going on behind the scenes that they could only guess at: police radio messages, police eyes on roads, railways and airports, secret warnings about certain criminals to watch. It was all strangely disturbing to Ernie. Even out in the desert it wasn't possible to get away from the greed and evil of men, and the sordidness of the cities in which they crowded and hid. Their avarice reached out over the land for a thousand miles like a claw.

'Whoever's in it isn't doing it for laughs,' he heard one of the detectives say. 'Wish we knew whether the engine had been tampered with or not.'

It was a new thought that hadn't even occurred to the boys: the idea that the crash might not have been an accident at all, that it might have been engineered. Sabotage.

By now it was getting late and the rays of the afternoon sun were streaming across the plain in rods of gold and brass. Most of the sifting and docketing of the crash seemed to be finished, and some of the men were packing up. Ernie knew that it wouldn't do for them to be seen hanging about too late in the day, so he made a show of leaving.

'Can we go now, Sarge?' he asked loudly. 'We've been here all day.'

'Yes, get going,' the sergeant said. 'We don't even want to see you around here anymore.'

'Thanks, Sarge! See you.'

The three of them set off in a line towards the town until they were hidden by some big bulldozer mounds. 'Down, down!' Ernie said then. 'We'll keep an eye on "Ryan's Riches" from here until the crowd has gone. Then we'll move in closer before dark.'

Dusk was a long time coming. The light lingered in the cloudless sky and the land took on its strange evening glow. Every stunted bush and mullock heap stood out in silhouette. It wasn't until the whole landscape was as sombre as shadow that Ernie moved. 'Quiet now,' he said. 'Make for the mullock heap on the right.'

He knew the country around the mine like his own hand so there was no danger from old shafts or abandoned cuts. They crept up silently and crouched down behind a low mound forty or fifty yards from the Bordini mine. 'This is as close as we can get,' Ernie said, 'but we can pick up anything that moves from here. There's only one shaft with a ladder.'

It started to get cold after a while so they pulled on the sweaters and sat close together, Nick holding the sugar bag over his bare knees. They rarely spoke, and then only in whispers. Sitting there with the vast openness of the land and sky all around him Ernie couldn't help feeling that everything was unreal. In his own heart he wondered whether their idea wasn't really quite crazy: the three of them hiding stealthily behind a mound of rock in the middle of Australia, waiting for someone who probably didn't even exist to pop up out of the ground like a rabbit from a burrow.

Nick stretched his legs from time to time with whispered complaints about stiff muscles and aching joints, but Willie stayed crouched in the same position, as soundless and immobile as a dark statue in the gloom. They hadn't really been waiting very long, but Nick was already impatient. 'Just a goose chase,' he said in a loud whisper. 'I reckon we're off our lollies.'

'Quiet!' Ernie said sharply. He needed a show of anger to keep down his own doubts. 'Keep your eye on the shaft.'

'I don't even know where to look,' Nick answered sulkily.

'Then look up your jumper.'

There was silence again, although Ernie was aware of Nick's shoulders shaking gently in the dark as he laughed to himself, presumably at Ernie's last instruction. His guess was right because a minute or two later Nick suddenly whispered, 'There isn't any room.'

'Room for what?'

'For a bloke up my jumper.'

Ernie gave him a jab in the ribs with his elbow. 'Stick your head up it, then.'

To bring their mood back to proper seriousness Ernie turned to Willie who was lying crouched on one elbow on the slope of the mullock heap, looking out over the top like a wartime scout on patrol. 'Nothing, Willie?'

168

'Nothing yet.'

'Won't be anything,' Nick whispered. He was trying to bait Ernie.

'Whether there is or not, we're going to stay here all night if we have to—to find out.'

That seemed to quieten Nick. A quarter of an hour went by. A half an hour. Now and again the distant headlights of a car or truck flared up in a sudden glow out of the darkness and sank away just as suddenly again. It gave them a queer eerie feeling as if will-o'-the-wisps were running about using torches like lightning flashes over the huge desolate landscape. There was a sliver of moon now, and a hint of starlight so thin that they could just pick out the position of the dips and mounds around them.

'Shhh!' It was more a soft outflow of breath from Willie than a command to be quiet; a silent exclamation of caution and surprise. Instantly all three of them were tense and alert.

'Watch!' Willie's whisper was so faint that it barely reached them. Ernie and Nick strained their eyes in the gloom.

'Where?'

'In the shaft.'

They waited for another second or two but Ernie still couldn't see a thing. He was on the point of asking Willie again when he saw it—a man's head and shoulders above the level of the ground, moving this way and that. He was obviously standing on the ladder in the shaft, looking about, spying out the land. A sudden thrill of fear swept Ernie, a deep sense of danger. Until now it had all been a little unreal, a make-believe, fun-and-games kind of thing. But watching the shadowy figure emerging like a snake from its hole filled him with dread and a kind of loathing. He was conscious of goose-pimples on the nape of his neck, and they weren't there from cold.

'Look!' Willie whispered again.

As if satisfied with its reconnoitring the head rose up stealthily, followed by the whole torso, and finally legs and feet. The man stood on the ladder for a final second and then stepped out quickly on to the surface. The first shock of surprise hadn't left Ernie when he was faced with another one. Instead of turning back and hauling up bags or bundles to take with him, the man walked straight off at a brisk pace towards the south. Ernie was nonplussed because he had assumed absolutely that if a man did emerge from the mine he would be carrying two cases full of opal with him.

'Quick, what'll we do?' Nick asked.

'Someone'll have to follow him,' Ernie said. 'And someone's got to stay here—to watch the mine.'

'I'll follow,' Willie said quietly. 'You and Nick keep guard.'

Ernie was glad. It was the kind of arrangement he would have wished for. Willie would trail the man like a shadow in the darkness—so swiftly and silently that he would never know he was being followed.

'Find out who he is,' Ernie whispered after Willie urgently. 'We've got to know who he is.'

'Be back,' Willie promised. 'You wait here.'

For a moment or two they could still pick up Willie's outline as he moved off quickly in pursuit, but then he faded into the gloom and they were alone. It had all happened very suddenly, and the renewed solitude was an anticlimax. They were still startled and on edge. Nick raised himself up on his knees, peering into the dark. 'Did you get a good look at him?'

'Give it a go,' Ernie answered. 'Barely even made out his shape.'

'Big man, I reckon.'

'Pretty big.'

170

'Wonder what he's done with the stuff.'

'If that's the bloke who took it.'

'That's him all right.'

Ernie paused, thinking. 'D'you reckon the stuff's still down there?'

'Must be.'

Ernie seemed to be trying to convince himelf. 'If Willie said he saw a bloke carrying something, then he saw a bloke all right, that's for sure.'

'With two cases.'

'Suitcases. And that's what the German buyer had the opals in at the motel when he left to get on the plane.'

They were silent momentarily. 'Then they must still be down there,' Ernie said at last, jerking his finger at the mine. Although neither was saying so, it was obvious that they were both thinking the same thing.

'Be pretty dark down there,' Nick ventured after a while.

'No darker than during the day, once you get in.'

Nick could tell that Ernie was bringing himself to a decision.

'One of us ought to go down,' he said suddenly. 'Might never get another chance. Not like this.'

'What if he's got a mate down there; an off-sider.' Nick's teeth weren't far from chattering.

'Not likely.'

'Don't like the idea, Ernie. This is for real, with these blokes. They don't muck around; they kill people.'

'I'll go,' Ernie said. 'I know the mine pretty well.'

'What about me?'

'You stay and wait for Willie. If something crops up, try to warn me.'

'You're starkers, Ernie. You never know what might be going on down there in the middle of the night.'

'Better find out, then.'

'What if there's some other bloke mining it now, and he thinks you're a poacher.' Nick's flesh was creeping just at the thought.

'Have to find out,' Ernie said doggedly. 'Simply have to find out.'

He took the torch, put a piece of candle and some matches into each pocket, and hurried over to the shaft. He swung his leg on to the second rung. 'Keep a good look-out,' he called in a loud whisper. Then he was gone. The mine shaft closed around him quickly as he descended and the darkness was impenetrable. He had to make every movement by touch and feel. Yet, although he felt his heart beating fast in his ears, it was from exertion and excitement rather than from fear. Now that he was actually doing something he could sink his anxiety in bodily action.

As soon as he reached the bottom of the shaft he switched on the torch and crawled into the lateral drive. A foot or two inside, he paused and listened long and carefully. Apart from his own breathing and the drum of his heartbeats in his ears, there wasn't a sound. 'As quiet as the grave!' he thought, and then shuddered at the idea.

Meanwhile Nick crouched behind his sheltering mound of mullock, cold and tense. He had the most horrible mental vision of Ernie trapped in the maze of catacombs below—long tortuous drives, dead-ends, sudden galleries filled with murderous conspirators, and concealed niches where there wasn't even enough space to turn around. But as time went by his tension eased and he concentrated less on the dark blob that was the almost indiscernible mouth of the shaft, than on the wide landscape around him, the night sky, and the fine far horizon. From time to time he got up and stretched his cramped legs, peering about for signs of Willie, but the plain was still and silent. He sat down finally with his back against the mound and pulled the sweater down over his knees for warmth.

Whether his wait from then on was long or short he didn't really know, because he was half asleep when he heard soft running footfalls coming out of the daze of his dozing, and the next moment Willie came loping up, panting and urgent.

'Quick, hide,' he whispered. 'He's coming back.'

Again it was something none of them had foreseen and even Willie, who had followed his quarry tenaciously all the way, hadn't guessed what he was up to until he has within a quarter of a mile of the mine on his way back.

'He went home to get some things,' Willie said.

Nick's heart went cold. 'Coming back? Oh gosh!'

Willie glanced about. 'Where's Ernie?'

Nick's forehead was damp. 'Down the mine.'

Willie's voice was a fierce horrified whisper. 'The mine? Ernie's down the mine?'

'Looking.'

'Warn him! You must warn him!'

Nick leapt up and was about to race forward to the mouth of the shaft when Willie hissed and gripped him hard by the wrist, forcing him back down behind the mound. For a second Nick couldn't see anything, but then he heard footsteps and a second later a man emerged carrying a bundle of some kind over his shoulder. He was walking heavily and incautiously, obviously certain that he was alone. As soon as he reached the head of the shaft he adjusted his load briefly, swung one leg on to the ladder, and climbed down rapidly out of sight.

Nick was still petrified. 'What about Ernie! He'll murder Ernie if he finds him down there.'

Nick was aware that Willie was trembling.

'Ernie'll be killed,' he said with terrifying simplicity. 'A bad man, this one.'

Nick turned to Willie. 'Did you get a look at him?'

'At his camp—I saw him light up the lamp.'

'Recognise him?'

'Know him,' Willie said, tensely. 'All of us.'

'Who, then?'

'Dobruzza.'

'Dobruzza?'

'Dosh Dobruzza.'

Chapter Fifteen

Back in the town the visitors and officials were having a busy night. The Civil Aviation investigators were piecing together their report on the crash, the insurance assessors were preparing the notice advertising the reward, and Sergeant Brogan and the detectives were once more checking the details of all known events from the moment the German buyer had left his room until the sergeant arrived at the burning plane.

'The pilot must have been in it,' one of the detectives said doggedly. 'How could he possibly think he was carrying two full cases of opal on his plane if he wasn't?'

'Do we know for certain that he wasn't?'

'If we believe the three lads, we do.'

'But how reliable are they?'

Sergeant Brogan shifted from one foot to the other. 'Pretty reliable, I'd say.'

'Then we're back with the pilot. Better list all his connections: miners he met, people he saw, motel staff, local hoods. Check for possible switching of suitcases—the blokes who took him to the airstrip, serviced his plane, got within spitting distance of him.'

The first detective stood up. 'I'll go out and start meeting some of those mates of yours, Brogan. Where's the list—

174

Cameron, Dobruzza, Donacelli. . . . The quicker the better on a job like this. Nice blokes, are they?'

Sergeant Brogan smiled wryly. 'You'll have to cope with the lot—silence, fear, resentment, language barriers, jealousy, family feuds. You'll have to be able to speak Yugoslav, Maltese, Spanish, Polish, Italian and German for a start. You'll need to watch out for a big boot in your ribs at one camp, and a rifle or a stiletto at the next. And here and there you might just lift up the corners of a shadow from a big crime syndicate back East.'

'Thanks for the encouragement.'

'My pleasure.'

And half-smiling, Sergeant Brogan led the way outside.

In the sitting-room of her dugout near Post Office Hill, Mrs Andropoulos looked at the clock and began to worry too. It was past midnight and there were no signs of Nick.

'I don't like him out so late,' she complained; 'one of these days he falls down a mine in the night.'

'One of these nights,' her eldest son, Con, corrected her.

'That's what I say; don't be cheeky, Con,' she said sharply.

'Not to worry. Nick knows the way.'

'That's just why I worry,' his mother answered. 'Home he should be by now if he knows the way. So something is wrong.'

'He saw the plane crash—he and some others. I heard it in the bar.'

'What others? Ernie, then?'

'I think Ernie.'

'So why aren't they both home now?'

'Been helping the police.'

'How would Nick be helping the police? I told him a hundred times, keep away from the police; you got no business there.'

'Telling what he saw.'

'So all day he has been telling what he saw? And now all night nearly he is still telling what he saw? How much did he see then?'

'He could still be with the police—with Sergeant Brogan.'

'Then I find Sergeant Brogan,' Mrs Andropoulos said with finality. 'And he will not like me when I find him.'

Con got up and reached for his coat. 'I'll go, mama; maybe they're still up in the motel.'

'Yes, you go,' his mother called after him, 'and you say if they no care about Nickie, then I do.'

Con emerged from the dugout and walked up the slope in the darkness with his mother's words still fresh in his ears. But Nick was fourteen. Almost a man. He could look after himself. Con smiled at sudden memories of his own boyhood, and then grew grim. Perhaps it was good to have someone to worry about you now and then. Boys needed mamas sometimes.

The dark landscape and the high bright stars surrounded him as he walked. But if Nick had someone to worry about him, there were others abroad that night who didn't. Willie Winowie, crouched behind a mullock heap out on the plain, was not being missed from the barren ground of the Reserve. And Ernie Ryan, in peril of his life, had no one to speak for him now. No one even to remember.

As soon as the figure of Dosh Dobruzza had disappeared down the mouth of the shaft Willie ran cautiously forward, motioning Nick behind him. They saw a light glow eerily for a second or two on the straight walls and then sink away. As they came up to the lip of the hole the ladder vibrated for a moment and was still, and a sound like a dull thud carried up softly to them. Very cautiously Willie

176

edged forward and peered down, Nick following closely at his side. They were just in time to see the light dance about for a moment at the bottom of the shaft before it plunged into the lateral drive and was completely doused in an instant.

'Ernie'll meet him,' Nick said over and over. 'So help me, he'll meet him face to face.'

Willie stood irresolute. 'Dobruzza's bad. And strong. He'll kill Ernie.'

'Ernie hasn't even got anything to defend himself with.'

'We haven't either.'

Nick shrank back from the hole for a second as if expecting an attack. 'What did Dobruzza bring back with him, d'you know?'

'No. Went to his camp and got a lamp lit. By the time I came close he had his bag full and was coming out again. When I could tell he was coming back here I ran ahead to give a warning.'

Nick bit his lip and kept peering down into the darkness that was surrounded by darkness. 'Ernie should never have gone down there till the coast was clear; till we knew where Dobruzza was.'

Willie was blaming himself for everything. 'I could have stopped him; headed him off.'

'Dobruzza? How?'

'Run past in the dark. Call out and laugh. Call out about opals.'

'By heck yes.'

'He's frightened too, Dobruzza is.'

Nick was exhilarated at Willie's idea. 'Of course; he's frightened too. And guilty. And suspicious.'

'Very frightened I reckon.'

'But wild too.'

'Mad-wild.'

'Especially if he finds out about us.'

'If he meets Ernie.'

'He wouldn't even bring him up. Just bury him down there.'

'No one would ever find the body.'

'Been done before.'

Nick's teeth were chattering faintly. Two or three minutes had passed since Dobruzza had disappeared and they hadn't heard or seen a thing. Suddenly the suspense and fear for Ernie were too strong for Willie and he grabbed the top of the ladder.

'I'm going to the bottom of the shaft,' he said; 'to look and listen down there.'

'Careful, Willie.'

'You keep watch here—in case someone else comes.'

Before Nick could say anything else Willie was gone, swallowed up in the darkness like a stone dropped into a well. Nick knew what such a decision must have meant for Willie. He didn't like darkness and he hated mines—so strongly that he'd never been underground in his life before he became friendly with Ernie. To go down that black hole into darkness and danger must have stretched his nerve to breaking point. It also told Nick something about Willie's friendship with Ernie—it was far stronger than anyone knew. For Willie to do a thing like this was almost like offering his life for Ernie.

Nick waited at the head of the shaft, alert and tense. Every few seconds he peered from side to side or turned round fearfully to glance behind him, but there were only the dim shapes of old mounds and cuts barely distinguishable in the gloom. Nothing moved except the wind that stirred the night beyond him and touched his cheek as it went by.

He had just looked round for the twentieth time and was bringing his gaze back to the mouth of the shaft again when a figure shot up in front of him. Nick recoiled, his hair seemingly as straight as sticks and his throat too tight to yell. It was Willie, coming up hand over hand like a gibbon and climbing so fast that he literally leaped off the ladder on to the surface. In his bare feet he hadn't made a sound.

'Somebody coming,' he whispered fiercely. 'Get back! Get back!'

'Who?'

'Dunno.'

'What's going on down there?'

'Dunno.'

'Didn't you hear anything?'

'Only scrabbling and scratching—just now.'

'See anything?'

'Torch flashing once or twice—far down the drive.'

'Couldn't see who?'

'Nuh. Only yellow light coming this way.'

Nick retreated further from the hole. 'Must be one of 'em then.'

Willie nodded, his eyes wide like a terrified horse's, but the movement and its message didn't reach Nick in the darkness.

'Point is, which one?' Nick said softly.

'Might be both—one bringing the other.'

'Gorrr!' It was a strangled sort of sound from Nick, but the icy clutch he seemed to feel was around his heart rather than his throat.

'Look there!' Willie nudged Nick's hand nervously as a patch of light danced for an instant in the mouth of the hole and disappeared. The touch of a foreign hand on his own almost made Nick leave the ground. 'He's...he's coming up!'

'Quick, behind the mullock heap.'

They raced off, Willie as swift and silent as a shadow. Nick blundering clumsily in panic.

'Down here,' Willie hissed. 'This side! This side!'

Nick was vaguely aware that Willie was giving the orders. If he hadn't been numb with fear he would have been amazed. Willie was always the one who said least and followed most, who waited for someone else to make the suggestions and take the lead. A follower, not a leader. But Nick was too dazed to take in the significance of what was happening to Willie.

They lay side by side, huffing and panting in a suppressed kind of way. Nick's heart was thumping so loudly in his ears that he felt certain it was going to give them away.

'Look!' Willie whispered. 'Light coming again.'

'Coming up,' Nick said softly.

Their breathing was still far too loud, he thought, but there was no way of silencing it. Willie raised himself on his hands like a goanna and peered down from the mullock mound.

'No more light,' he whispered after a while. 'Must be coming up in the dark now.'

Nick was trembling. 'Must be Dobruzza.'

'Must be him.'

A faint thud, a thump like something bumping against rock, reached them.

'Ah, there!' Willie whispered.

'What . . . what was it?'

'He's nearly to the top; turning to come out.'

'Can you see him?'

'Not yet.'

Willie's goanna position was more tense than ever, poised far forward as if ready to thrust off like a rocket. His eyes fairly needled the darkness.

'Here he comes!'

'Who . . . who is it?'

A figure emerged dimly from the shaft. It was squat and

180

grotesque looking with a hump on its back. It clambered carefully on to the surface and stood there for a second looking about uncertainly.

'Gor,' said Nick. 'What the . . .'

'Ernie!' For once Willie's quietness left him. He yelled and leaped forward at the same time racing across towards the shaft so fast that Nick hadn't even climbed down from the mound before Willie had reached Ernie and was wringing his arm and gripping his shoulder. 'Ernie! You safe, Ernie!' he kept saying. 'You safe.'

'I'm okay,' Ernie said, slightly overwhelmed. Then he pointed excitedly at his back. 'See what I've got.'

Nick came up at that moment. 'Cripes, Ernie! You frightened the daylights out of us. Looked like a hunchback.'

But Ernie was too full of his news to notice Nick. 'See!'

'See what?'

'The case!' Ernie said gleefully. 'One of the missing cases.'

He had a suitcase tied to his shoulders by a bit of cord.

'Here, help me off with it.' He struggled to free his arm and get the cord over his head. Nick helped by grabbing the case from behind and lifting. He paused in surprise. 'It's light. Hey, it's empty.'

Ernie was impatient. 'Of course it's empty. You don't think I'd be climbing up the shaft with it hanging round my neck if it was full, do you?'

Willie was still agog. 'Where you find it, Ernie?'

'At the end of my drive—the one I made. How's that for luck?'

'Buried?'

'Half buried. There was a sort of lump there, pretty new looking, so I just scratched a bit and there it was, just an inch or two down. Hidden in a hurry, I reckon.'

'Empty?'

181

'Empty. He must have stashed all the opal somewhere else first.'

Willie held the case in wonderment. 'Two, I reckon,' he said. 'Must be another one.'

'Sure to be,' Ernie said. 'In one of the other drives.' He wound up the piece of cord and put it in his pocket. 'Got to go back in a minute and look for it.'

Willie and Nick recoiled so much that even in the darkness Ernie was aware of it. 'What's up?' he asked. Then, as if realising for the first time that Willie was back from his chase, he added quickly, 'Hey, did you find out who he was?'

Willie wasn't one to beat about the bush. 'Dosh Dobruzza.'

'Dosh Dobruzza!' Ernie said tensely. 'Might've guessed it.'

'Him all right.'

'Well, we'll fix him this time.' Ernie took the case from Willie. 'We've got this on him for a start; and we'll find the opals too, before we're through.' He lowered his voice like a conspirator in the wind and darkness. 'And we're the only blokes that know about it.'

'Ought to tell the police, don't you reckon?' Nick said.

'Not yet. When we've got more proof.' Ernie put the case down. 'We've got to find the other one of these—and the stuff that was in them.'

'Be in canvas bags,' Nick said. 'The opals.'

'Lot's of 'em, probably. He's buried 'em somewhere.'

'Is now, I reckon,' Willie said.

Ernie still missed Willie's meaning. 'He'll come back, I'll bet; when things have died down a bit.'

'You didn't see him?' Willie's words were meant to be a question, but Ernie took them as a statement.

'Why, what did he do when he got home?'

182

Willie was puzzled. 'Lit the lamp and filled a bag with stuff.'

'What stuff?'

'Don't know. He was finished when I got up close.'

'Probably full of empty bags—to carry the stuff away in.' Ernie looked away across the landscape in the direction of Dobruzza's camp. 'Wonder when he'll be back.'

Nick was beginning to realise too that they were talking at cross purposes. 'You didn't see him down there?' he asked again, indicating the mouth of the shaft.

Ernie was impatient. 'Listen, what are you two going on about?'

'Dobruzza,' Willie said earnestly. 'He's not home now.'

'Where, then?'

'Down there,' Nick answered, prodding his finger up and down in the air above the shaft. 'Down the mine.'

Ernie blanched so much that it was surprising his face didn't glow white even in the darkness.

'Dosh . . . Dosh Dobruzza?' he said weakly. 'Down there? Down there *now*?'

'Down there now.'

'When?'

'Fifteen, twenty minutes ago.'

'Holy Moses.' Ernie swallowed. His throat was so dry that it hurt. 'Why didn't you warn a bloke,' he said accusingly. 'Could've been killed. What if I'd met him face to face in one of the drives?'

'That's what we thought,' Nick said.

'Tried to come fast to give a warning,' Willie said, 'but not enough time.' There was such a note of apology and agony in his voice that Ernie felt sorry for what he'd said. Nevertheless, the more he thought about the awful possibilities, the more appalled he was.

'You must've been crawling around down there within a few yards of him,' Nick said.

'Probably was.'

'Can't see how you didn't run slap bang into him.'

'I must've been right at the end of the side drive when he went past up the main tunnel. Bit lucky, struth.'

'Lucky!' Nick rolled his eyes at the dark. 'You ought to take out a lottery ticket.'

There was a lull for a minute in their talk, and they were aware of the wind moving in the silence.

'What now?' Nick asked.

'Wait, I guess,' Ernie answered. 'Can't go back while he's still down there.'

'You can say that again.'

'Might stay a long time,' Willie said. 'All night, could be.'

'I reckon we ought to get the police now,' Nick said vehemently.

'You're hot on this police bit,' Ernie said impatiently. 'What could they do except wait, the same as us?'

Nick paused. 'Guess you're right.'

'Even to arrest him they'd have to pin something on him.' Ernie stood thinking. 'What we need is a day or two to go right through the mine without being interrupted.'

'And with no worries about him coming down on top of us,' Nick added feelingly.

'Police lock-up,' Willie said.

'By gosh, that's it,' Ernie said jubilantly. 'We'll get Sergeant Brogan to lock him up.'

Nick was sceptical. 'For what?'

'Suspicion,' Ernie said airily.'

'You've lost me. Why don't you just tell 'em to go down after him now. Catch him red-handed.'

'Don't be a clot; we want to find the opal first. There's going to be a reward, didn't you hear 'em say today.'

Nick wasn't convinced. 'Be a lot easier to call the police now, I reckon. Catch him down there.'

184

'Tell you what,' Ernie said urgently. 'You stay here, Nick, and keep watch. I've got an idea.'

'Great. Leave me on my own again, waiting to get a knife in my back.'

'When Dobruzza comes out, if he does, follow him like a dingo—especially if he's carrying something.'

Nick was more than lukewarm. 'What the heck are you two going to do?'

'I want Willie to take me to Dobruzza's camp.'

'Now?'

'Yes, now. And on the way back we'll drop this in at the police station.' Ernie held up the case.

'What if Dobruzza comes out in a minute or two and catches you at his camp?'

'You'll have to warn us. Throw a stone on the roof.'

'Very funny.' Nick wasn't in the mood for silly jokes. 'Better be quick, then,' he said. 'Are you coming back here?'

'After we've told Sergeant Brogan.'

'He'll be asleep by now.'

'Then we'll wake him up.'

'Well don't be too long. I hate being alone out here in the middle of the night.'

'Dobruzza's busy down there,' Willie said consolingly. 'Won't come up for a long time.'

'Keep a good watch all the same,' Ernie said. 'And let's hope he doesn't know of another way out.'

'That's for sure,' Nick said fervently. 'I don't want him coming up behind me in the dark, I tell you.'

'No worries,' Ernie said. 'You'd hear him before he could get you.'

'Goodbye, Nick,' Willie said, sidling after Ernie. 'Stay behind the mullock heap, then you're okay.' He disappeared into the gloom.

'Don't forget to hurry,' Nick called plaintively. But the

other two had already gone.

Nick looked at the dull aperture of the open shaft lying like a darker patch on the dark ground, and was horrified at its nearness. He could picture Dobruzza coming up secretively at this moment, preparing to pounce out and take him by surprise. Looking back constantly he made for the shelter of the mullock mound where he could lie hidden and safe. But even then he had no real peace. Ernie's parting comment had sown the awful doubt in his mind that there might be another outlet among the maze of drives; and if that were so the first thing he, Nick, might know about it would be heavy breathing behind him and a knife in his back.

Ernie and Willie ran and walked, walked and ran, covering the ground at such a fast clip that even if Dobruzza had risen from the mine immediately after their departure he would have been far behind. Willie led the way, picking the route quickly and shrewdly past cuts and obstacles, avoiding miners' camps where men might be lying awake or dogs might be dozing. And he warned Ernie uncannily where test shafts lay open and unmarked in their paths like deadly traps.

Old Red Ned O'Keefe had often complained about them, saying that it wasn't safe to walk about any more within twenty miles of the place without fear of disappearing suddenly down a ninety-foot hole as straight and smooth as a cylinder. 'Mechanical diggers,' he always snorted. 'Monstrosities. They're covering the ground with more pock-holes than the moon. And so close that you can step into two of 'em at the same time and fall to your death with a leg in each hole!' So Ernie was glad of Willie's guidance and the swift sure way he picked out the track.

Although Dobruzza's camp was nearly three miles away they reached it in less than half an hour. They approached

186

cautiously, even though it was deserted, somehow feeling the malevolent presence of its owner even in the junk that lay about. But everything was peaceful and still. Willie hung back a little now, and it was Ernie who led the way into the filthy and littered lean-to at the mouth of the dug-out. He shone his torch quickly over everything. The dug-out itself was even worse than the lean-to—an indescribable chaos of boxes, mining tools, empty cans and rubbish. And it stank. An old mattress lay on the floor in a corner where there was just enough space for it between great dumps of cartons and empty bottles.

Ernie was downcast. 'Take us a month to find the stuff if he's hidden any of it here,' he said. He moved over towards the mattress. 'Try his bed first.' He realised that he still had the suitcase in his hand and called Willie over. 'Take this, Willie, and put it down somewhere while we look the place over.' He shone the torch on the case. 'It's taken a bashing all right; look at the thing.' Although strongly made, with metal ribbing and safety latches and locks, the case was scarred and twisted out of shape.

'Was not like that at the motel,' Willie said. 'Nice then.'

'Probably dropped down the shaft when it was still full.'

'Don't think he brought anything back here tonight,' Willie said confidently. 'Walked too easy. Not carrying much, I reckon.'

'Let's go through this place all the same.'

'Better be quick.'

'Sure. Don't want him back here to cut our throats.'

'Would too,' said Willie uneasily.

They searched hastily for five to ten minutes but found nothing. After a while they worked their way back to the lean-to. Ernie kept flicking the torch over the junk as methodically as he could.

'What a dump,' he said.

They were about to move outside when the light fell on

something near the far wall. Ernie's memory stirred and he brought the beam back, peering carefully.

'Gosh,' he said excitedly.

It was a tin, a rectangular tin with a purple thistle painted on the lid and a dent in one side.

'What you find?' Willie asked, puzzled.

Ernie leapt forward over boxes, bottles and litter. 'My tin! My opal tin!'

'Your tin?' Willie was still nonplussed.

Ernie snatched it up and turned it over eagerly in the torchlight.

'It's mine all right. I'm certain of it.'

'How did it come here?'

'He stole it, that's how.' For Ernie the mysterious battle between Dobruzza and the boys had suddenly become an intensely personal one. 'When I made my strike and had a good parcel stashed in this tin under my bunk, someone ratted it before I could sell it. It was this creep, that's who it was.'

'Sold it by now I reckon,' Willie said laconically; 'the opal.'

'I'll bet he has.'

'Never get it back,' Willie observed.

'No? Well, I'll make certain he doesn't get away with this lot, then.'

'Better get going now; might come back.'

'I wish he would. I'd use a jack-pick on him.'

'He'd kill you, no fear. 'Specially now.'

Ernie was still scrutinising the tin in the torchlight when Willie grabbed his arm. 'Lights coming,' he warned. 'Heading this way.'

'Car?'

'Maybe a ute or Landy.'

'Who on earth, I wonder? Couldn't be Dobruzza.'

Willie stood watching the distant lights intently as they

approached. 'Could be police, I reckon.'

Ernie didn't wait any longer. 'Quick, run! No matter who it is, if they catch us here we're gone. They'll reckon we're in it up to our necks with Dobruzza.'

They raced off into the darkness, leaping and dodging. 'If they pick us up in their headlights we're done for— sitting shots like kangaroos in a spotlight.'

'This way, this way,' Willie called, leading off cleverly to the right, behind cuts and mullock heaps. 'Be all right this way.'

It was then that Ernie suddenly remembered something and stopped short. 'The case! We left the suitcase back in the dugout!'

'Too late,' Willie said. 'Someone stopping; police, I reckon. Got a big light.'

'Then Dobruzza's done for. They'll find the case and nab him the minute he shows his nose.'

'Find the case all right.'

'We've done him in, Willie. Framed him, in a sort of way.' Ernie was silent for a while, as if regretting what had happened.

'Could tell the sergeant.'

But Ernie wasn't yet willing to rush into confessions. 'Don't want to dob him in yet. But I could if I wanted to.'

'You could.'

'Could tell Sergeant Brogan what I've got to say.'

Willie wasn't quite following Ernie's point. 'What you got to say?'

'That my opal tin was in Dobruzza's camp.'

'But you won't say it?'

'No need. Not now, when he's got the suitcase there.'

'So police catch him anyway.'

'It'll do to put him out of the way while we search the mine.'

Willie suddenly understood. 'That'll do, I reckon,' he said.

Ernie tugged his elbow. 'Better be getting back to Nick,' he said. 'His eyeballs must be popping out of his head by now.'

Chapter Sixteen

Things worked out as Ernie had hoped. The police kept watch on Dobruzza's camp and arrested him as soon as he returned. But though they searched the place from rubbish top to rubbish bottom and found all kinds of other things suspected of having been stolen, the suitcase was the only piece that was connected with missing opals.

'We're holding you on suspicion,' they said. 'We'll need you for further questioning.'

Ernie heard about it shortly before noon the following day. He wondered what Dobruzza must have thought when the police said they'd discovered the suitcase in his dugout. But if nothing further could be found against him they wouldn't be able to hold him a prisoner on suspicion for very long, and even if they charged him they might grant him bail. Ernie had goose-pimples at the thought. One thing was clear. They had to explore the Bordini mine while Dobruzza was still safely locked up.

But it wasn't easy to begin at once. There was no quick way of contacting Willie; and Mrs Andropoulos was so upset about Nick's staying out for most of the night that she wouldn't let him get out of bed till after lunch. In the end Ernie had to plead with her to let Nick come.

'I'll look after him, Mrs Andropoulos, cross my heart I will,' he said.

'Cross *my* heart,' she answered tartly; 'my heart is on the cross all night, waiting.'

'It just couldn't be helped last night; but today I'll watch it.'

'You watch him?' she said scornfully. 'You are the one who leads him to d'ash-tray.'

Ernie was hurt. 'I don't lead him astray. So help me, I don't.'

It was a new situation for Ernie. He had always seen himself as a quiet fellow who minded his own business; and he believed that other people had seen him that way too. Perhaps even as a bit of a no-hoper like his father. It came as a jolt to realise that someone now saw him as a menace who ought to be kept away from other boys. Even Nick wasn't very happy at having been left sitting by himself for half the night, guarding the old mine. He thought Ernie and Willie had left him in the lurch.

It was after one o'clock when they finally got away from Nick's mother, and Ernie was beside himself with impatience. Then, for once, Willie's uncanny kind of telepathy didn't seem to be working because there was no sign of him; and so they had to walk all the way out to the Reserve.

As Ernie and Nick came up they could see most of Willie's people sitting in the sun playing cards, gambling away any money they happened to have made by working or noodling.

'G'day Ernie,' Uncle Winelli said with a wide smile, pointing at the things the boys were carrying. 'You get opal?'

'Maybe.'

'Got mine?'

Ernie was cautious. 'Registered mine last Christmas,' he said truthfully.

'Yours now, eh?'

'I reckon.'

The others all stopped their card-playing for a minute—old Grandpa Yirri, Aunt Merna and half a dozen more.

'Fellow in jail,' Aunt Merna said suddenly. 'Got arrested last night.'

'Yes,' Ernie murmured non-committally.

'Dosh Dobruzza, that fellow I reckon,' Uncle Winelli said.

'Yes.'

Aunt Merna looked up at Ernie sharply. 'You know about that?'

'I heard.'

'Tip off,' she said. 'Tip off, I reckon.' Aunt Merna could speak English best of all, but she was full of words from American films.

Ernie felt very uncomfortable. 'Willie around?' he asked.

'What you want with Willie?' Tom Winowie asked. He was Merna's brother, a big man with muscles like whip-lashes.

'Just mucking about together,' Nick said in appeasement.

'More better let him go.'

'Ain't here anyway,' Merna said. 'Up store, I reckon.'

'Thanks. We'll go looking.'

Ernie and Nick retreated quickly. 'Wonder what's got into them,' Ernie said. 'Sore as a heat rash.'

'Trouble last night, so Con said. He went up looking for me, and ran right into it. Drinking and fighting as usual. Merna nearly got arrested again. And Tom Winowie too.'

'No wonder.'

'And then Dobruzza being caught. And Willie out there last night.'

'How'd they find out?'

'Ask me. They've got radar.'

Ernie glanced up at the sun and increased his speed. 'We'll never get a proper look at the mine if we keep this up,' he said urgently. 'And it's got to be today.'

'Why don't we go straight over from here?' Nick suggested.

'Without Willie?' Ernie's tone showed what he thought. 'Not on your life.'

'What's with Willie?' Nick asked sourly. 'His crowd weren't too keen on us just now.'

Ernie kept his eyes on the ground. 'That's grown ups,' he said, and there was bitterness in his voice. 'They're always going on; same on both sides.'

'Willie's not too keen on working below anyway; bit scared I think.'

Ernie suddenly stopped short. 'He's not scared. Never been scared. Just not used to it, that's all. Down below.'

'Maybe he doesn't want to be in it, though.'

'What's that supposed to mean?'

'Doesn't want to go down the Bordini mine, looking. So he's gone away.'

'Gone away? What's this 'gone away' business?' Ernie was getting angrier and angrier.

'Gone walkabout. So he doesn't have to face it.'

'Why don't you shut your big mouth!' Ernie yelled it out so furiously that Nick was taken back.

'All right! All right!' he muttered.

'You talk such damn silly rot.'

'I only said . . .'

'Yea! Yea! You only said, you only said.'

Nick felt silent. He could see that it was no use going on about it any more. In fact, the whole thing puzzled him more than it hurt him. He had never seen Ernie like this in his life before, and he could only guess that something between Ernie and Willie was at the bottom of it.

193

'Let's go straight to the mine, then,' Nick suggested again. 'Like I said.'

'Not without Willie,' Ernie answered quietly and stubbornly. 'If he doesn't go, we don't go.'

Nick was getting angry too. 'Well I wish you'd make up your mind. First you're in such a tearing rush to go, and then you don't want to go.'

''Course I want to go—but not without Willie.'

'Why? Because he's *black*, is that it?'

Ernie spun round at him, and for a second Nick thought he was going to get a clout between the eyes. 'Because there's a reward of ten thousand dollars,' he said, 'and Willie's going to get some of it, so help me!'

'Why?'

'Why d'you think?' Ernie turned away in disgust. 'Don't be so dense, Nick.'

Nick was stubborn now. 'Well how am I supposed to know? So I still say why?'

'Why, why, why! Why don't you turn the record?'

'I'm telling you I don't know why! What else d'you want me to do—get down on my hands and knees or something?'

Ernie stood stock still and looked Nick square in the eyes. 'Why should Willie have some of the money? You tell me, Einstein.'

Nick gave up angrily. 'So he can bust it up, like the rest of his mob.'

Ernie clenched his fists but he didn't hit Nick. Instead he took a deep noisy breath and then spoke very quietly—so quietly that Nick could hear the tremor in his voice. He was aware that Ernie hated him for having made him say what he desperately didn't want to say.

'So Willie can go down South, and get some training, and . . . and get a proper job.' Ernie turned away. 'Now, will you *shut up*!'

194

A light went up in Nick's mind. 'Oh,' he said. 'I get it.' He stood silent for a while, thinking. 'He wouldn't get kicked around so much down there, would he? At least, not by the likes of Dobruzza.'

The mention of Dobruzza stirred Ernie from his soapbox and he walked off quickly towards town. Nick said nothing and followed. But they hadn't gone far when a figure came towards them from the direction of the Bordini mine. It was slim and dark and travelling very fast. They both noticed it simultaneously.

'Willie!' Ernie stopped and waved his hand wildly. 'Willie! Willie!' Willie waved back and continued to come on like a racer. Within minutes he was beside them, his chest heaving and his breath panting. 'Where you been?' he said.

'Where *you* been?' Nick answered. 'We've been looking all over.'

'Been waiting.'

Ernie looked at Willie in admiration. 'By the mine?'

'Yes.'

'You had more sense than the two of us together. We should have thought of that.'

'Thought of what?' asked Nick.

'By Jove, you're bright today, Nick,' said Ernie irritably. 'Of meeting at the mine, dumb-dumb!'

'How were we to know?'

But Ernie brushed him aside. 'Never mind that now. Let's get going.'

Nick was still nettled. 'That's what I've been saying all the time,' he said. 'Before they let Dobruzza out.'

The word was enough to spur on all three; they grabbed their things and headed for the mine at a trot.

As soon as they reached the shaft Ernie called the other two over and started diving his hands into the bag he was carrying. 'You both got candles and matches?'

'No.'

'Here, then. Take some each. In your pockets.'

'Might break—in a bloke's pocket,' Nick said.

'Doesn't matter. Long as you've got some in an emergency.' Ernie fossicked further. 'A torch for you, Willie, and one for me. And I'll take the tucker and water-bottle in the bag till we get down there.' He looked around. 'We've only got one gouging pick and shovel between us, but it'll have to do.'

'Shouldn't be much digging anway,' Nick said. 'Not if we find the spot.'

'Hope no one's watching,' Ernie said uneasily. 'What d'you say, Willie? Coast clear?'

Willie peered about carefully. 'Clear, I reckon.'

'Good. Let's go. I'll lead off, Willie in the middle, Nick last. I reckon we've only got three or four hours left. If we don't find the stuff in that time, we're done.' Ernie swung the bag over his shoulder and started the descent.

The shock of the underground darkness and the narrowness of the tunnels caught them again, as it always did and always would, even though they lived to do it a thousand times. Ernie led on purposefully with his torch beam probing ahead, noting each chute and cross-drive, but rarely stopping until they reached the big gallery far over towards the other shaft.

'Right,' he said, straightening up. 'We'll make this our headquarters.' He lit a candle and stood it upright on the floor. The flame wavered very gently, indicating an air-draft.

Nick stretched his arms and rubbed his elbows. 'Good.'

'Don't like them tunnels,' Willie said. 'Too dark and skinny.'

'Tell you what.' Ernie was brisk and eager now. 'You blokes take the drive between here and the next shaft. There are some side chutes and a few little dead-end pros-

196

pects. Watch for loose stuff where he might have buried something.'

'What you going to do?' Nick asked.

'I'm going back to my old spot to look for the other case. And then I'll start on all the cross-drives.'

'What do we do if we find something? Sing out?'

'Unless it's Dobruzza you find.'

Nick rolled his eyes. 'Gorrhhh!'

'Come back here and wait. This'll be our meeting place.'

Nick and Willie looked less than comfortable. 'We won't blow this candle out, will we?' Nick asked.

'Be good to leave,' Willie suggested. 'Know where we are.'

'All right then. We've got plenty of candles.' Ernie picked up the gouge. 'I'll take the pick, you take the spade. The rest can stay here.' And he put the bag with the water-bottle, food, and spare candles in the corner. 'See you.'

Willie watched him as he crawled back into the tunnel, the yellow candle-light throwing brightness and shadow on his face and tousled hair. 'Be careful Ernie.'

'I'll be right.' Already Ernie's voice was muffled, flung about inside the close walls of the tunnel. 'Good luck!'

Ernie moved methodically down the drive till he came to the one he'd dug himself. He turned into it and worked his way to the end, checking the niches and pockets he'd left here and there in the walls, but there was nothing to see. At the end of the drive there was such a great mess of mullock that he could hardly crawl. This was where the thief who had ratted his find had originally left a big hole, and where Ernie had found the first suit-case. It all suddenly made sense. If Dobruzza was the person concerned both times—and of course he was—then he would naturally have gone back to bury the case where he knew a handy hole was already waiting.

197

Ernie lay on one elbow and flashed his light over the spot. He wondered why Dobruzza hadn't hidden both cases there. Was there a reason, or was it just chance? Perhaps he ought to be trying to understand how Dobruzza's mind worked. A cruel, greedy, ruthless man. He'd taken the opals out of the cases because they were easier to hide that way—in dozens of separate canvas bags. And he was clever, cunning. Would he have hidden all the bags in one spot, or were they now scattered about all over the mine? He had also been in a hurry—on the run. He might not have had time to spread them about too much.

Ernie decided that the opals were more likely to be in one spot. There was too much trouble involved in memorising a dozen different places, and too much danger of forgetting some of them. In any case, this was only a temporary measure. Dobruzza had certainly planned to pick them up and flee South with his haul as soon as he could.

A loose stone was pressing into Ernie's hip and he heaved himself forward on his elbow to change his position. As he did so the torch fell from his hand and lay for a second with its beam shining full face on the loose rock around the hole. There was a sudden flash of iridescence, and his heart jumped. Opal! He scrabbled feverishly forward, wild thoughts in his mind of Dobruzza emptying the bags into the hole in a great cascade of coloured fire. But it was only a single piece, a splinter left behind from his own find. He put it in his pocket. It would still be worth a few dollars; and there was some kind of ironic justice in the last piece going to the original finder.

He searched about for a while, using the sharp end of the gouge to rake through the rubble on the floor around him, but it was fruitless. So much for that. There were no more answers in this drive. He turned laboriously to go back, reaching up on an impulse at the last minute to pull out the old wire spider he'd used for his candle. It might be handy later on.

There was an enormous amount of mullock lying about on the floor and in the drives nearby where he'd shovelled back rubbish from his own digging. He remembered that in the early stages he had thrown a lot of it into an old drive opposite his own—almost filled it, in fact. He scrambled back and started worrying at it, his head and shoulders in the shallow chute, his behind sticking out into the main tunnel. He scraped the loose rock back with his bare hands, throwing it out between his legs like a terrier digging for rabbits.

He didn't have far to go. Almost at once he struck something wide and smooth—the side of the second suitcase. Although certain that it would be empty like the first, he still felt a pulse of excitement as he worked furiously to dig away enough of the back-filling around it to expose the handle. Then he heaved strongly and pulled the case free. It was even more badly damaged than the first, one latch completely torn away and one corner smashed in. There seemed no doubt that it had been dropped down the shaft, heavily weighted with opal. But, as expected, it was empty, and Ernie felt a real sense of anticlimax as he shut it and prepared to crawl back to the rendezvous.

Willie and Nick were waiting when he arrived. They had seen and found nothing, and the sight of Ernie emerging with the second case gave them a minute of excitement too; it seemed at least as if they were getting somewhere. In fact all their senses were still tingling from the sound of Ernie's scrabbling in the tunnel and the flash of his approaching torch.

'Gives a fellow the creeps,' Nick said feelingly. 'Having lights and snufflings coming towards you under the ground, and not knowing what's going to come along behind.'

'Don't like it,' Willie added with a shudder.

'You blokes,' Ernie said, rubbing his sore knees, 'you'll be wetting your pants next.' But in his heart he knew that he was just as scared as they were; he was only putting on a front for their sakes.

They spent some time handling the case, turning it over and over, bewailing the fact that it was empty. But even as they were doing it they knew it wasn't getting them anywhere. Nick was the first to speak his mind openly. 'Come on, detectives! What's next?'

Ernie picked up his torch. 'There are still a fair few drives we haven't looked at. You take the nearest ones, and I'll take the ones further back.'

'How do we know whether we've done the same ones or not?'

'Won't matter if we do. Double check.'

Nick wasn't impressed. 'And what if we meet head-on in one of 'em; how do we tell whether it's you or not?'

'Who else is it going to be?'

'Dobruzza maybe—escaped from the police?'

The suggestion, half-joking though it was, stopped all three of them like an icy hand. 'Scare a fellow to death,' Willie said.

Nick agreed shakily. 'We . . . we ought to have a signal.'

Ernie recovered from his pulse of fear and took on his role of morale-booster again. 'I'll sing God Save the Queen,' he said, 'as soon as I hear anyone coming.' It did the trick. Nick and Willie laughed and got ready to go back into the tunnel.

This time it was a long slow job for all of them. Ernie felt the loneliness more than ever, perhaps because he didn't seem to be getting anywhere. Going from drive to drive, each one narrow and hard-surfaced and low, he became convinced that no one could hide a hundredweight of opal in these clean sides. It would have to be in dead-ends like platypus burrows, or in niches or sudden pockets. But no matter how much he explored each one there wasn't the faintest trace. He became unsure of himself too; twice he lost his sense of direction and fell into a panic before he found his way again, and constantly an oppressive feeling of imprisonment, of being entombed, seemed to hem him in. Claustrophobia, he said to himself; that's what it is.

But worse than any of these was his conviction that someone else was in the tunnels watching him. Nick's comment about Dobruzza had stuck in his mind like a splinter, and now it was beginning to fester, so to speak. He remembered a horrible passage in the story about Tom Sawyer that Mr Martindale had read to them, where down in the labyrinth of the caves Tom had suddenly come face to face with Injun Joe. Mr Martindale was something of an actor, and just at that spot he had let out a yell and jumped back; it had frightened the daylights out of half the class and Ernie had had nightmares for a week.

And so now, as he crawled about in the darkness of the narrow tunnels, he became petrified lest Dobruzza's face should leap from the next dark nook or lest Dobruzza should be following stealthily behind him waiting for the moment when he could drive a knife into his back. After a while the feeling that he was being followed became so strong that Ernie was certain he could hear breathing immediately behind him, and he would suddenly whip round and shine the torch hard and long straight down the tunnel into the far darkness. There was never anything there but Ernie could see his hand shaking and hear the blood thumping in his ears. It was the same uncontrollable urge, he remembered, that had made him look under the bed when he was a little boy, as soon as his mother had said goodnight and left the room.

No one, least of all Willie and Nick, knew the agony

Ernie had been through when they finally joined up again in the big gallery. His face shone white and damp in the torch-light, but they put it down to warm perspiration rather than cold-sweat. All three of them were tired and dispirited.

'What do we do now?' Nick asked tonelessly.

'Dunno.' Ernie sat down against the wall with his wrists on his knees, his hands hanging down listlessly.

Willie was quick to see the erosion of Ernie's spirit, the loss of his leadership. 'Still other places to look,' he suggested. 'Not time to give up yet for long time.'

Ernie roused himself and looked at Willie. 'Who're you kidding?' he meant to say, but he stopped himself at the last minute when he realised that Willie had reversed their roles and was now the one trying to lift up his partners. Ernie was filled with sudden admiration for Willie. 'You're right, mate,' he said. 'We'll give her another go in a minute.'

'Have to hurry,' Nick said pessimistically. 'Must be getting late.'

'Still time yet,' Ernie answered, though he knew Nick was right.

'We'll have a bite to eat and then start the last big search.'

'With a fine tooth,' suggested Nick.

'With a comb, nong,' Ernie corrected him. 'A fine comb.'

'With a tooth or a comb, it doesn't matter,' Nick answered.

They sat munching biscuits and swigging briefly from the water-bottle.

'You know,' Ernie said slowly, 'a bloke ought to be able to work out what a crim like Dobruzza would do with a stash of stolen opal.'

'Sell it,' Nick said.

202

'Down here, I mean. What would he be thinking of? What sort of spot would he pick?'

'One that no other fellow would ever find,' Willie said.

'One where no one could get them even if they did,' Nick added.

'Can't think of any such place,' Ernie said slowly. 'Not down here.'

Nick considered the idea for a minute. 'Maybe they're not here at all,' he suggested. 'Maybe he emptied the cases up top before he got to the shaft. Behind a stone or in a bit of a cut. Maybe this business is all a blind.'

They were all silent, somewhat uncomfortable at the thought.

'We should've looked at his footprints,' Nick went on. 'Could you tell if he was carrying a heavy load from the depth of his footprints, Willie?'

Willie shrugged. 'Not me. Grandpa Yirri maybe, or Uncle Winelli. They could do it.'

'Dobruzza's left everything down here,' Ernie said firmly. 'He would've gone over to pick it all up on his way home last night if he hadn't. He didn't know Willie was following him.'

'That's right, I reckon,' Willie agreed.

'That's right, I reckon too,' Nick said. He rolled his eyes round the gallery and got to his feet. 'Then they're down here, the opals. So all we've got to do is to find them.'

'Need a compressor and jack-pick, maybe,' Willie said.

Nick took up the spade. 'Or a plug or two of gelly.'

Ernie shuddered. 'Just let Dobruzza go free,' he said ominously, 'and you'll get all the gelly you want. Dropped down on your head quick smart. All finished up.'

The thought was enough to galvanise Nick. 'Come on, then. Hurry up.'

So they took shovel and gouge, torches and candles

again, ready for another sortie into the drives. Around them the walls of the gallery, and beyond that the solid fastnesses of rock, the seams of potch, the age-old unknown history of gems unimaginable, lay hidden and silent.

Hidden and silent, too, lay the peril that waited for them, the imminent danger, the final disaster. But for these last late moments they could sense nothing of that, and so they went on with their searching unknowing.

Chapter Seventeen

The final search of the drives was no more successful than the others had been. In the end Ernie himself went over all the parts that Willie and Nick had covered, including the short sections from the gallery to the second shaft, but there wasn't even a bug's eye of opal to be seen in the whole tortuous maze. They were tired and depressed when they gathered in the gallery again.

'It isn't down here,' Nick said for the dozenth time. 'It can't be.'

'Where, then?' Willie asked.

'He must have dumped it somewhere else.'

'It's down here all right,' Ernie said doggedly.

'Where, for crying out?'

'Don't know. But it's down here.'

'Better come back tomorrow, maybe,' Willie suggested. 'Nearly night time now, I reckon.'

The thought startled Nick like a needle prick. 'Gosh, I've got to get back home. Mum'll murder me if I'm late again today.'

'We can't wait till tomorrow,' Ernie said desperately.

'We don't know how much longer they're going to keep Dobruzza locked up.'

'Well, we'd better pull our fingers out,' Nick said firmly. 'I can't stay much longer.'

They were sitting with their backs to the wall, eating the last of the biscuits.

'Drink?' Ernie asked, holding up the water-bottle.

'Thanks.'

Ernie leaned over, stretching to pass the bottle across to Nick. He winced as a small sharp stone pressed into the side of his buttock, pinching the flesh through his thin pants. He shifted position quickly and put down his hand to move the stone; but there were others, a whole jumble of them, and it was hard to sit comfortably. Ernie scrabbled about with his hands, trying to smooth them down, then stopped suddenly and looked about him at the floor.

'Hey,' he said slowly, 'd'you reckon the floor was always covered with as much mullock as this?' He turned sharply to Nick. 'D'you reckon, Nick? Compared with the way it was when we came down here the first time?'

Nick looked about him deliberately. 'Don't think. Used to be pretty clean, didn't it?'

'That's what I reckon. Smooth compared to this.'

Ernie scrambled to his feet, grabbing the candle from the floor and holding it up high to throw light all over the gallery.

'More this side, more mullock,' Wilie said, pointing to where they'd been sitting.

Ernie was electrified. He strode over to the short tunnel leading to the second shaft and shone the light into the entrance. 'Loose rubble in here too,' he said. 'But only for the first six feet or so. As if someone's been spreading the stuff to get rid of it.'

Nick ran over and knelt beside him, peering. 'Hey,' he said excitedly, 'd'you reckon?'

Ernie was up on his feet again, moving the light around the gallery. 'Not much altogether, though—only a drum full or two.'

They were all suddenly making the connection.

'Would be enough,' Willie said.

'To make room for a case full of opal!' Nick did a war-whoop round the gallery.

Ernie grabbed the old spider he'd brought back from his own drive, hammered it hastily head-high into the wall with the pick, and thrust the candle into it. 'The floor,' he said, raking feverishly with the tine of the gouge. 'Under the floor here. It must be.'

'Been sitting on it,' Nick said. 'So help me, don't say we've been sitting on it.' He seized the shovel and started scraping away the loose surface mullock near the mouth of the drive.

Willie was down on his hands and knees, rooting away the loose stuff with a sharp stone like a hand-axe. 'Try in the corners,' he said. 'Try in the corner of the floor against the wall.'

Ernie was ripping deep with the pick like a madman. 'It's loose underneath,' he cried. 'Real loose. Just stamped down a bit on top.'

'We're on to it.'

Willie was scraping out a deepening trench in Ernie's wake.

'Whee!' They were both yelling to each other in excitement.

'Here's something,' Ernie shouted. 'I'm on to something. Look.'

He had exposed a length of wire in the trench, six inches down, and running towards the wall. He was about to heave on it triumphantly when Willie gave a wild shout. 'Mustn't!' he yelled, and leapt back with all his strength, colliding with Ernie and sending him flying across the gal-

206

lery on his face. The pick, its tine hooked under the wire, fell across Willie's foot and was jerked back by his movement. Then the whole world ended. The floor heaved up, the wall came down, and tons of darkness crashed and rolled above and over them, obliterating light and time, hurling and pummelling space, crushing cavities, booming down distant drives, and finally rumbling and swirling slowly into stillness.

Darkness.

Darkness and silence.

Ernie stirred. He moved an arm and lay still again. Long silence. He stirred again, more purposefully, bringing one leg up in a froglike movement, thrusting himself forwards and upwards. Finally he turned over on his side. A cascade of stones and rubble tumbled from his neck and shoulders and back. He was vaguely aware that he wasn't in his own bed. He shook his head and blinked his eyes. Darkness. Utter darkness. Utter, blind, mind-destroying darkness. He lay still with his eyes shut. Something thin and wet and warm ran down his forehead and crawled across his cheek. Like a wet, warm eel. He put up his hand quickly, grabbed it, and squashed it between his fingers. It had no body and left a slightly sticky mess. Presently another one ran down the same spot. He put his hand up to the place where it had started on his forehead and squashed it hard. A sudden shaft of pain shot through his head and his mind started working. He had a cut on his forehead. It was blood.

He sat up suddenly, his hands feeling the coarse rock and rubble all around, his eyes blinking unseeingly again. He shook himself, the movement hurting his head and bringing more dust and bits of stone tumbling from his hair and shoulders. Then, at last, came memory. A tangled flood of remembering. Dobruzza, opals, Willie, Nick, discovery. And black chaos. His mind was recovering quickly now. Explosion. There'd been an explosion. And with it, darkness. Black-out.

The realisation that he had the means of making light came quickly with his panic and his need. He had a piece of candle in his pocket. And matches. The old precaution. Although he was fully conscious and aware now, he was still trembling and fumbling, and it took a long time to get a match out of the box and actually strike it into flame. But he did it at last, the first sudden flare coming so sharply and fiercely that it hurt his eyes. He held the shaking match to the wick for a long time before it caught, the flame burning down so close to his fingers that he had to throw it away hastily. Then he slowly held up the candle.

The light brought the shock of reality. The place was a shambles. Loads of mullock, so it seemed, had been brought down on the far side of the gallery, and in one place the corner of the floor and wall had been blown out in a crater. The drives were sealed off by a rock fall.

Ernie got to his feet shakily, looking about dazed and appalled, then dropped to his knees and crawled frantically forward. Willie was lying on his back near the far wall, spreadeagled and motionless. Even as he reached him, Ernie was looking about for Nick, but there was no sign of him. He brushed some of the rubble and dust from Willie, put his arm under his shoulders, and raised his head.

'Willie!' he said urgently and passionately. 'Willie, are you all right?' But Willie lay limp and silent. There was a dribble of blood oozing slowly from the corner of his mouth, but otherwise Ernie couldn't see any outward signs. 'Willie! Willie!' Ernie looked down at the motionless face, terrified lest he was already looking down on death. 'Oh God!' he said despairingly.

He lowered Willie's head and lifted his wrist, trying to feel for signs of a pulse. But he had never been any good at it and couldn't make out anything one way or the other. Desperate, he put his ear down against Willie's chest, trying to detect a heart beat, a flutter, a movement of breathing, anything that might indicate whether Willie was still alive. But he detected nothing. Nothing at all. Numbed, shattered, entombed and alone he knelt with his cheek still pressed against Willie's chest, tears welling slowly from his eyes, running down the dusty curve of his face.

'Willie,' he kept repeating in anguish. 'Willie! Oh God! Oh God! Oh God!'

Ernie had no idea of time. He didn't know how long he had been in the mine, how long he had been kneeling at Willie's side. But he roused himself at last, crawled over to the candle, and shone the light around the gallery. Vaguely he knew that he had to do something. Action. Escape. Escape to get help for Willie. And for Nick, if he could find out where he was.

He got to his feet and staggered forward, holding up the candle. As the light fell on the angle of the opposite wall near the crater the broken floor suddenly gleamed with colour—mosaics of it, fiery and blue and green, chunks of it, pebbles, edges, angles, hard sharp surfaces of it, beads and pin-points of it as bright as tiny eyes, shafts and beams of it, gleams of it, masses like unreal flowers suddenly blooming in the dark, embers and coals and flames of it burning strangely and wildly in the rock.

Opal! The stolen opal!

Ernie stumbled forward crazily, wavering and tripping, scrabbling over the mounds of rock and mullock that half filled the chamber and brought the ceiling down close to his head. But he reached it at last, sliding down the slope of the mound on his elbows towards the gleaming treasure.

Opals! Dobruzza's opals!

He set the candle upright in the mullock and picked up one of the glowing stones. It was as big as his fist and as fiery as coal. He turned it over and over in the light; then put it aside and picked up another. He scooped up two whole handfuls of smaller stones and let them run through his fingers in a waterfall of blue and green and red. It was miraculous, incredible. He began scraping them together and, as he did so, came upon something soft and pliable underneath. Cloth, he thought. No, canvas—the bag that had held the stones—shattered in the explosion. He pulled it out, and saw another one beyond it. He tugged and strained until he hauled it free too; it was almost intact, except for a small split on one side. Beyond it were others again—Dobruzza's cache, all stacked neatly like small butts of grain waiting to be picked up by the reaper.

Ernie got up and crawled back over the mullock heap, nursing the candle as he went. They'd found the treasure, if that was what they wanted. But nobody knew they'd done it, nobody knew they were here. They could die here and lie here a thousand years, and nobody on earth would even find their bones.

The wound on his head was throbbing badly, but the bleeding had almost stopped, the cut clotted up with dirt and hair and drying blood. Despite the pain he could think more clearly now. He had to dig a way out. There was no sign of the pick or shovel—they were probably buried under the mullock—so he would have to use his bare hands. But first he had to work out where the tunnel was. He took the candle and shambled about, reconnoitring. Both tunnels were sealed, the one to the second shaft less badly. He wondered whether Nick could possibly be in it because he had been crawling about in the entrance a moment before the blast and might have been flung forward by it. Ernie knelt in front of the spot where he thought it must be and called. 'Nick! You there, Nick?'

The sound of his voice echoed hollowly around the chamber. 'Nick! Can you hear me?'

The echoes vibrated and died away slowly. Ernie turned away. If Nick was inside the drive and still alive he must either be unconscious or out of earshot. But if he was alive at least there ought to be fresh air for him from the second shaft. Which perhaps was more than could be said for the prison he was in. If everything was sealed, as it seemed to be, he wondered how long the air would last.

He crawled back towards the other side, trying to pin-point the position of the tunnel there. Using his body and his bare hands he started pushing and heaving the mullock aside, lifting the bigger chunks of rock piece by piece and shoving at the rest of the heap with his shoulders and elbows. He worked until his arms were sore and bruised, but even then he'd hardly made an impression on the mound. It was hopeless without a tool of some kind. He searched about for a thin flat piece of stone that he could use in his hand like a scraper or an Aboriginal artefact, and attacked the heap again. This time it was more effective for the smaller stuff, but all the bigger stones still had to be shifted singly by hand.

His head and arms ached unbearably now and he started to get spasms of the shakes when his whole body shivered uncontrollably. He knew he was starting to suffer from shock which he'd heard the Sister at the hospital describe one day after a mining accident at the Eight Mile. But he drove himself on. If he gave up now, if once he accepted excuses for himself that he was tired or hurt or sick, if he told himself it was impossible to do it, then it really would be impossible and he might as well lie down and die.

So piece by piece, scrape by scrape, he worried at the mullock till he had made a dint in the side of the heap. And scrape by scrape, handful by handful, he shifted rubble and chips until he'd cleared part of the wall. But even then he was only just approaching the lip of the tunnel. And his strength was running out.

He left the candle, what was left of it, burning on top of the mound. What was left of it! The sight of the stump, almost burnt down to nothing, filled him with sudden unimaginable terror. For when it was gone he would be in the dark. Permanently and irretrievably in the dark. When that happened he knew he would go mad in an hour. No escape, no hope of finding the way, the end coming slowly and horribly by starvation and madness—in a tomb, sealed up with a treasure worth a queen's ransom. It always seemed to be the way. Greedy riches and dead bodies went side by side.

He was crawling about looking for a better hand tool when he heard a sound. It was not much more than a breath, a faint exhalation of human pain, but it made him jerk round, nape tingling and eyes wide. Something was alive in the chamber with him. He listened again and then rushed forward, scrambling back over the mullock. It was Willie.

Ernie bent down over his face, ears to his lips. Willie was breathing; barely breathing perhaps, but certainly alive. 'Willie! Willie!' he whispered urgently. 'You hear me?'

Still there was no response, nothing but a faint hush of breath for a second time, a half-formed moan that died as it was made. But Willie was alive. Ernie knew it now, knew it in his mind as well as his heart. He lifted Willie's head a little and rested it more comfortably on the rubble. 'Don't worry, Will,' he whispered; 'I'll get you out of this. I'll get you out of this.' And as if in answer to such a promise, there beyond Willie's head was a sudden glint of metal and wood, an arc of shovel-blade and a hint of the buried handle. Ernie flung himself on it, his throat sobbing dryly. 'The shovel!'

Now he scrambled back to the mound again feeling stronger, like an unarmed soldier unexpectedly given a weapon to defend himself with. He attacked the mullock again, much more effectively this time, working down the face of the wall by the tunnel mouth. The tips of his fingers were badly blistered and the pain in his head grew worse as he worked, but he kept on doggedly. He began to feel light-headed and the spasms of shivering increased, coming on in waves that wracked his whole body. But he kept on. The sight of the candle drove him relentlessly— not much more than half an inch of it left, and even that shrinking steadily every time he paused to look. It was not only a race to clear the tunnel, or to try to save Willie and Nick. It was a grim race against darkness. And that was death.

At last he could drive his body no longer. His breath was coming in great hot gulps till he was wheezing and choking with it. The muscles in his legs were quivering so much that he could hardly stand up. He half collapsed, half sat, on the side of the mound, his head hanging forward on his chest. But only for a moment or two. The dwindling candle was like a cancer eating away his life behind his back, so he roused himself and scrambled up laboriously till he could reach out and lift it down. He looked at it half-mesmerised for a second, the light falling brightly on his damp feverish face; then he blew it out and lay slumped in the darkness. If he couldn't work he couldn't afford light. That had to be his motto from now on.

For a short time he lay half-conscious, his eyes shut and his body drained. But as his awareness returned, so did his horror and fear of everlasting dark, perpetual entombment. He opened his eyes and shut them again quickly. It was far more horrifying with them open than shut because then there was no more illusion, no more assumption that light was just an eye-blink away. The reality of it numbed his mind. He wondered if it was night in the world above him. It must be. Midnight perhaps, or early morning. Night-time and darkness. No, not darkness. For what kind of darkness was it when there was light everywhere—stars like shining ice, moonlight on the hills, the gleam of headlights and campfires.

He opened his eyes again and the blank blackness was more then he could bear. He fumbled for his matches, almost dropping them in his haste. 'Careful, careful,' he said to himself. If once he dropped them, or lost the bit of candle, he might never find them again. The match didn't ignite at once, but even the spit of fire as he struck it on the box was like salve to his mind. It suggested sanity once more. When it finally flared he held it trembling against the wick. Instantly the candle flame grew up again, tapering and shapely with just a hint of yellow edging the white. He had never realised how beautiful a candle flame really was. But, like a living thing, the moment it came into being it was slowly draining its life away.

He got to his feet quickly and clambered up to find a spot for it again. The glint of opal came up at him as before, but he ignored it. Riches without life were worthless. Like Midas. He was just putting down the candle when something beyond the opals caught his eye. He took a step downwards and held the light far forwards, peering uncertainly. Something cylindrical like a short thick stick. He couldn't make it out, and bent even closer. The next instant he recoiled in horror. It was gelignite, a stick of gelignite with detonator attached, apparently exposed in the rock-fall, and by some miracle left unexploded. There was a wire too, bent and half-hidden from view. Carefully, very carefully, he began to withdraw, keeping watch as if it was a snake poised ready to strike. Every time he dislodged a stone or lump of rubble he sat frozen for a second, then breathed out and continued his retreat across the mound.

214

He realised everything very clearly now. It had all been a trap, a booby trap. Cleverly set on all sides of the cache. Dobruzza was going to have the last laugh after all, or so he'd planned. The person who came to take the treasure would die doing so.

Ernie suddenly remembered the last second before the explosion: Willie's shout, and the push that had sent him sprawling across the floor. Willie must have seen the danger, must have sensed it, in that last split second, but hadn't had time to get clear himself. Poor Willie. And now what was anyone doing for him?

Ernie reached the far side of the mound safely and set the candle on a rock. Then he took the spade and started digging carefully again. He had to work from one side now, hoping even then that he wouldn't cause a rock fall on the other side. It was like being in a room with a cobra and not knowing what it was going to do. His hope, he told himself, was the solid wall he was working against; already six inches of the tunnel was exposed and before long he would be able to start clearing mullock from inside.

He shovelled steadily for a while but gradually the pain in his head and his body started burning more fiercely again till he sobbed as he dug. But he didn't give up. This was the final assault, the crisis. The flame was eating the last of the candle now, and the darkness seemed to be tensing itself in the dim corners ready for the moment when it could leap out over everything in one suffocating rush. Ernie dug on. He drove the shovel down the wall, levering away the bigger stones, exposing more and more of the tunnel outline.

His legs began trembling again, and twice he stumbled forward as if he was going to faint. But he checked himself each time, his hand on the shovel, his head bent forward for a second, resting against the wall. Then he went on

215

digging. He was becoming less effective as he grew more and more exhausted, sometimes heaving hopelessly with the blade locked behind a rock, sometimes missing altogether and shovelling air. But stone by stone and grain by grain he dug downwards. After a while there were red colours all round him, a strange sea of red that he was working in, waist deep sometimes and at other times so deep that it was over his head, with sharp bright spearguns that darted into his forehead and went deep into the flesh of his arms and body, thrusting through to his bones like slim needles. But still he dug on, in the red sea and under it, while great buoys swayed above him and swung their bells against his temples until red alarms of agony rang and vibrated through his mind.

But he dug on.

The candle mocked him when he tried to look up at it. There were rows of almond kernels, upright and white like candle flames, on the mullock heap, and sometimes tiny yellow leaves sprouting from the rubble reef where it broke through the red surface of the sea. There were discs under the flames and the almond kernels and the leaves—squat discs half an inch thick, round discs a quarter of an inch thick, thin discs like wide flat wafers or buttons. But he dug on under the white almonds and buttons until, when he heaved at a protruding stone, a whole avalanche came down almost knocking him off his feet. And there, right beside him, was the tunnel outline, with a foot of the drive exposed at the top.

Ernie reeled back to get his balance and looked again. Miraculous. He advanced straight at it, scratching and scraping to enlarge the hole. When his senses came back a little more clearly he saw that it was better to shovel from below, driving in the blade along the floor and letting it fill from above. Despite his staggering stance and his weakness he made headway. In a little while he had a gap eighteen inches wide. He fell to his hands and knees then and looked into the hole. The blockage was shallow, extending no more than three or four feet inside. He could almost crawl through it as it was.

He got to his feet but fell forward to his knees again. His head was swimming so badly that for a minute the candle, the mullock heap and the cavern all moved around him sickeningly on a slow tide. But they and the world slowly grew stable once more and he groped about for the shovel to clear the tunnel for the last time. It was a pitiful effort, however, and after two or three minutes of swaying and scraping he hadn't really widened it at all. It would have to do. The candle was going, he kept telling himself, and he had to get Willie out before it did. So he put aside the shovel and crawled over to Willie. He was still lying just as he had been, and Ernie couldn't tell about his breathing. In any case there wasn't time. So he took a grip under Willie's arms and started to drag him over to the tunnel.

It was agonising work. Because he had to duck-wall backwards as he dragged, he fell back on his rump every time he struck a stone with his heels. And each time it was harder to get started again. He was at the end of his tether, played out, finished. He would have to rest before trying to get Willie to the other end of the tunnel. But first the light. He put down his burden and went to scrabble back to the candle for the last time when he noticed Willie's pocket and suddenly laughed. It was a queer hysterical gurgle. Willie had a candle; he himself had given it to him.

Emergency lighting, out of the bag! He knelt down and took the candle from Willie's pocket, a strong new piece three inches long, never used before. 'Dear God,' he said. 'Been there all the time.' And he laughed again till the laugh turned into a sob that choked in his throat and he fell forwards with his head across Willie's legs. He lay there for a long time while the candle on the stones above

217

him guttered and sputtered, shrank slowly like a living thing frightened to die, and finally winked out. And the darkness which he had fought so long lay over the two of them, thick and suffocating; lay over the hiding place of one man's greed, over the fortune whose fires it quenched as soon as it snuffed out the light.

It was a long time before Ernie stirred again. But memory and awareness came at last and he sat up, the candle still clutched in his hand. There was the torture of match-striking then, the long trial and failure of igniting the new wick, the re-striking and trial again. But in the end he did it and crawled forward, peering into the tunnel. It needed more clearing, so he stood the candle nearby and scraped and shovelled again. And then, at long last, he could crawl in backwards and drag Willie after him, foot by foot.

And so a new agony began. First Ernie crawled ahead for ten or fifteen feet and set down the candle carefully. Then he crawled back to Willie and dragged him bit by bit from the darkness into the light. Then on with the candle again and back to Willie, on and back, on and back, on and back. Over and over again. Once he was tempted to leave Willie and go on ahead on his own, but he put down the idea sternly and struggled on. And so, crawling and shambling, collapsing and rising, dragging and resting, wincing and hauling, Ernie Ryan reached the end of his *via dolorosa* with Willie, and stood up shakily at the bottom of the shaft by the ladder. There, above him, was light. He blew out the candle, half delirious with pain and joy and exhaustion, and clung to the rungs of the ladder, laughing and crying and talking aloud to the still form of Willie lying at his feet.

'We did it, Will! We did it!'

He laughed again, a queer dry croak that died away at the back of his throat. 'You stay there while I go and get help.'

Then he clutched the ladder and, rung by rung, hauled himself up, swaying back perilously sometimes, clinging above the brink of disaster, but always battling his way upwards, steadily upwards, until in the end he struggled out on to the surface and lay there panting.

It was a new day. The morning was full of sunrise, long warm beams of it shooting clear through his floating body, and touching the hills with light. And there was no darkness. The plains wide with air, the golden dust rising on the roads, the high high arch of the sky—all were bright and brimming.

Ernie took a deep breath and smiled. For want of a better way to express his joy, he smiled. And the smile stayed on his face, foolishly, rigidly, like the pasted mask of a clown, while he stood up at the head of the shaft and turned his gaze to the sun. And so Ernie Ryan walked unsteadily down the rim of the morning towards the town; walked from darkness into the rinsing light; walked in a sense from the clutches of his own tomb back into life again.

Chapter Eighteen

The news of Ernie's emergence from the ground like a ghost from the grave spread quickly. He had barely gasped out his message to old Red Ned O'Keefe, whose camp was the first one he came to, before Red Ned was driving like a maniac in a willy-willy of dust to get the police; and he in turn had hardly wheezed out the news before police and detectives were thundering out to the Bordini mine. There they brought out the inert form of Willie and—miracle of miracles—Nick too, from the other shaft where he'd been lying bruised and shaken, but quite safe, hollering up the straight smooth sides of his prison for fourteen hours. Sergeant Brogan led the detectives to the hidden gallery where carefully, very carefully, they removed the unexploded charge and finally brought out the cache of opals—bag after bag of it, until rumours ran madly up and down the Fields that the plane had crashed from the sheer weight of its load.

But Ernie knew little of this. Red Ned took him down to Sister Williams as soon as he'd alerted the police, and the Sister put him straight into hospital. There she bathed the gash on his head, cleaning it of the clotted mess of blood and hair and dirt, bathed his blistered and bleeding hands, bathed his body which was so blackened with huge bruises from the explosion that Ernie, looking down feebly, couldn't believe that it was his own.

Then Sister Williams gave him an anti-tetanus injection, bandaged his wounds, made a long hot drink for him and gave him a sedative. And so, as soon as she eased his head back on the hospital pillow, the whole bed with its soft mattress and beautiful, clean, white sheets rose up gently and floated out through the window. It rocked and swung there on waves of air, sinking and swaying, dipping and rising, until it carried him far away where all movement stopped and there was nothing.

He was so curled up in the goodness of the bed that he didn't hear Nick call to him cheekily when the Sister discharged 'that Andropoulos boy' into the care of his talking mother. He was drifting so deeply that he didn't even hear the Flying Doctor plane roaring overhead, didn't see the sad look on the Sister's face as she watched it fading southwards, didn't know it was hurrying Willie desperately to a big hospital in Adelaide.

Time passed, but it meant nothing to Ernie. All that morning he slept unmoving, and all through the afternoon, and far into the night. And when phantasms started to surround him at last in the deep locked prison of the darkness so that he began tossing and whimpering and flinging his arms about to ward them off, Sister Williams was at his bedside in a flash, with gentle firmness and more sedatives. To Ernie she was his mother, emerging silently out of the shadowy gloom of his boyhood when he needed her long ago. And then he lapsed back into a long blank sleep again until the sunlight was fairly hammering at the walls outside and even his sheltered room was brimming with it.

'Better?'

It took a while to fit sights and sounds together again, even after he had opened his eyes.

'Feeling better?'

He still wasn't aware that someone was speaking to him; it was an unbodied question floating about loosely in the air.

'Feeling better this morning, Ernie?'

There it was. The whole world swooping into focus—time, place, and memory coming together with the suddenness of a physical jolt. He moved quickly and his head hurt, but only for a moment.

'Willie! Where's Willie?' He looked about feverishly.

The Sister's voice was very quiet. 'He's very sick, Ernie. He's been taken to Adelaide. By the Flying Doctor.'

'Will . . . will he be all right?'

'I don't know. Nobody knows yet.'

'What about Nick?'

She moved forward. 'Nick's quite all right. As good as gold. He's gone home already.' She paused. 'And what about you? Better?'

'Yes thanks, Sister.'

She was standing at the foot of the bed with a smile on her face and a thermometer in her hand. 'Good! I think you look better too.'

221

She kept Ernie in hospital for five more days all the same. 'As a precaution,' she told him. But it was really because she knew he had no one to look after him and wanted to make sure he was strong enough to fend for himself when he was discharged.

Even in hospital he couldn't escape the outside world. Sergeant Brogan and two detectives came to see him on the second day, asking more questions and taking more notes, until his head started to spin and Sister Williams bundled them out. The Flying Doctor called in too, peering into his eyes and talking mysteriously about delayed concussion and shock, but he was pleasant enough and seemed satisfied in the end. He brought copies of the city newspapers with him, and Ernie crawled down into the sheets with embarrassment as he saw the headlines the reporters had written about his exploit. Sister Williams arranged for him to have a copy of his own, and whenever he thought no one was about he secretly read the story over again.

On the third day there was even bigger news. A man from the insurance company called at the hospital to say that the reward would be divided into three parts, each of about three thousand three hundred dollars, and given to Ernie, Nick, and Willie — or their families. But Ernie was sad rather than happy. For there was no real news of Willie. He was still lying in a coma, they said, and nothing more could be done until he recovered consciousness. To gain publicity the insurance company had wanted to arrange a special ceremony where the three boys could be photographed as they were given their reward, but under the circumstances it was considered best to do the thing quietly. Nick and Ernie each received a cheque privately, and Willie's share was handed to his family.

Dosh Dobruzza was brought up for trial on the day Ernie was released from hospital. The first hearing was held before a special magistrate in the dining-room of the

222

motel, and people crowded everywhere. If they were hoping for a spectacle they were disappointed because the whole business only lasted a few minutes before the magistrate remanded the prisoner to be tried in Adelaide at a later date.

Ernie and Nick were standing near the door trying to get a better view of what was going on when Sergeant Brogan and another policeman led Dobruzza away. All three of them were handcuffed together. As they went by, Dobruzza suddenly leant over towards the two boys. "I kill you," he said thickly. "I come back, maybe four year, five year, and then I kill you."

Sergeant Brogan jerked him forward violently. "Get moving," he said. "No talking!"

But Ernie felt sick. He suddenly realised that the spectre of Dosh Dobruzza was going to follow him for the rest of his life. Even the sight of the police plane flying overhead an hour or two later on its way to Adelaide with the prisoner didn't make things any better.

For a whole week after that Ernie drifted about listlessly, waiting for news of Willie. He didn't go back to school. Whenever the mail came in, whenever a bundle of newspapers arrived, or a bus filled with tourists roared out of its own dust-cloud, Ernie was there hanging about the motel for news. Sometimes, when he knew one of the men, he would ask questions—hesitant, plaintive questions—but there were never any answers. Once he overheard two of the barmen talking about him.

'That Ryan kid's always hanging about here these days.'

'Yes.'

'Makes you cry to look at him.'

'Yes.'

'Waiting for news of that Aboriginal kid—what was his name?'

'The one got blown up in the mine?'

'Yes.'

'Willie.'

'Yes, Willie. Poor devil. Had his chips, I'd say. Still unconscious, they reckon.'

Ernie turned and plunged away blindly. He couldn't bear to listen to talk that was so casual, so unconcerned and heartless; talk that treated Willie like an animal or a package.

The following day he couldn't stand it any longer. He went to see Nick and told him that he was going to Adelaide to find out about Willie for himself. He would use some of his reward money and stay as long as Willie needed him. Nick came over to the motel with him to make arrangements.

Just as they walked up past the store they heard Andy Bishop, one of the transport drivers, talking loudly as he filled his tank with petrol.

'Ain't got no time for dingoes that lay booby traps. Ought to string 'em up.' He hung the hose back on the pump and screwed the cap on the tank. 'Still unconscious, the kid. Ten days or more since it happened. Sure hanging on, ain't he?'

Ernie stood stock still. For a second or two he looked up at Andy Bishop, then turned slowly towards Nick. 'Willie's still alive,' he said, as if announcing the news to himself for the first time. They stood together in the middle of the dusty road.

'It'd be in the paper if he wasn't,' Nick said.

Ernie's eyes blazed as if he was suddenly furious with Nick. 'Don't talk like that,' he said. For in his heart Ernie knew what would be in the paper if Willie died. An inch of space on a back page saying that Willie Winowie, the Aboriginal boy who had lain in a coma for two weeks after an explosion on the opal fields, had died this morning. There would be bigger headlines for a dead racehorse.

A commotion over at the motel roused them — the sound of a bottle being smashed, followed by a babel of voices shouting and swearing loudly. Aunt Merna was in the middle of the group, violently drunk, flailing about with her arms, shouting abuse.

'Same old crowd,' Nick said resignedly. 'Have a spree on Willie's money.'

'Willie's money!' Ernie spun round on Nick with a fierce cry, and for a minute Nick thought he was going to rush at the drunken group and lash out at them like a madman. But instead he caught his breath in a kind of sob, turned round abruptly, and ran off towards his own dugout. Nick tried to keep up with him for a while.

'Hey, Ernie, come and stay the night with us,' he called. 'We've got a bed ready. Ain't no bus till tomorrow.'

But Ernie didn't even hear him. He charged on ahead until Nick dropped back further and further and finally gave up.

Ernie ran straight into his dugout and flung himself down on his rickety old bunk, his face pressed hard into the rough hessian. For a long time he stayed there without moving, his eyes dry but his throat choked and his heart burning. It wasn't until the dugout grew dark and his body ached that he got up slowly, walked to the entrance, and looked out.

The sunset had almost faded into night. The last hints of light were falling away in the west and the stars were out in a moonless sky. The wind was cold, colder than he had ever known it before. He shivered. Far, far ahead of him was the dark landscape he had watched a thousand times—the dim slopes, the hump of a hill, the pin-points of light here and there on the Fields, and beyond them for ever and ever the vast inscrutable silence.

Where, he wondered sadly, did it all add up? His own life, and his mother's and father's; Dobruzza's and Nick's

225

and Mr Martindale's—and Willie's. Willie's that was still hanging in the balance. And all the other things: his lost opal find, Nick's long journey on the stretcher, the cruel plight of Willie's people, Aunt Merna using the reward to buy cheap wine, and his own unknown future. . . .

He stood watching it all in his mind's eye, hardly aware of the silence and loneliness and the cold wind. But at last he turned and went inside. He had made up his mind. He would go to Adelaide as he had planned, to see Willie. After that he would decide about himself.

He packed an old sugar bag by the light of the blackened hurricane lamp in the dugout—his last bits of clothing, a water-bottle, a few tins of food, a pair of sandshoes, a plate, knife and fork—and set off down the slope towards the town. Ahead of him the headlights of a heavy truck bored through the darkness and dust like two narrow tunnels of dirty ice as it roared up out of the South and slowed down as it reached the motel. But Ernie didn't go into the town. Instead he veered off to the left until he struck the main Adelaide road; then he turned his back on the Fields and headed South.

Back at the motel the truck driver eased himself out of the cabin and stretched his arms hugely. A couple of miners were standing outside the store, watching.

'Good run?'

'Terrible run.' The driver's back cracked as if the bones were jumping back into place. 'That haul is enough to send you screaming; enough to make you see snakes and salamanders crawling over the windscreen.' The miners watched as he started untying the tarpaulin ropes.

'What's news down South?'

'Nothing's news.'

'Nothing?'

'Strikes, demos, marches, and footy. Lot of ratbags down there.'

He loosened the ropes and flung back the corner of the tarpaulin. 'And the kid's dead.'

'What kid?'

'The Aboriginal one—from up here. Haven't you heard about it?'

'The one in the mine?'

'Yes.'

'Willie whatever?'

'That's him. Heard it on the radio—an hour out of Port Augusta.'

'Best thing.'

'Guess you're right. Died about lunch time today.'

'Didn't have a chance anyway.'

'Not a chance.'

The driver started throwing things down from the back of the truck.

A mile down the track Ernie found the going easy. The road was barely distinguishable, a darker corridor in the darkness, but he knew it was there—more than six hundred miles of it—stretching away ahead of him. He strode out strongly. By morning perhaps, or sometime during the next day, he hoped he might be picked up by a traveller or a transport driver; but if not he wouldn't be concerned—he would walk. And at the end of it he'd find Willie.

After a while he paused to look back. The lights of the Fields were still winking thinly, one or two of them here and there, and for just a moment he felt faintly sad and homesick. He was leaving part of his life behind him forever—a strange wild frontier of heat and hardship, cold, dirt, thirst, and dust. And a human frontier too, of greed and generosity, cruelty and kindness, envy, malice, stealth, and hatred. A long unending struggle of man against nature, and man against man, and, hardest of all, man against himself. For though changes were sweeping

227

across the Fields and turning the old ways of mining upside down, men were not changing. They never would.

The huge curve of the sky cupped him round, the stars gleamed icily, the wind marbled his cheeks. And beneath him, under his footsteps as he trod, lay the ancient seas of rock that had changed his life—the bands and wavering threads of potch and the sudden unspeakable fire still locked there in the stone.

ABOUT THE AUTHOR

Colin Thiele was born in Eudunda, South Australia, in 1920. He was educated in various country schools and at the University of Adelaide. He served in the Royal Australian Air Force during the second world war and has taught in high schools and colleges of advanced education. He is currently Director of Wattle Park Teachers Centre.

Colin Thiele has published almost fifty books, including *Storm Boy*, *The Sun on the Stubble*, *Blue Fin* and *Magpie Island*. He has written in various fields—poetry, prose, fiction, drama, history, criticism and biography. His work has won many awards and citations of merit and has been translated and published extensively overseas. He is a Companion of the Order of Australia.

Dingo Boy

Michael Dugan

Carl, a fourteen-year-old from an orphanage, is fostered by a farmer who values him only as a source of unpaid labour. As Carl's disappointment and resentment intensifies, his sympathy grows for a pack of hunted, starving dingoes beyond the farm's dog-proof fence. A final act of defiance in their support would almost certainly mean Carl's return to the Boy's Home where, he ironically learns, he had greater freedom. Would he have the guts to carry it out?

King of the Sticks

Ivan Southall

There was a stillness and a listening–Custard could feel it all. He knew someone was spying on him, he could feel their eyes as he worked along the rows of beans. But who would believe him. They all thought he was vague, pixilated, dreamy . . .

Especially Seth. He always looked at Custard with a disappointment that this weedy kid was his brother. But Seth had gone to market and would not be home for two whole days.

Bella didn't have much faith in Custard either—but what else could you expect from a sister?

But Rebecca, his mother, did believe him. So she ventured forth, musket in hand, to face the enemy that threatened family and home.

So the day went crazy.

For Custard this was a beginning and not the end.

Dominic

Mary White

Meg Curnow, sculptor, isn't the usual sort of mother. She doesn't make Dominic go to school; treats him as an equal; doesn't talk to him about his father, whom he's never seen. He's happy with this; spends a lot of time working on the puppet theatre he's created; goes long-distance running; plays with the kids next door.

Meg's friend John is the only flaw in his existence and Dominic suspects his increasing influence on Meg. When she suddenly decides to send him to school, that's when everything begins to go wrong.

The Circus Runaways

Margaret Pearce

Sawdust flying from the hooves of dancing horses, glittering acrobats swinging high up on the trapeze, fanfares and braided jackets—the excitement of the circus was to turn a miserable winter into a season of surprises for runaway John, his dog Blue and his horse Roanie.

And life out of the circus ring was to be just as eventful, for circus folk are different, wonderful, funny . . . and sometimes dangerous.

Tallarook was only a short stop for the circus but it was long enough for someone to try to burn the circus down. Who could it be and why? As the days and towns roll by, John finds out—not only about the saboteur but also about growing up.

Whispering in the Wind

Alan Marshall

Peter and the old man Crooked Mick lived in a bark hut with two windows and a chimney. Peter had a white pony, Moonlight, that could gallop faster than the wind.

Peter and Moonlight left the hut to search for the last surviving Beautiful Princess. Their adventures took them through the Land of Clutching Grass, over mountains and through the Watchful Forest. They met Greyfur, the kangaroo with a magical pouch, the Willy Willy Man, the Jarrah Giant, and the Pale Witch who took them to the moon. But they still had to deal with the Bunyip who guarded the castle where the Princess lived.

Tales of Tuttle

Doug MacLeod

Professor Tuttle has an interesting life in Tantoon Town. There is no time to be bored when you are a great inventor with friends like Miss Purdie, Old Bill and MacTavish.

If you suddenly find yourself wrapped up like a birthday present or chased by a pair of bionic teeth, you can be sure that Professor Tuttle is in town.

Professor Tuttle is a genius, forever trying to invent the perfect machine. So far, his inventions have been anything but perfect—however, the one thing about the Professor is that he *never* gives up.

HEARD ABOUT THE PUFFIN CLUB?

...it's a way of finding out more about Puffin books and authors, of winning prizes (in competitions), sharing jokes, a secret code, and perhaps seeing your name in print! When you join you get a copy of our magazine, *Puffinalia*, sent to you four times a year, a badge and a membership book.

For details of subscription and an application form, send a stamped addressed envelope to:

The Australian Puffin Club
Penguin Books Australia Limited
P.O. Box 527
Ringwood
Victoria 3134